**Rick Gekoski** came from his native America to do a DPhil at Oxford and went on to teach English at the University of Warwick. In 1982, he decided to become a full-time rare book dealer, specialising in important twentieth-century first editions and manuscripts. He lives in Salisbury and spends time each year in New Zealand.

**Praise for *After Darke***

'A riot of eloquent bigotry and bluster . . . What Gekoski excels at is the hard, witty, shouty – yes, masculine – business of creating a literary hero like James Darke' *The Times*

'Unbroken, unbowed and raging against the wokeness of the modern world' *Mail on Sunday*

'[A] masterpiece of negative catharsis. The novel's antihero, Dr James Darke – a reclusive, misanthropic bibliophile, filled with general rancour towards the world – gives paradoxical pleasure by venting so biliously on our behalf. For readers weary of earnest piety and emotion easily bought' *The Australian*

By the same author

*Darke*
*Darke Matter*

# AFTER DARKE

*A Novel*

## RICK GEKOSKI

CONSTABLE

CONSTABLE

First published in Great Britain in 2022 by Constable
This paperback edition published in 2023 by Constable

1 3 5 7 9 10 8 6 4 2

Copyright © Rick Gekoski, 2022

'Fifteen Coins', *The Gold of the Tigers*, Jorge Luis Borges, 1977, p191
*Steptoe and Son*, Ray Galton and Alan Simpson, 1962, p217

A CIP catalogue record for this book
is available from the British Library.

ISBN: 978-0-34913-493-2

Typeset in Bembo by Hewer Text UK Ltd, Edinburgh
Printed and bound in Great Britain by Clays Ltd, Elcograf S.p.A.

Papers used by Constable are from well-managed forests and other responsible sources.

MIX
Paper from
responsible sources
FSC® C104740

Constable
An imprint of
Little, Brown Book Group
Carmelite House
50 Victoria Embankment
London EC4Y 0DZ

An Hachette UK Company
www.hachette.co.uk

www.littlebrown.co.uk

For Matthew Greenberg

# PART ONE

# *Darke Times*

Oh, gentlemen, perhaps I really regard myself as an intelligent man only because throughout my entire life I've never been able to start or finish anything. Granted, granted I'm a babbler, a harmless, irksome babbler, as we all are. But what's to be done if the sole and express purpose of every intelligent man is babble – that is, a deliberate pouring from empty into void.

Fyodor Dostoyevsky, Notes from Underground

# Chapter 1

'Dr Darke! Good to see you again, sir!'

I do not know his name, this casual retainer, just his agency. I call him Driver. Scarcely aged in the intervening years, he was standing to the side of the black Mercedes 500, his suit no worse for wear than he was, thinned slightly perhaps, creased but not careworn. He wore a peaked cap over his peaky face, which gave him the appropriate status, as so many of his clients might have wished. I didn't care, the only thing I had always required of him was that he be silent. I had made this request when first we met, and he acceded immediately, though whether this was done gracefully I would not venture to say. I'm not interested.

Aware of taking some slight risk even with his formal salutation, to which I did not respond, he opened the door to let me in. Putting my slight bag of possessions beside me, I sank into the wonderful soft leather, one of the very many simple luxuries that I had done without, while spending my allotted time at Her Majesty's pleasure doing without. Without privacy or provision, or anything to please eye or ear. I could go on and on, but soon won't.

There'd been no cinematic gate-clanking as I was released. Led through a series of gravy-grease corridors and poached linoleum floors to a side exit, I was then left to make my way to the front. I hadn't walked that far in years, and had to stop regularly to put my hands on my knees to catch my breath. My surprising early release was due to a fortunate coincidence of bad luck: a viral outbreak in the prison, plus my deteriorating health were deemed sufficient to secure an early ticket of leave from the nitwits and jobsworths who decide such things. I was deemed no threat to the community. That was right. Nor was I likely to re-offend. That was wrong. What was it called? The long walk to freedom? It didn't feel much different, prison isn't something you can just walk out of, or away from. Not a place, a state of mind.

The light was fading, the streets emptied of persons, a few cars straggled by. In front of the prison were neither journalists nor gawpers, though some might have been expected, but there was more pressing news than my slinking back into the world, my sentence served, my debt to society fully paid. Neither was there my daughter, nor grandson, nor friends, if I still had any. Just Driver and his car, better even than I could have hoped. It was of course raining, and cold. I had no overcoat, just the creased and faded black linen suit with which I first entered these premises, and which now hangs from me as if cut for another man, as indeed it was. I was shivering, but warmed up as we drove away. I didn't need to look back. I knew what I was leaving, though unaware that what I was leaving cannot be left.

I must have fallen asleep in the fug, my head cradled, snuffling the rich oily leather, for I was awoken sharply by the whoosh of a bus, the stop and start that told me we were now in London. Befuddled, I sat up and looked out the front window. I could see, of all edifices, only the ground floor, since the car's visor blocked my view. I can imagine Driver calling out the names of the invisible sights to a carful of Japanese businessmen, football players or Israeli diplomats: *Buckingham Palace, gentlemen, on the left. Marble Arch! St Paul's Cathedral!* I am unused to movement on such a scale, at such a pace, have resided in a plodding world, looking neither left nor right, for neither offers anything more congenial than the soiled surfaces beneath my feet. Like the damned I did not meet eyes, eyes were best left to themselves.

I peered out the tiny window of my cell, seeing truncated portions, half a tree, an expanse of tarmac with a few cars on it, people disappearing off to the sides. I was more interested in the cars than the people, though both were soiled and ordinary, and bruised one's spirit. A few hunched and battered wives, some equally damaged Fords and rusty formerly white vans.

Everything in prison, at least at first, set off a countervailing memory:

*My hands shake, my eyes wouldn't pass an O-Level test. My beloved Jaguar 3.8 is languishing elegantly in storage, its crackled leather and unsullied British racing green an unavailable delight, ah, the pleasureful effort of piloting it through traffic, it takes some doing, having no power steering. I couldn't hoick it about any more, not strong enough. I will instruct my garage to sell it.*

*Suzy said I preferred driving it to driving her, which was true much of the time, until it was true all of it. She refused to drive it herself, would barely get in, scorned it as the choice of elderly white-haired gentlemen wearing suits. She preferred the self-definition of her red Mini, which I equally contemptuously regarded as fit only for It-girls in miniskirts. I could barely bend and shuffle into its tiny space. We didn't go out much, and when we did, compromised and used a car service.*

We slowed down, the car alit smoothly outside my house. A newly installed light burnished the ebony of its entrance. I had my key ready to hand. Driver opened the car door, and stood to the side deferentially.

'Good luck, sir.'

The hallway lights have been left on, the windows reveal lamps and the shadowy presence of my possessions, my former home, my home once again. In my absence it had been tenanted by Lucy and her children, and turned into offices for her Foundation! I have no idea why I agreed to this, indeed have no memory of having done so. Lucy has been instructed to remove all traces of their tenure. Rudy slept in Suzy's former study, and I have a horror of opening the door and seeing childish stuff blu-tacked to the wall: Sheffield United FC scarves, school photographs, posters of rockers and rollers. As for Amelie's four-year-old residue, I cannot bear to think of it.

I want my house exactly as I left it. Once it was mine and Suzy's, now it is mine alone. I stand in the warm hallway hoping that her presence will mote the air. Her voice no longer calls to me, nor can I summon it, as so often I tried in those first searing months in prison. Why have you abandoned me, I would cry, why, when I most need you? But if Suzy was most assuredly not there – she loathed ugly places and people – might I find her, something of her, an echo or fugitive message, find her now if only I attended sufficiently? I was listening intently, as if she might whisper her presence.

Standing in the hallway, I put my small bag on the floor, and peered about myopically as nothing came into focus, the pattern of the Hamadan runner at my feet seemed unable to keep still, as if some ghostly hand were shaking it gently. Inert and lost, I was unable to summon so much as a plod. I had naively presumed that my coming home would be both literal and metaphoric, that the rightness, the inevitability, of the place, my place, would be immediate and enthralling. After some discussion, let me call it, Lucy had acceded to my desire to make this transition on my own. In any case, as things worked out, she was not allowed either to pick me up or to accompany me home. Or to visit.

I was shaken by the discontinuities. The feeling of my returned shoes – my lovely Ducker's brogues, an unaccustomed weight – against the carpet, the tight enclosure of walls and ceiling, the importuning blues of the signed Matisse prints on the walls, so inappropriate in their Georgian situation. Suzy bought them one afternoon at a West End gallery, carted them home in a taxi, and by the time I arrived at the end of the school day, she had removed my Piranesis from their place in the hallway, banged in a couple of nails, and hung their replacements.

'Darling, look!' she'd said. 'Aren't they wonderful! They brighten up the hallway. They're so welcoming!' She'd always hated the Piranesis, which she found dour and class-bound: 'You only find them in upper-middle-class houses where the people have no idea about art!' Apparently I was one such. I have good taste, if conventional. You need conventions to decide what is worth valuing, and what is not, to supply context and comparators, to avoid the lure of the merely original. Suzy, on the other hand, approached every work of art anew: it did not matter who it was by or what the subject, the only question was whether it had 'quality', a term that she was aggressively unwilling either to define or to defend. 'You get it, or you don't: you need to have seen a lot of art, and to have an open mind and spirit!' In my experience, openness of mind and (whatever this signifies) spirit often lead to no good. The old roads lead to the safest and best destinations. Suzy teased me. Good taste is what the upwardly mobile cultivate. It signifies. But if you're already up, you don't think about it at all, it's vulgar.

Some years later, exactly to spite me, she'd bought a dreadful picture, of which she was apparently a 'studio co-creator' by one Rimington, S., a graduate of our school, who became one of the stars of the YBA movement. She hung it in her study, and when she died it was the first item on my clear-out pile. It did very well at Sotheby's, which certainly did not confirm that her judgement about its 'quality' was correct.

The air in the hallway was odourless, save for a faint whiff of perfumed polishes, and my nose twitched missing the usual offences of acrid cleaning materials, cooking oil, poor tobacco, human sweat and farts. And despair, that has a smell too. It was the first time in these years that I had been alone in a quiet space, sufficient at first to still my heart, then to set it beating frantically. I managed to get my breathing under control, swayed and righted myself. I opened the door into the drawing room, and made timid entrance, seeking anxiously to locate not the comfort of the old but the intrusion of the new: something discordant, unexpected, *other*. It looked safe: my armchair was in its proper place, almost to the inch, the Indian cushions were plumped on the sofa, the corners of the carpet aligned, no dust appeared on surfaces or edges of the frames of my Samuel Palmers, the lamp was carefully centred on the Pembroke table, its shade perfectly aligned, seam to the rear. What alarmed me, though, was the noxious smell of lilies, a vase filled with vulgar pink blooms perched on the side table. Underneath it was an envelope, with 'Dad' written on the front. I left it there, and retreated from the smell and memories. Suzy liked lilies, especially after she died.

The kitchen, too, was an almost exact replica: when she moved in, Lucy – at my suggestion – had taken myriad phone-photographs of the contents of every room, and had forensically replicated their former incarnations. Gazing round carefully, though, it looked as if the walls had been repainted, none of the former streaks and blemishes could be located. The colour almost matched, though it was tonally inferior to the subtle Farrow & Ball original, too matt, rather vulgar really. I suppressed a moment of indignation, for what had I to indignate about? I was fortunate to be so well served, was I not?

When Lucy and her children moved in, the first thing she did, telling me only afterwards, was to reinstall the letterbox that I had removed when I reformatted the door after Suzy's death, when I wished to be left alone, entirely alone: no post, no doorbell, no phone or email, no comings and no goings. This might have been regarded as good preparation for the more severe incarceration to come, but it was not. The movement from locked in to locked up to (now) locked down was not seamless: each of the stages of my journey was separate, and led neither to nor from the other, though there's no denying that I've chosen to spend a lot of time behind closed doors. That's what doors are for.

The fridge was adequately stocked for the coming days, with a couple of bottles of Ferret Pouilly-Fuissé, and a variety of treats from Selfridges' Food Hall: Jersey milk and cream, Greek organic yoghurt, country pâtés and fish paste, mature brie and cheddar, Normandy butter, jams, preserves and pickles, smoked trout and oysters, prosciutto and salami. In the freezer were some fillets of beef and chicken breasts, and the vegetable drawers revealed cos lettuce and cucumber, new potatoes, courgettes and aubergines, apples and pears. And tomatoes, which should never go in the fridge, I'd told Lucy this far too many times, but her ex, Sam, always insisted that his be served cold, which is to say tasteless, which he is.

In the bread bin were a small baguette and a seeded sourdough loaf, and the cupboards revealed a range of tinned goods, dry biscuits, and jars of white asparagus. A carved wooden bowl filled with dainty fair-trade bananas and lustrous purple Buffalo grapes, the size of marbles, sat on the sideboard like a work of art. Braque perhaps. The grapes emanated, I was touched that Lucy should have remembered, from the Japanese counter at Harrods. I was once addicted to them, in small quantities; you do not stuff these into your mouth willy-nilly, like something from Waitrose's fruit counters, these were, each one, a perfect and intense experience. I rarely ate more than four or five, often with a sliver of Montgomery's Cheddar.

I picked one up, and rolled it very gently on my fingertips, put it between my lips and slowly into my mouth, interrogating the sensation of skin against skin, bit gently and almost gasped as the initial spray of sweetness was released, after which the tip of my tongue felt assaulted and singed by acidity. I found it hard to accommodate the empty fold of tannic grape skin, and spat it out into the garbage bin, but the taste in my mouth lingered, curiously unfounded and disagreeable.

I was touched, and appalled, that Lucy should have provided so copiously. Of course she had no idea how the mere sight of the foodstuffs would make my stomach, which had over the last four years no exposure to such riches, turn over, put its legs up and roil. It's worth mixing metaphors sometimes to convey extra shock.

In prison I'd eaten enough, just, to keep myself out of trouble, and alive.

*I sit in the dining room morning noon night, to consume my statutory £1.87-a-day of nourishment. Breakfast I limit to thin porridge and toast with yellow goo. Occasionally there will be apples (soft) or bananas (brown). Perhaps some slices of ham at lunch. I cut the fat off, and if there's some meat left, pink or brown, it makes my teeth tingle in rebellion and my gorge rise.*

*I have passed beyond hunger, like Gandhi into a spiritual fast, light-headed and righteous. I fart and my heart flutters unbearably. Yesterday I sat amongst my fellows, trying to ingest a few bites of 'chicken supreme' (we get other food with pseudo-bistro names, like 'lasagne bake') and grey vegetables boiled within an inch of their former lives. I eat in very small bites, each an effort, it takes time, and courage.*

I sliced a piece of sourdough, considered and quickly rejected butter, and sat at the kitchen table to eat it slowly. Though my wonderful Gaggia gleamed on the kitchen bench, and a bag of my bespoke beans from H. R. Higgins sat beside it, I resisted their call. There will be time yet for a hundred indecisions, and for a hundred visions and revisions, before the taking of toast and coffee. Night had drawn in, the window showed the black of night, shimmering like a Mark Rothko.

I tried to remember his room at the Tate Modern, but nothing emerged, everything is lost. It was now time, in the natural course of things, for a drink. A glass of that white wine, a whisky perhaps. Glenmorangie in its crystal glass, tiny amount of mineral water, no ice. My stomach delivered an immediate rejection. I left the kitchen and turned to go upstairs, increasingly certain of what I would not find there.

Lucy needed the house restored to full receptivity, of mail and persons, because for the more than three years it was to serve as the home of the Suzy Moulton Foundation, the charity that she had created to honour her mother's memory, defend and celebrate her father's character, and to advance the cause of assisted dying. For the first year the Foundation, like most such, had been tied together by a variety of shoestrings, but as occasionally happens in the crimped charity world, it got lucky. On his death my friend Philip Massingham, co-member of our Poetry Group of Grievers, left the Foundation what the newspapers called 'a significant sum', because unbeknownst to us all he was a rich man, and a charitable one. Lucy's project was one of many that benefited from his largesse. Further bequests from other supporters followed, and within a year or two the SMF had two full-time employees, one of African descent and the other of indeterminate sexuality, as well, of course, as the pro bono legal services of her new partner Jonathan.

Presumably the upstairs rooms had been reformatted into offices and meeting rooms. I trudged up fearfully with my bag of scant possessions, though what I had discovered so far confirmed Lucy's powers of recreating the past, like some domestic Marcel Proust. Given her general slovenliness and pedestrian taste, I wondered if she'd had the advantage of someone else's eyes, opinions, and hard work.

My study is the most important room, where my all too occasional moments of peace were generated. Though my Dickens first editions had long been transformed by Sotheby's into a trust fund for dear Rudy, the bookshelves were as I had arranged them. Alphabetical order was hardly disturbed, though one of my J. G. Farrell first editions had migrated into the William Goldings. I put it back. Next to my computer on the desk was a new small upright machine with a screen, and a holograph note beside it, which I did not read.

I needed first to unpack my few bits, of which only one mattered, the thick scraggy notebook that I had kept in prison. I sat down in my armchair, and took it from the bag. The pages were yellowed, the covers grimy and soiled by grease-fingering. It had a lot of entries in the first year, fewer as time went by. I cradled the notebook as if it could settle me and provide some peace, if only in remembering the exacting past.

> *I'm able to write in this little notebook to make my occasional observations, but I cringe at the very thought of being recurrently obliged to write a letter to Lucy, or to Rudy ... and then to Philip, Miles, Dorothea, George, various acquaintances and old boys, all those moved by my plight, who would like to join me in spirit, if not in prison.*
>
> *We are forbidden access to computers, so I cannot reply with generic emails. 'Thank you so much for being in touch, please do not do so again.' This injunction against computers seems unnecessarily punitive, though I can quite understand why we are not allowed access to the Internet, lest the clever amongst us look up recipes for making an incendiary device out of stale white bread, gruel and farts.*

I could barely make out my words, not because of their grimy veneer, but because my handwriting, once italic and gracious, had shrunk, and deteriorated so comprehensively. Whole sentences in my minuscule script were often incomprehensible, and I have had to guess in transcribing them. I felt this loss of my formerly elegant hand most keenly, and at first ascribed it to inferior conditions, instruments, and paper. But the real cause was an emerging tremor in my right hand, which I can no longer hold horizontally without it beginning its palsied shakes.

Yet another case of the Oscars. He put this harrowing gaol-house malady poignantly: 'My writing has gone to bits – like my character. I am simply a self-conscious nerve in pain.' A promising phrase! I'm good at titles: *A Nerve in Pain: The Incarceration and Tragic Decline of Oscar Wilde, a Monograph by Dr James Darke*. It could go in the back of my desk drawer, unfinished like my former project, *Scalded and Boiled: The Indignations of Charles Dickens*.

I know enough about myself, by now, to recognise lack and incapacity where they are evident and long-standing. I am not a writer, and my post-Oxbridge attempt at a study of a major author was dilettantish in the extreme, my incapacity to write or to finish it a testimony to the discrimination of my unconscious. The only exception to this was my composition of a new ending for *Gulliver's Travels,* which I wrote for Rudy when he was eight, and which, I very much hope, gave him both pleasure and the capacity to deal with my prolonged absence from his life.

I had promised myself that I would destroy the execrable testimony of my prison diary, but did not, and though I am once again tempted, it seems I cannot. Can one destroy a diary without injuring oneself in the process? Philip Larkin couldn't, he had to die first and get someone else to do it for him. Someone who had to promise not to read it. It was a bit naughty, diaries are like that. My fellow inmates were constantly curious about what was in mine, though the few of them sufficiently literate to read could hardly have deciphered my handwriting.

Perusing the various entries makes me feel more at home, if I might put it that way, and I can feel the sensory underload of prison life re-entering my mind and body. Sitting in this room, with its foreign and unwonted order and gentility, I feel myself coming alive only in the memory of things past, which I thought could not pass soon enough, and I am unmanned by the process.

Might returning to my desk, and to this, my true and ongoing journal, might that put things right? Lucy left my computer ready to go. It's a relief now to be able to type these entries, however many errors I make. Who cares? Though I wonder, as ever, why I bother? What did that snitbag Woolf, herself a mean diarist, say about her compulsive inward stocktaking? 'Do I ever write, even here, for my own eye? If not, for whose eye?' My own answers: 'No, not for mine. And no, not for yours.' Then what for? The desire to make this journal grew out of my failure to live a life, and the least I can do is record the process.

These passages are not the story of my life, they are my life, my life's work, disordered, unruly, suffused with loss, unsolaced, unbalanced, lost in wordiness, lost. Rather fun, I suppose, if you like this sort of thing. I don't, not just now, I lack the requisite ease, the contemplative reflexes of a recorder of life's minutiae, I return to my old computer and writerly activity out of a sense of ... what? Duty? Nonsense. Habit? Not at all, if it were I would break it. Nothing as grand as any obligation other than the most pedestrian: I write not to record the times, but to fill them. And when, eventually, they are done, I will be. Or perhaps it is merely the other way round?

It's only just past eight, time enough to read, perhaps turn to Radio 3 on the wireless, consider a draught of Armagnac, smoke a cigar. My cherrywood humidor from Fox of St James was in its accustomed place on the small Georgian table next to me. I opened the lid to discover a selection of Montecristos, from the welcoming petit Number Fours to the torpedo Number Twos, neatly laid out, the immediate smell sufficient to make me dizzy and nauseous.

*I have taken up cigarette smoking, the viler the better. If there were Woodbines I'd have had those. Instead I am learning to do roll-ups. Rollies. My Glaswegian tutor Jock can do them with one hand, while playing the bagpipes with the other. He thinks my attempts hilarious, but I'm improving. I hold the thin result between thumb and finger, as unglued as its creator, wisps of tobacco hanging at both ends, and inhale as greedily as a gangster. Three puffs, done, four, burnt fingers.*

It's time only for bed, for – if I can manage it – a few hours of oblivion, to awake early in the morning. We rose at six to face the humiliations of a new day: the showers, the toilets, the breakfast.

On my bedside table are a plastic bottle of water and a strip of Valium tablets. My freshly laundered paisley pyjamas are laid out at the foot of the bed, my maroon leather Moroccan slippers tucked under. I am too bewildered to feel comforted or grateful, take off my clothes and hang them over the armchair. Slip on the pyjamas, the silky feeling makes my skin crawl, as if it wished to slink away somewhere to be on its own. I sit on the edge of the bed, the mattress both firm and yielding, unscrew the plastic top of the water, take a five-milligram pill of Valium from the strip, should be plenty after all these years, and swallow it, hoping it might be adequate to still my spirit and stifle my dreams, knowing it would do neither. I'd need twenty milligrams to do that, a thought that led me to pop another couple of pills, wondering how many I might need to ...? But that was in the old days, when people could knock themselves out and off with an overdose of sleeping pills. It was so easy to do that, sometimes it was, or was claimed to be, accidental, a badly judged mix of alcohol and Nembutal. Marilyn Monroe was either a suicide or an unfortunate over-taker in quick need of an undertaker. Silly damn woman. Foolish Arthur Miller bit off a lot more than he could chew, nice Jewish boy, she was the one with all the teeth. It would have been worth it for a while: he making her smart, and she making him crazy.

The sheets were as creepy as the pyjamas, the 800-thread count Egyptian cotton unsettlingly smooth and accommodating. I'm used to a nightly battle with my bedclothes, squirming to establish the least scratchy relationship with the demotic fabric, until at last one posture and connection is preferable to the others, the relief a small pleasure. I have not touched cotton or silk for many years, they have no pride, accommodate and yield as easily as a high-class tart, not that I ever visited any such. My metaphors are getting as drowsy as I. In another few minutes my mind flits round in random associations, presaging the sleep to come, and perhaps the dreams.

The Christmas before I was tried and convicted, I hosted the family celebrations, such as they were, or could be. It was the first since Suzy's death, and Rudy insisted tearfully that she have a chair at the dinner table, and I demurred harshly and fearfully. I didn't tell Lucy, but over that entire week, the most regular company and visitor in the house was Suzy. I mean this, almost, literally. During the day her words and her image filled my mind, tormented my heart, and disordered my spirit. During the evenings, trying to sleep, phantasmagorical images of her embodied and disembodied body flooded my consciousness until I thought I might drown.

The family came, and stayed, oblivious. Suzy came, and stayed, threatening and surreally invasive, calling to me. I could not ascertain whether I wanted her to go away, to restore my sanity and peace, or to stay to continue my connection with her, however painful. And now, returned to the very bed in which these struggles took place, I twist and lie and turn seeking some glimmer of that connection, yearning to be haunted if only briefly, to hear her voice whisper and see her body reappear, and fade, reappear and be gone. I understand, lying there, what is so mysterious and unsettling about this empty re-entered house, this place of absence. What has gone missing is both me, and her.

I turned on the bedside lamp, aware that sleep would not return for some time. My sleeping, like my stools, comes only in occasional fitful bits. In prison I learned not even to sit up when I awoke prematurely, trained myself simply to lie there, trying not to think, or to feel, to remember or to plan, to entertain thoughts of neither the living nor the dead. Suzy wouldn't make a nocturnal appearance, had instructed me not even to try to contact her, like a spouse after a combative divorce. I tried to breathe slowly, as recommended by the self-improvement books that Lucy sent me, to listen to the sound of the sea whooshing in my ears, until it filled me up and I tossed with anxiety about my poor beleaguered heart.

I awake to feel my toes and legs, unaccustomed to their efforts yesterday, cramping, knotted in complaint, agonising. I push my feet against the bed board, but the relief is only momentary, stand up moaning and walk round the room, push my toes firmly into the softness of the Moroccan woollen carpet. Nothing helps. I struggle round the room, then to the bathroom, moaning. Apparently cold water may ease the spasms. I half-fill the bath, and stand in it, clutching at the rail, waiting for relief. Sometime later, I have no idea how long, I found myself on the floor, having slipped or fainted perhaps, my head throbbing. I struggled up to look in the mirror and located a large red welt on my forehead, vivid streaks of blood down my cheeks. The sight was captivating: I turned my head to the side, imaging a crown of thorns, and was tempted to put my arms out and feet together. Suzy used to call such an image the crucial fiction. The dazed and emaciated figure in my mirror recalled poor abandoned Jesus on His agonising return to the arms of His Father, who ostensibly loved Him.

I'm no longer at war with God, as I most assuredly was when He tormented and took Suzy from me, yet another example, amongst millions, of His failure to provide loving kindness. I believe, though, in His so-called son Jesus, who seems a sound chap, if a bit earnest. He had a hard life from start to finish. His mother was a virgin, His Father having withdrawn, He was biologically an orphan, and spent His life trying to find a working paternal relationship. At the end He complained, as He had His whole life, that His Father had abandoned Him.

As for this Father, this Nobodaddy, He's hooey, a psychological project and projection. I employ Him as a metaphoric progenitor for the largest processes of being, the comings and of goings, and wish Him well with His most recent project, the extinction of mankind. The reason that God never shone the light of His panoptic benevolence on humans was simply that we never deserved it, being, as the King of Brobdingnag sagely observed, the vilest species of vermin ever to inhabit the Earth. Soon enough we will be no more. That will be ample confirmation of God's benevolence, sufficient indeed to create believers, were there any people left to believe.

I remember this, by the exhausting Mr Lawrence:

'But,' she objected, 'you'd be dead yourself, so what good would it do you?'

'I would die like a shot, to know that the Earth would really be cleaned of all the people. It is the most beautiful and freeing thought. Then there would never be another foul humanity created, for a universal defilement.'

'No . . . there would be nothing.'

'What! Nothing? Just because humanity was wiped out? You flatter yourself. There'd be everything.'

'But how, if there were no people?'

'Do you think that creation depends on man! There are the trees and the grass and birds.'

I swabbed the blood and cleaned my face, dried myself, put on my dressing gown, and walked about, my cramps in abeyance. The house felt empty, desolate and abandoned, an outward exemplar of my inward state. I felt a turning that might be hunger, and descended to the kitchen to see what remedy my system might accommodate. In the cupboard is a glass jar filled with Flahavan's organic oats, another with Dorset Cereals muesli. From the open shelves of the dresser I selected a small blue Chinese bowl, extracted a spoon from the silver drawer, emptied a few oats and a small handful of muesli into it, added a dollop of yoghurt and sliced a banana finely on top, with a swish of Jersey milk, and mixed thoughtfully. Sat at the table, and looked curiously at the result, lifted it to my nose and sniffed, put it down, got up and walked into the sitting room, to return in a moment with the envelope that Lucy had left for me. Unsealed it, took out the folded page, straightened its edges, and placed it by the side of the unaccustomed abstract mixture in the bowl.

*Dear Dad, dearest,*

*I'm so desperately sorry not to be able to pick you up, to hug you fiercely and to bring you home. I suppose it is just as well. Damn fucking virus, who knew this was coming, or where it will go? And now we're locked down, which will ironically be easier for you than for me and for poor Rudy, who misses you terribly, and still feels aggrieved that you didn't write to him. I have tried to explain, though I'm not sure I understand it either, I just say Grandpa has his funny ways. You will hardly believe how changed he is! I know you've seen the pictures, but his voice! Almost manly, and (yes, am I sad or what?) a little bit posh now. You of course will love that.*

*Upstairs on your desk I have left an ALEXA machine. Do NOT be alarmed! I have programmed it, and you don't even have to turn it on. You can ask it questions or give it orders just by saying 'Alexa, what is the time?' Or 'Alexa play me Beethoven's Fifth Symphony.' And she will! But of course you won't. BUT the one thing you please (!!) must do is just say 'Alexa, ring Lucy.' And hey presto I will be there! Or even 'Alexa, ring Rudy' and he will be! We're always there because we are virtually never anywhere else. The children are home-schooling, as you know. Kill me!*

*I've also got you a new iPhone and it's on your desk, fully charged. I wrote its number on a sticker and put it on the back so you won't forget it. Our numbers too. So now I can ring you, and we can all text. But Alexa is best to really see each other, it makes it so real!*

*The other thing is that your computer is now plugged in and ready to go. On your desktop I've put some stuff you might need. Tax and financial records, further correspondence about your trial and (horrid word) incarceration, and various bits and pieces from people to whom you may wish to respond, though knowing you, you won't, which is not to say that you shouldn't.*

*Oh, dear, I'm babbling, I'm so sorry, it's hard doing even this, writing this, thinking of you reading it.*

*I feel so anxious that the house won't be perfect, as you remember and need it. It took ages to get our stuff out, yours back in and in the right orderliness. I could hardly have done this on my own – you know me! – but Jonathan and especially Bronya helped so much. Rudy too. They all send their love.*

*So! You're home. I hope you sink into it and love it and exult in its many comforts and pleasures, and in the love that we all feel for you. You deserve it all, and more. I'm so proud of you!*

*Love you so much my dear brave father, there's so much to say, to catch up on, and to plan.*

*Lucy xxxxx*

It was hardly breakfast time, but I filled my spoon with the unappetising goop before me, put a tiny bit in my mouth, the yoghurt coated my gums, seeds and sog filled my mouth, I gagged and rushed to the sink to spit it out, before rinsing my mouth and returning to bed.

# Chapter 2

In the morning, I sat for a time in the sitting room with the curtains open, unusual for me even in my former state. I prefer to be in my study, and as for light, there's too much of it about already. You can overdo light. I am more at home in the darkness, and during the hours of daylight prefer domestic gloom, which suits me, with curtains closed and only a few lamps lit. I pace like an animal in a zoo, my natural habitat. In a cage. Unable to escape. That is how I felt before I went to prison, and it is how I feel now that I am (bad word!) released, under house arrest.

And the peculiar and rather wonderful thing is: so is everyone else! I see them on the telly and hear them on the radio complaining relentlessly, until after a few minutes they disgust me and I turn them off: *OOOH, I can't go out, I'm bored, I don't get any exercise or company, the kids are driving me crazy, it's so scary and unfair, I'm incarcerated and can't escape!* Well, what suits some doesn't suit all. The playwright Mr Stoppard was quoted saying that social distancing without social disapproval was what he had always yearned for, and that he was enjoying it. I wonder why he worried so about being disapproved of?

I'm not exactly enjoying it, but am as happy as can be, which is to say neither happy nor unhappy, slouching and napping in my cage like a drugged animal, a state easily obtained with a combination of Valium, alcohol and cigars. My head spins, and my balance is sufficiently uncertain that I spend most of my time in a chair or bed. When I walk through the house, I keep one hand on the wall. My relative contentment is not because I have 'inner resources', but because I have outer ones: enough space, enough money, enough amelioration by way of drink and food and comfort. And thank God I am unaccompanied by others: if you put too many animals in a cage eventually they will disagree, then fight, then kill each other. It's natural. Nature is rough stuff.

I don't wish to Alexa my darling daughter, I dread it. When in prison, I tried to dissuade Lucy from visiting, but she came and came, however painful it was to us both, and it was like the script of some absurdist drama, with few words and many silences.

*For the first weeks, when Lucy arrived, I refused to come out to the visitors' room. She was desolate, then furious, sent me a letter accusing me of reverting to Plan A. I shredded it neatly, and threw it away.*

*Our first meeting was not a success. She sat in the chair opposite me at the table, weeping, holding her hand out for reassurance. Tried to say a few things. Failed. My heart was full and I could not speak, looking into the silence. We sat for some minutes, and then she left.*

Following this unhappy un-meeting, I had a letter from Lucy:

*Dearest Dad,*

*I don't know what to say, or if I did how to say it. I will come again next Thursday afternoon, and no doubt the words will come too. And the tears. I am sorry to add to your distress, I'll try to be brave. After all, you are. I try to think of you and all this positively. It's what you chose. For yourself. For us. I'm determined that something good may come of it. I need to talk to you about this.*

*Rudy sends his love, and is writing a story, which I have helped him with, but not too much. He printed it out. I hope you like it, it helps*

him in your absence, though being an eight-year-old he is perfectly able
to retreat into a solipsistic fug much of the time. Lucky him.

*I love you,*

*Lucy xx*

Enclosed was a story from Rudy, which I supposed was cute, a
category I detest. I put it aside to read, later. I would have to
compose myself to compose a reply, two replies, but I was in no
mood to correspond. I did not wish to end up as a character in an
epistolary novel, a genre I detest. *Dearest Florence, Well, it seems
trouble is afoot in Melfont Manor, where dear Sophie is finding herself in
a curious and unseemly predicament . . .*

Rudy's story was no doubt prompted by his mother as a way of
storming the gates of my heart, in which she knew that he held a
special place. He was cunning enough to devise an adventure in
tacit response to the one I had written for him the previous year,
in which Captain Gulliver made his final voyage, and his grandson
Reuben turned out to be the hero.

### GAMPY'S BEST VOYAGE

*When Gampy went away he was not sad. He had gone on voyages
before. He always came back safe, because he had superpowers. He was
super smart, and super strong because he was a trained fighter. When he
wanted to he could transform himself. Then he was not Gampy but The
Gampster, and then he was really scary. Nobody knew this, but they
were going to find out soon. The Gampster had lots of things to do. He
was a Great Writer, and he was going to write a book about his
adventures, and it would be exciting.*

*He was going away. He went there on a bus, with the other travellers.
When they got to the camp they were all given special uniforms, and had
nice rooms. They were going to stay there for a long time, so they had to
bring stuff. Gampy brought his pens and paper and a book to write in.*

### NOT THE END

I read and reread this. It's resourceful of him in so many ways that I can hardly bear it, unbearably sad, both precocious and regressed, the sort of nonsense he adored when he was six. If I had any lefto-ver heart, it would be breaking. I suppose the poor tyke has no idea of what to say and how to say it; it was foolish of Lucy to encourage him.

When I was alone, later, I tore the page slowly and geometri-cally such that the emerging pieces were of a size, and put them in the bin, fluttering them from my hand like snowflakes. I could not bring myself to write in acknowledgement, for fear of encouraging the process, but told Lucy to convey my thanks.

She had developed a morbid fear that I am dying. Each ensuing visit I was interrogated about my health. I'd obviously lost weight. How is my heart? Which medications am I on? How should I know! I get fed my pills every morning, and watched to make sure I swallow. A prison, I tried to explain, is very unlike a private hospital.

Lucy insisted I have a 'thorough' screening, as if that were likely: that I see a cardiologist, get checked for diabetes – there's a lot of it about, like Polish plumbers – and other internal disar-rangements. And have a colonoscopy! It doesn't bear thinking about, she certainly shouldn't, and I most assuredly won't. What's inside my bowels – this is a matter of profound personal policy – is my own business. When I made the mistake of saying so, Lucy began to quiz me about my chronic constipation, which she was inclined to regard as some sort of metaphor. It is not: nothing in, nothing out. I have no internal contents either to excrete or to express.

When my time comes – I can feel its fetid breath – I will have neither fear nor regrets. I do not in the least mind being dead, a world without James Darke in it could hardly be called diminished. But being dead, and dying, are separate categories:

*I am nearly seventy-three, and I confess myself afraid of the very disagreeable methods by which we leave this world; the long death of palsy, or the degraded spectacle of aged idiotism.*

Being dead? Excellent. An efficient cerebral haemorrhage. An efficient heart attack. A comprehensive stroke. Marvellous. But to lie abed declining, physically humiliated, someone washing me, wiping my bottom, turning me this way and that? In pain, then worse pain, then agony of body and spirit? Like Suzy? No.

Suzy has finally departed, leaving only faint whiffs and images, not her, not the photographs, the words on her pages, the home movies, the YouTube clips. They are someone else, not her, not my wife, not my Suzy. My not Suzy. The more I consulted such images the more quickly they died, and now they are incontrovertibly nothing to do with Suzy Moulton, or with me. Suzy has still residence in the world, friends speak of her, sometimes fondly, and offer memories that I neither share nor wish to indulge. Her daughter has a comprehensive Suzy dossier in her heart. I gave Lucy the albums, and what was left of her mother's diaries and papers. I want nothing more to do with her, as she has nothing to do with me.

I confess this knowing that it is not true, not entirely, no more than it is true that I can envisage my own demise with the ironic poise that my words have suggested. I wake in the night, now four years from her death and four years closer to mine, I wake trembling with fear, shouting NO!, rolling onto my side and sometimes off the bed itself, sheared off by terror. I feel my throat constrict, my heart beats wildly, for hours the blood thumps me awake. In this state I drift off for a few minutes, until it repeats and I awake with another shout, the Everlasting NO! And yet another image prefiguring my poor desiccated final days, alone and inconsolably lost, frightened to death.

Since I cannot rely on an overwhelming physical event to sweep me away, I will do it myself, I've done it before to Suzy's profit and mine own. I am ready, and have my final remedy to hand, thanks to dear Philip. My final solution. Everyman his own Hitler.

I may be released and out, but luckily cannot be about, being probed, tested and internally interviewed. The hospitals are stuffed with gasping ventilated patients, there's hardly room for a not entirely decrepit old man whose daughter is neurotic. I'm safe, for the duration, which may be long enough to see me out.

But my hesitation, my cowardly and cruel reluctance to do an Alexa – at last a woman who will do entirely as I demand – is not based merely on an unwillingness to be physiologically interrogated and fussed over, but by the implication of the phrase in her letter: '*there's so much to say, to catch up on, and to plan.*' The answers to which are: Go right ahead, if you must, and fuck that. It's the 'planning', apparently a bit of a throwaway, that alarms me the most.

During the years of my incarceration, as the echoes of my trial and sentencing receded, I remained a subject of public interest as the Suzy Moulton Foundation grew in strength, size, and public exposure. Jonathan Cooper, having signally and usefully failed to defend me from the charge of murdering my dear wife, subsequently won several high-profile cases with regard to various issues about assisted dying, and the coverage of these cases never failed to mention mine. I am the elderly progenitor of this moral progress, for those who feel it to be such. My early release reflected my special circumstances; a case where life did not mean life.

And those that did wrote to me constantly during my years in prison, sent me gifts, flowers and foodstuffs (many of which I was not allowed to receive), cards, letters of support and occasional expressions of erotic interest. One dewy American admirer sent me an ill-designed and amateurishly executed silk embroidery carrying Ralph Waldo Emerson's lofty sentiment: 'The martyr cannot be dishonored. Every lash inflicted is a tongue of fame; every prison a more illustrious abode.'

*This transcendental Yankee Waldosap had never been in prison, nor did he know anything about it, the pompous arse. I considered wiping mine with the soft and silky panel, to have such relief if only for one movement, but refrained. Instead and as ever wipe myself with paper that scrapes, apologise once again to my suffering anus, pull up pants and trousers so rough and so irritating that I scratch the resultant rashes until the blood runs down my leg dampening and soon stiffening my socks. My lower legs have stripes, as if I had been flogged or flayed.*

I rarely opened the letters or occasional gifts, too many of which had offerings not of sweetmeats and myrrh, but encapsulations of wisdom: improving books, collections of homilies and exhortations, religious offerings. I detested all of them, and it was from these gratuitous and unwelcome gifts that I began to formulate my project to eviscerate the wise men, reduce them to rubble. Interrogating the depths of my despair, no amelioration was evident, or possible. There is no relief. Does this make me wiser, then, than the sages, the great and the good of spiritual life? I think so. We all inhabit and acknowledge the dark, but I'm not whistling in it. Nothing provides consolation. Nothing is good enough for me.

Yet there are days and days, and they pass and have to be passed. What are days for? My dispositions have always been founded on the belief that some forms of being are preferable to others, else my contempt for the vast majority of my fellow man would be illogical. If we are merely passengers on a rock hurtling into oblivion, then what does it matter? Whistling, do I hear the faint whisper of a whistle? Do I still seek some solution to the simple question: how to be?

I shunned the company of my daughter, rejected all amelioration of my isolation and discomfort. Nothing, nothing comes of nothing. But the more cunning entreaties and communications were sent not to me, but care of Lucy or Jonathan at the

Foundation. These fell into several unwelcome categories: requests for interviews, invitations to speak or to write. None, of course, could happen until my release, but the correspondents wanted to get their requests on the table early, and they reiterated them frequently. Miles the dapper literary agent pressed a claim on the prison diary that, he was certain, I would or should be composing. Could he see it as soon as possible? There would be a strong market!

Lucy and I discussed many of these requests during her visits, and to her surprise, I preferred these topics to a discussion of my blood and bowels, both of which thundered and roiled at her intimate and impertinent enquiries. I am sorely aware of the inexorable decline of my viscera; it is pain to be me. I do not share this information, keep it not to but from myself, as something to be both endured and ignored, until the day, until the day. If Lucy had the means, she would insert herself down my gullet and wander about, interrogating my pancreas, visiting with my liver, cosying up to my heart, poking about my stomach and trawling my bowels like some miniaturised visitor in a disgusting Disney film. *Hello, organic folks! Everything all right down here?*

Better to fend off the various requests, to which I simply reiterated that whatever the entreaty, I was against it. Just say NO, I insisted. Simple enough really? Except that it wasn't, not to Lucy. She knew I would be keeping a diary, though I demurred when asked about it. Diaries, like bowels, are private and often mucky. But she saw the possibilities of the publication of such, for it might confirm me as a spokesman, even a martyr, for the Cause. After all, had I not wittingly gone to court to plead not guilty to murdering her mother, simply to be able to make my case publicly? It was doomed to failure, and I to prison. And I never even got to make my case, the prosecution and hostile judge saw to that, as I spluttered and failed to justify my behaviour.

Lucy was in regular contact with Miles, and colluded with his

continued interest in the contents of my supposed diary. She was
not the only one: it intrigued those both outside and in.

*I carry my notebook in my pocket, and made the mistake of writing in
it after lunch today. My fellows were intrigued: Whatcha writing about?
Why don't you read it to us? The tones were greedy: Could it be taken
from me and monetised in some way? Awake and asleep I resolved to
keep my notebook safely to hand and pocket.*

*My fellows quickly observed that I was the wrong sort, that is, the
right one. And there's me thinking that uniforms erase class differences.
Though ostensibly indistinguishable from my peers it took no discrimination whatsoever to identify me as Other. How? The usual. Accent.
Carriage. Background. A toff. That toff. They'd heard of me. The word
got round. Some of them thought it quite acceptable to murder one's
missus. More than a few had. But mine was dying anyway, so why
knock her off? And if you do, why not just the old pillow-face? Quick,
foolproof even for such a fool as I. Then cop a plea, out in six months.*

They couldn't have read my diary entries even if they'd managed
to steal it, and had they done so, what value could they find in it,
or from it? Sell it to a newspaper with the sensational divulgations
that I hated the food, disdained the warden, and suffered from a
variety of digestive maladies, described so exactingly that even the
*Mail* would have rejected it, and me.

But to Miles, all such would be welcome, the messier the better.
What honour has a tragic hero if the circumstances of his fall are
diminished? Prometheus, pecked by a budgie? Ahab, casting for
trout? Miles would be keen to know the details exactly as I
recorded them, but I've been sufficiently humiliated during these
last years of trial and incarceration. I deserve a rest.

I made this point to Lucy, but like her mother, once an idea is
ensconced in her brain, it, she is relentless. And though I am rather
good at saying no, having done so much of it, even I get weary, and

anxious to have a simple life. I did not discourage Lucy sufficiently, and through her, Miles. Now that I am out if not about, he will pursue the subject, and me. I have had to promise Lucy, at least, to speak with him, thank God it couldn't be over lunch. If I cannot consistently say no to Lucy, I certainly can to the bloated preening Miles, whose eyes dew up at any mention of Suzy. Not grief, but memory, sufficiently pressing to keep my ire alive and my brain ticking over, and over again.

I stand under the shower for long minutes, the large glass fronted space, the opalescent white tiles, astonished by the reliable, adjustable heat of the water, the density, strength and arc of its spray, let it cover my scalp and ripple down my body, lean my forehead for a moment against the wall, almost smile. A new bar of Jo Malone soap is on the tray, and I lather myself with it liberally, before washing and conditioning my hair, rinsing and luxuriating. I am cleansed at last, dry myself with a large bath towel that is a miracle of whiteness and absorbent fluff, soon stand naked and, curiously, hopeful.

If I am to find Suzy, might this work, this foolish last resort? I leant against the bathroom door, and pressed my forehead to it, tried to breathe evenly. After a time I shifted my feet, put my heels closer together and my toes outwards, and soon pressed my groin to it as well. I grimaced at the emerging memory.

Suzy and I met and fell in love mind and body, but the arrival of the bawling Lucy comprehensively disturbed our emotional and physical attachment. Sleepless and unsettled, we would sometimes smirk at each other, to ask what it was we used to do with our days – whole days! – much less our nights. She was always more highly sexed than I – women are keener in bed – but even she desisted from making any demands. For some time after the birth her vagina was sore and her breasts ached, and my scant needs must have been a relief. Very occasionally I would look after myself, feeling mild humiliation after discharging my duty.

We were living in a flat in Winchester, ancient and attractive if you were an American tourist, but with all the attendant leakages and stoppages. The walls were damp, the plumbing unreliable, the draughts under the doors so constant that not even a plethora of stuffed sausage dogs could repel them. It was cold even when warmed by oil and storage heaters in the sitting room and bedroom. My duties at the College were less than onerous, teaching for some fifteen hours, deftly avoiding various administrative responsibilities, preferring even the confined life of a new parent to the clustered silliness of the senior common room and the dreary recurrent duties of a schoolmaster. One afternoon I popped home, having forgotten one of my exercise books, to find Suzy naked, forehead and groin pressed against the closed door to the bathroom, her buttocks weaving slowly.

'Shhh!' she said, as if there was something that I could possibly say, having discovered my wife having sex with a door. I watched for a few minutes, aware that it would be inappropriate and unwelcome to make any sort of movement, except perhaps to leave, which I most sincerely wished to do. But as I began to turn away, she whispered urgently.

'Get on the other side of the door! Take your clothes off, and press against it like I'm doing! Make our bodies align. Trust me. Do it now!'

She moved aside, and I went into the bathroom, dutifully removed my clothes, I'm quite biddable really, and replicated her posture, forehead and groin aligned where I supposed hers might be. It hurt, and I moved my head back a few inches so that my penis was conjugate with the paintwork, breathed deeply, did a few buttock sways, tried to fever my imagination and perhaps my body. Only connect. My neck hurt, my dick retracted, my mind recoiled. Having given this ludicrous posture a full five minutes, fully aware of Suzy's close and pressing invisible presence, but unexcited by it, I sat on the toilet seat, and leafed through a copy of the *TLS* from the magazine rack at its side, as any literate Tantric dropout might. From the other side of the door I soon heard a loud moan. Lucky Suzy, lucky door.

Repeating the posture these many decades later, what remains of my poor shrivelled appendage once again retreated further into my belly, but of Suzy there wasn't the slightest trace. Hardly a surprise, but the absurd re-enactment has been curiously agreeable. If no trace of her can be summoned, memories certainly can. I'll have to settle for those.

I clean my teeth with the new soft brush and tube of Aēsop toothpaste to soothe my aching gums, take out my soap and lather my face. The mirror reveals a skeletal mask, inversions and pockets of thin covering, blotch and pallor. My skin, which formerly adhered so warmly and intimate with my bone, now poached and separated, hangs from it. My arms and legs wattle, my buttocks are saggy folds semi-attached to my rear portions. Thank God I don't have breasts, it's disgusting to remember what they can become. Even mine, on my shrunken chest, reveal nipples no longer properly settled into their mooring, which is itself awry, and jiggles to the touch. I think of my former self. Of Suzy, young and replete, then lying on her deathbed, looking almost as I do now, with death dancing on my frame in anticipation.

I am now insufficiently steady to risk using my straight shaving razor. We weren't allowed them in prison, it would have caused daily showers of blood from the many slit throats. Even a safety razor, though, is better than a damned electric one, and I soon pat on some aftershave, the smell of which makes me heave, don my dressing gown, ready for the unanticipated trials of freedom.

The next of which is to dress myself. In my own choice of my own clothes, which are deployed exactly as they once were: my trousers, shirts, suits and jackets freshly pressed and hanging in my wardrobe, socks and underwear in my drawers, pullovers in the drawers below, shoes polished and aligned on the floor of the wardrobe. I gaze at these riches dumbfounded, as if they were props in some Edwardian theatrical performance.

I dress slowly, smoothing each garment, my fingertips encountering distant memories, put on soft underpants, a fine cotton shirt from Turnbull & Asser, mid-blue, and a pair of moleskin trousers, grey, cashmere socks, charcoal, and a pair of lighter-weight leather slip-ons, black. I'd put away the brogues, which felt heavy and unnatural when I took my first steps, unsteady as a toddler. An easy metaphor offered itself: could I take these first steps, can I step back, or forward, into my old, or new, life? Care once again whether I should have chosen one sort of shoe or another, to go with the grey trousers? Stride once again into the life of an elderly aesthete, savouring the many things which made up my former life, and self?

My gait is not entirely to be trusted, my shanks attenuated to the point of atrophy, my balance unreliable. On her final visit before I was released, Lucy was distressed by my physical state – 'decline', she labelled it – and insisted that when I got home I must go for a walk every day. But ascending the single flight of stairs yesterday left me breathless, and today my legs ache. Going outside in a spirit of adventure, even of compliance, is rather beyond me.

I looked in the full-length mirror on the inside door of the wardrobe and studied the reflection, unrecognisable. I don't mean some vapidity of 'the clothes maketh a new man' variety. I mean I saw *someone else*. A stranger. The former James Darke is unreflected, perhaps never to return. Who am I to say? Who am I, now? What have I become? What ghost now inhabits this faltering machine?

But even machines have to eat, that's how they keep functioning. Fuel. Eat something, as ever and previous. My bowl of cereal gloop sits on the kitchen table, soggier now, perhaps more digestible. I put on the kettle, drop two teaspoons of Assam tea into my teapot, coffee unimaginable, add boiling water, stir gently and leave it for five minutes while I contemplate my breakfast, which sits accusingly on the table. I'd hardly had enough in the middle of the night to give it a fair go, woozy as I was.

Oats, raisins, sultanas, dates, hazel and Brazil nuts, deep creamy yoghurt, bananas that will taste like banana. I stare at the bowl, differentiating the one from the other, as if studying a chessboard, lean forward as if it were my move, peer so closely that I risk getting yoghurt on my nose, sniff deeply, and lift my head, puzzled. There's a phrase for the sensation, isn't there, though I've had little use for it. The cereal *smells good.*

I put a bit of stuff into my mouth, held my breath as I interrogated the unaccustomed mixture of textures and flavours burdening my tongue, moved them about from side to side and front to back, swallowed. If I could have repeated the process for the next hour I would have, not because I was starting to enjoy the cereals, remembering things past, but because with every slow mouthful I could delay calling Lucy. She is an early riser, as most parents with four-year-olds are, and will be waiting impatiently for my call. If she felt obliged to ring me first I would regret it.

What's that infernal machine called? I consult Lucy's note to remind myself. *Alexa.* I sit at my desk, stare at the screen, does one need to make eye contact, and speak as slowly as if to a foreigner, a child, or a robot.

'Alexa, ring Lucy.'

A blue light whirls, and a ringing sound ensues. The screen lights up, and to my astonishment and horror there is Lucy's face.

'Dad! Is that you? I can't see you, you're too much to the side, try to sit in front of the screen ...'

She can see me? It's painful enough seeing her squashed disproportionate face – has her nose grown? – cramped onto the tiny screen, but I cringe at the thought that mine may appear similarly on hers. I'm hardly dressed for this occasion, and have a huge abrasion on my forehead that I do not wish to explain.

I will certainly fluff my lines. I hate the telephone at any time, and this new variety is purgatorial, yet another gadget for children.

'Dad? Dad! Can you hear me?'

I moved further to the side, presumably out of the range of the hidden camera, and at a sufficient angle that I hardly see Lucy either.

'Yes, yes, I can. Damn machine, I'm not used to . . .'

'You'll get the hang of it soon! It's so great. Hold on a sec and I'll call Rudy, he's having one of his usual lie-ins . . .'

'No, please. Wait! Lucy, this is all too new, I don't feel comfortable . . .'

'You will, you'll get used to it! It's going to be all that we have for the next whatever. Isn't it horrible? I feel so dreadful that we can't hug and be together and celebrate and hug some more . . .'

At which point, fortuitously, my stomach began to growl and to cramp, a response I suppose both to the unaccustomed ingestion of the cereal, and the incipient emotional intimacy.

'Lucy! Darling! I'll ring you right back!'

'Dad? Dad!'

I don't know how you hang up an Alexa, there doesn't seem to be any button that says OFF, so I switched it off at the mains, and rushed to the lavatory, about which I will write no more, though there is much I might say. The blessed privacy, the firm wooden seat, the luxury of the paper . . . It gave me sufficient time to compose myself, and to make a plan. However much I wished to avoid talking with Lucy – too soon, too new, too raw, too unaccustomed – I could hardly fail to ring her back. I would use the new mobile for that.

'Darling Lucy, sorry about that. Can you hear me OK now?'

There was one of those tiny pauses that signals a big feeling.

'Yes, I can. I'm sorry . . .'

'So am I but . . .'

'. . . that you don't like Alexa. It takes getting used to but that can wait. The main thing is you're home! Tell me how you're feeling and getting on?'

'Darling, the thing I feel most is abject gratitude for the way you've left the house, and for all the goodies. It's so kind of you, no, not kind, so loving, it made all the difference . . .'

'I'm so glad, thanks.'

'. . . because it's been surprisingly complex, and odd, and unsettling, being transported so abruptly from that to this. I thought it would be simple, and simply delightful, but it's hard, re-entering this form of life that I had almost forgotten.'

The slight pause suggested that she didn't understand what I meant. I wasn't saying, was I, that I had actually forgotten how I once lived? Yet that is almost what occurred: my body had forgotten its former circumstances. My nose, my eyes, my skin, my fingers, my stomach, quailed at the unaccustomed newness, yes, newness, of my homecoming. Lucy would be sensing that this panoptic unease included her, certainly seeing her, even talking to her. Oh, so I needed a period of quiet and withdrawal? *Again!* I could hear her exclaiming inwardly.

'I'm so sorry, Dad. I knew it would be hard, I've been reading a book about it.'

'A book? About what?'

'Well, you know. Being released. It can be a difficult process . . .'

Horrid term, horrid process, horrid phone call.

'It is. Let's leave it to unfold. I'll ring you tomorrow, and I'm sure it will be getting smoother . . .'

It won't be. She knew it.

'All right, of course. I love you.'

'I love you too.'

What to do, do next? I had a day in front of me unburdened by routine or requirement, free to do whatever I wished, I could even go out the door into the viral air, go for a walk, or to forage for provisions. But I have no need of either. No need of anything, or nothing. I had supposed it would suit me, but instead I feel as if I've been abandoned, no one to tell me what to do and when, and how to do it, neither rule nor structure. I suppose I might try to read something, better yet try to write, this perhaps.

I descended to the kitchen to pour myself a large glass of Vichy water, as salty as the wretched Perrier, but with an underlying and balancing minerality that suggested the back notes of good Meursault. To call this 'water', like the tap residue that filled our cups in prison, is a serious category mistake. I was swishing this liquid round my mouth contemplatively when interrupted by the ringing of the phone upstairs. I did not answer it. The water pooled on my palate until with an effort I swallowed it. Water, just water. What is happening to me?

It was surely Lucy, ringing my new phone number, but the message revealed that it was, in fact, Jonathan Cooper. I'd hardly seen him during my years of incarceration, because it took the first two of them for his relationship with Lucy to prosper, and in any case I was not disposed to meet him. He felt himself responsible for my plight, and his presence made us both feel worse. Though he was my lawyer, and had argued my case, it was I who insisted, against his passionate advice, to plead not guilty to a charge of murdering Suzy on her deathbed, rather than accepting and pleading guilty to the lesser charge of manslaughter.

I went to prison because I chose to defend an indefensible position, and in paying the cost felt that I had at least tried to make my point, and got some publicity for it. The ways in which we allow our loved ones to suffer at the last is morally intolerable; we don't let our pets suffer in such a manner. We English love our dogs more than our spouses, not only when one or the other is dying. A dog is so much less trouble than a loved one, infinitely faithful and adoring, begging to be bidden, single and simple-minded in fealty. Most owners admire these canine qualities, I detest them. I have no need of a fawning companion, an adoring acolyte.

So, a moral example, was I? A bit of a martyr? It was a mistake, as all friends and family had insisted. I wonder if lurking at the back of my mind, as so frequently in those days, was the figure of Oscar, who was offered the opportunity to catch the night train to France and to evade his sentence, but instead lingered over drinks with friends at the Cadogan Hotel, until he was collared and led away. Damn fool. He came to regret it bitterly. So did I.

Jonathan and Lucy were careful to keep their growing attachment secret, to save Rudy the double trauma, I think it's called, of losing his father and his precipitate replacement with a stranger. Lucy was never likely to forgive Sam his role in my exposure and arrest: if he hadn't blabbed about his father-in-law's mercy killing of his wife, in the presence of the therapy group of grievers that he was leading, then I would never have been charged. Once I went to prison, Sam had to go.

It was for the best, it worked out well. Sam had been so comprehensively ostracised and humiliated by Lucy that the separation, much as it hurt, must have been a relief. He moved back to Sheffield, which he should never have left, indeed which he never did leave, and married some local lass. Lucy tells me that his career is flourishing, and that he has published a guide to the grieving process – his speciality, though he knows little enough about it – entitled *Good Grief.* I now think of him as SamWise, after that fat stupid hobbit.

This being the modern world, and SamWise having his fair share of Northern canniness, he soon located a way of monetising his speciality. Not by charging by the hour or day for accessing his wisdom-skills, exorbitant though such charges would have been. No, he and an architect friend invented a form of, I'm not sure what to call it, not 'dwelling' but a prefabricated wooden construction of a four-metre-square room, without windows but with a sloping glass roof. It was a meeting place, chairs went round the sides, and the occupants communed together to express their sorrows. At first it was called a Grief Module, but there is a market for more than grief, there is also misery, narcissism, self-absorption, schizophrenia, personality and anxiety disorder, premature ejaculation or none at all, sex or substance addiction, low or high self-esteem, and numerous further varieties of mental or physical dysfunction, many of whose adherents enjoy an intense get-together. *Thank you for sharing!*

The name of the prefab room was soon changed to Recovery Module, and sales tripled. To my astonishment it was highly profitable, and got a lot of publicity. That SamWise could have an idea at all was rather surprising, and though this was hardly a good one (it was fatuous and exploitative) at least it caught on. The newly bereaved and/or neurotic rather like getting together in such austere circumstances, though unlike Quakers in their spare environments, these occupants are unsuited for quiet contemplation. They are moved to talk, a lot, and to listen, a little. I gather this is common in the group therapy world. Sam's cube caught on, various institutions, sanatoria and religious groups bought one, even the occasional daft celebrity had one for purposes of spiritual withdrawal and contemplation. All reported excellent psychic and spiritual results, though how you would quantify them is unclear. SamWise would gaze into the distance thoughtfully, and say, *On a scale of one to ten.*

It went jolly well, until it went into liquidation: once the pandemic spread, and rules about social distancing were strictly enforced, there was hardly anything more likely to spread the virus than a dozen people crying and choking and sputtering about their many trials. Tears and orders dried up, it was all over.

Sam wrote to me several times when I first went to prison, letters full of goodwill and contrition that I didn't answer, of course. I'd told him that I forgave him before my trial, there was no need to repeat the sentiment. But within a week of arriving home I had a letter from him which expressed the hope that, given my new freedom from care, I might consider answering him. I can forgive him the stupidity of supposing that once the prison gates are opened, care is banished. What would he know about it? But in his new incarnation as entrepreneur (failed) and author (banal) he is increasingly inclined to treat his many and portentous pronouncements reverently. He sees himself as a leading light in the grief darkness, and respects himself accordingly.

The letter contained a proposal. He was setting up – 'curating', he called it – a weekend workshop based on his 'highly regarded' *Good Grief* volume, at which there would be various important speakers, the major one of whom would be himself. Would I care to join him, he enquired, in presenting a session about Assisted Dying, based on The Case of Suzy Moulton, in which both of us described our roles in the drama, and subsequent reflections about them?

The good thing about receiving a letter, rather than an email, is that you can tear it up, or crumple it and aim for the wastepaper basket, processes more physically and psychologically satisfying than hitting a DELETE button. I crumpled and tossed (missed, of course, I always miss) and would have thought no more of it, except that I did. It put me into a spin so prolonged that I spent part of it looking at Sam's laughable new website, which his letter had referenced: *drsamparkincounsellor.com*. I didn't, of course, read the bilge. As if it were a comic book – it was! it was! – I concentrated on the pictures. There were images of multiple versions of his Module, in various locations and inhabited by rows of seated representatives of the emotionally wretched. But most arrestingly there were pictures of SamWise himself, giving lectures, leading seminars, walking, talking, and (yes, truly, that is how he described it) just *being* – meditating, communing, and self-actualising (I don't know what this means, as I can't work out what its opposite is).

He had lost weight, and now cultivated a lean, honed look, and most arrestingly, had grown a beard. Wise men have beards: sages, prophets, and seers are universally hairy. And so are therapists, who would like to be included in the pantheon of the truly enlightened, and are not. But then again no one is. There is no enlightenment, there's not enough light to enable anyone to hog a fat portion, the most any of us can do is to escape momentarily from the darkness. Except those of us who are content to reside there. It is harder to be blinded by the darkness than by the light.

I did not, of course, answer his letter. If I am an inaccurate tosser, he is a major one. It is, I suppose, a sign of a new-found confidence, or arrogance, in him that he should presume to suggest, *Let's get together: you can describe how and why you killed your wife, and I will convey how I dobbed you in.* He is now even more comprehensively objectionable than when married to my dear deluded Lucy, who once thought him manly and real, with a thoroughbred integrity born in the North Country. But he has at least maintained his close attachment to Rudy, who is now old enough to make train trips to Sheffield on occasional Saturday mornings to watch his beloved Blades, after which he spends the rest of the weekend with his father and new stepmother, whom he likes.

He is teased about this unworthy sporting attachment by the boys at his school, all either Arsenal or Spurs supporters. The first term he wore his Blades scarf to school until one morning he was almost strangled with it before it was taken from him, and its replacements regularly disappeared from the cloakroom.

He hates Arsenal and despises Spurs. I warn him that this may be taken as a sign of anti-Semitism in North London, but he has little idea what I mean, or perhaps he doesn't care. Most of his new friends are Jews. In the coming months he will be spending a great deal of his time, and my money, on the bar mitzvahs of his various brainy friends. Though he sympathises with the faith, he's shown no sign yet of wishing to convert, much as he resents his time going to school chapel and singing stupid hymns. At least they're in English, I observe, though he thinks they are all the worse for that, so fatuous are they. Except for 'Jerusalem'. He loves Blake, whom he regards as an old hippy, which to his generation is usually a term of disapprobation, though he uses it fondly. For his last birthday I bought him a facsimile edition of *Songs of Innocence and Experience,* many of which he can already recite by heart.

I made myself a pot of tea, and put it on a tray with a tiny ceramic jug of full milk, and carried it upstairs. I no more wished to speak with Jonathan than with my daughter – why was it not apparent to them that I would need, do need, some time to settle in and down? They know me. I'm like that: my own way and on my own terms. Thank goodness for the prevalent plague, which supplies the physical distances that I require, if not the emotional ones.

'Jonathan? It's James. I'm sorry I missed your call.'

'Thanks for ringing back.'

'Of course ... What can I do for you?'

'Well, first of all, welcome home! We're all so thrilled for you, and can't wait to get together.'

'Thank you. It's good to be home, and you've left it in the most welcoming condition ...'

'Of course!'

'But, this homecoming? It has rather surprised me, it's rather a shock.'

There was a silence at the end of the line, he was sensitively giving me time to explain myself, except that I had no desire to do so in further detail.

'I suppose it would be.'

'Yes.'

'Well, James, I'm ringing really just to say that Lucy, you know, she's very upset ...'

'I dare say. We all are. It doesn't just end, you know, getting out, getting home ...'

'I think I understand. We both do, but Lucy feels ...'

'I know how she feels, and she knows how I do. We will get

through this in good time, let's trust to that, and each other. She and I always find a way.'

'You're right, of course. It would have been so much easier if we could all be together physically!'

'It wouldn't. It's best this way. Let's let it unfold.'

'I think I understand . . .'

'Thank you. Give Lucy my love, and Rudy.'

'Goodbye, James.'

Alexa watched forlornly, abandoned. I switched on my computer, and gazed at the desktop files. If I couldn't or wouldn't talk to Lucy, I could at least read the stuff she'd organised for me. I'd need to stay clear of the file labelled 'HEALTH: URGENT', and check out the one that said 'CORRESPONDENCE AND THINGS TO DO'. I suppose that is what her letter referred to vaguely as 'plans', best get it over with: I neither have nor want any such.

I clicked on the yellow folder, and various document names appeared. 'MILES' I had no desire to open, 'PUBLISHERS' was unpromising. 'INTERVIEW REQUESTS', though, piqued my interest. Before my trial, when I was pursued by admirers, howling mobs, and various journalists, I rather enjoyed the occasional interview in the newspapers, and appearances on the telly. Schoolmasters, however retiring or retired, rather like a stage, we're used to captive audiences who write down what we say, however nonsensical. Though the presiding judge was unlikely to find my loquaciousness tolerable or even forgivable, I had nothing to lose.

Journalists, though, are not students, they cannot be dictated to. I was enjoined to be careful in their presence, as an unguarded phrase, taken out of context, can be damning. I didn't care. My whole effort was to be found guilty, and I had nothing to hide. Had I killed my wife? Yes. How did I justify that? She was dying and in great pain. I was proud of what I did. I wrote an essay entitled *Do You Love Your Dog More Than Your Wife?* which made the point rather elegantly, and served as a talking point for interviews.

I'd rather enjoy another bit of exposure. Not so much in support of the activities of the SMF, about which I am (though I would never say so to Lucy) indifferent. Suzy was gone, now she is goner still, and whatever attachment I had to her cause has faded with her memory. I cannot press myself against that door for ever, she's no longer on the other side. *Suzy doesn't live here any more.* And for the cause of Easeful Death, well, good luck to it, it can carry on without me.

Which doesn't mean that I have nothing further to say.

# Chapter 3

'I'm so glad you've agreed to do this, Dad! It will give you a chance to express yourself publicly, and to re-enter the world!'

I hardly knew what to say in the face of such provocative nonsense, so didn't respond. I do that a lot.

'The key thing is to pick the right person and the right medium for your interviews. I don't think you'd be comfortable on camera or Zoom, so maybe on the phone? Or, wait a minute, that's a bad idea, maybe it'd be best if they submit questions, and then you can answer them at your leisure, carefully?'

'I suppose so.'

I was expected, I imagine, to add some witless truism of the 'that will give me time to think' sort, but I'd had plenty of that. I know what I think. And I know what Lucy wants me to think: to foreground my commitment to the cause of assisted dying, to demonstrate that the price that I had paid was worth it, and that my fervour for the cause is undiminished. Enhanced, really.

'Thanks for sending me that list of journalists. I have a few ideas. First of all, no to the tabloids: they're the ones that attacked me so viciously when I was arrested and tried. Fuck them.'

'I quite agree!'

Not that I got wholehearted support from the broadsheets either. The *Guardian* was sniffy and superior, and the bloody

*Telegraph* patronised me. You know what? Mr Murdoch may be one of the Oz-beasties, but I have an atavistic respect for *The Times*, as if it were still the paper of record. I had a former teaching colleague at school, an orotund classicist of the wittiest, dullest sort, who was an ogler and surreptitious fondler of boys at a period in English culture when such activities garnered a shrug of amused toleration. We called him the Blimp of the Perverse, and often addressed him as 'Colonel', which he was mildly amused by, thinking it a reference to something upright in his bearing, not knowing the inwardness of the joke, or its happy relation to his name, Horniman.

My former colleague had written to me during my trial, to express admiration, solidarity, and warm regards, which of course I did not answer. I could now use our thin relations to approach his son Archibald, Features Editor at *The Times*, to whom I wrote to suggest that, perhaps, they might like to do something with me. Archibald took after his father. He had married well and conspicuously, fathered the occasional child, but spent his life foraging in the sexual undergrowth. His father was wont to confess, over a few glasses of sherry, that the boy was often in a touch of bother. I'm not clear why, but this seemed to me a good reason to choose him as my journalistic interlocutor. If things got tough, I could get tougher.

Horniman *fils* replied to my enquiry immediately and enthusiastically. What about an interview for their Sunday supplement? That would give me sufficient space, and exposure. Their features 'get picked up round the world!' He would 'hand over' the assignment to one Juliette Mayberry, 'a sensitive and intelligent girl with a congratulatory First from Oxford', a phrase that confirms that pompous arsery is genetically transmitted. She would soon 'make contact', as if she were some sort of visiting alien.

Which I suspect she is: calling a girl 'sensitive' waves the red flag, in a way that it would not do for a boy. We schoolmasters were aware of this on a daily basis. Boys are simple, and not in the least sensitive. Propelled by a lust for masturbation, large quantities of food and sport, they are easy enough to deal with. Occasionally the odd one would exhibit a taste for poetry or sodomy, often together, but they usually withdrew from both.

But girls, on the other hand, are – the alien metaphor is inescapable – a different form of life entirely, a different species. Obsessed by self-expression and presentation, they wear their clothes and accoutrements as if costumed, paint their faces as heavily as members of an Amazonian tribe in one of their obscure rituals. Unlike their male, what I would not call equivalents or even fellows, they do not have interests and enthusiasms, but opinions, feelings, beliefs and grievances, which align exactly with their *values*. I have never heard a boy put his hands on his hips and say, 'I find that offensive!' as if the very fact of an aggrieved response were sufficient reason for the offender to change his opinion. When I occasionally and mildly responded to such disapproval by saying that no one has a right not to be offended, I was greeted with the same incredulity and disdain that would result if I defined a woman as a person with a vagina.

I will be interested to hear from this quivering Mayfly, there may be some fun to be had in our supposed 'interview'. Of course, Lucy thinks I am in danger, and likely to be dangerous, because of my (former!) ignorance regarding politics and world affairs, where I am – or was – inclined to opinions which had little basis in either fact or thought. 'As long as they sound good!' Lucy would say, disapprovingly. And I have, to be fair, always preferred a well-turned phrase and an elegant narrative arc to something more prosaic, like a fact or an argument.

A mouthpiece, that's what she hopes I will be, that's the plan. For the last week she has been sending me lists of the achievements of the Foundation, their 'mission statements' and contacts with other such organisations in forty-eight countries 'round the world'. Where else would they be, round the moon? The website of the Suzy Moulton Foundation is full of this semi-literate corporate-speak, in itself sufficient to make me disavow any contact with them. I think it preferable if people are spared an agonising death, but after all, people die, whereas painful prose lives on and on.

What Lucy does not know, nor have I made it apparent to her, is that I am now, after four years of enforced idleness, tolerably well-informed about world affairs. There's not much to do in prison, except read, talk, listen to the wireless or gawp at the telly, and learn who is objecting to what. For someone as angry, desperate and indignant as I, this new world of the Gleefully Aggrieved was a revelation. What it lacked in intelligence and discrimination was compensated for by volume.

A few of my fellow inmates were surprisingly knowledgeable about the bleeding sores of the day. Their company and concerns were more congenial than the endless round of chatter about football and the racing results, and rubbish about their families, though curiously it was through a bit of family blather that my political appetite was sharpened.

*I am attempting to read Martin Luther King's memoirs from prison, trying not to look up, when I am joined by a large (very) West Indian, who plonks his tray down carelessly, water spilling from his glass. He is called Wally, though whether that is his name or nature is unclear.*

*Names get rearranged here, it's quite impossible to know who anyone actually is. Not that I care. I am already known as Darky, which may have drawn Wally to me in the first place. One glance at my reading matter rather confirms that we are of the same persuasion. He is serving time for 'aggravated assault', which is what he does when he's very aggravated. He says this with a rueful smile. I don't know the details, nor will I enquire.*

*Suzy would be studying his face. I use her eyes to bring her in, since she has so far refused even a moment's entry. I think she's sulking, she hates ugliness and poverty and lack. I look up at Wally, just a peek, nothing encouraging, capture the lustrous purple black of his cheeks, the eyes that want to laugh, the white teeth displayed between bites and smiles. He is unbearably friendly, it's impossible to put him off. I'm an object of interest. He wants to talk, he needs to talk, he hardly stops talking. And what he talks about is his family. He has no interest in mine, thank God. Neither have I.*

I am not expert in the *triste topiques du jour*, but I know a little, plenty really, and I have a lot of opinions. More than previously, just as well-framed, now with an adequate leavening of facts. Not alternative facts, such as a politician or indeed a novelist might have, but real ones, which are yet another endangered species. Like our former Jamaican immigrants.

Writing this makes me laugh. Not so much at my unexpected transformation, but at the trouble that it may cause. If I'm lucky.

*Wally wants to write his life's story. Too many of them would, if they could write, which Thank God they cannot, sometimes literally. Wally is the son of immigrants imported to do the work no Englishman was willing to do. Blacks. The new Irish. He thinks it's a great story, and that no one has told it. Which of course they have. I tried to dissuade him from what would be both a painful and a fruitless exercise, unaccompanied by catharsis, a term I explained to him, and that he rightly disdained.*

*Wally was volubly exercised by the case of Mr Floyd, a poor Black chap whose understandable reaction to having a policeman leaning on his neck for nine minutes was to announce repeatedly that he could not breathe, and then to demonstrate that this was true. An outpouring of sentiment accrued, and an inevitable new slogan was coined.* **Black Lives Matter!** *It was immediately made clear that the rejoinder* **All Lives Matter!** *– the very basis of received religion – must be regarded as a form of racism. I didn't entirely follow the line of thought, which had the clear* *implication that some lives matter more than others, and some races more than others. Only a nitwit could agree with this.* **BLM** *Buttons appeared around the prison, who knows how, and as soon as they are displayed they are quickly confiscated, soon to reappear. I refused to wear one. No, thank you: I would only wear one that read* **NLM**.

*Soon enough there will be the great culling, as the winds and the seas and the temperatures rise and the great dispossessions begin. It will be preponderantly Blacks who die in their hundreds of millions. Their lives will not have mattered sufficiently, and no sanctimonious 'taking the knee', no slogans, would have saved them.*

Wally is only in prison temporarily, after which he will be deported to somewhere in the West Indies that he has never seen or resided in. He has no adequate paperwork, dating back for the requisite number of years, to make his case, and after repeated entreaties to the officials of the Home Office, when he was told that his appeal had been rejected and that he was subject to deportation, he punched the offending jobsworth on the nose. You wouldn't wish to be punched on the nose by Wally, you'd have some trouble finding it again.

I've had an email from Jonathan, confirming that *The Times* has accepted my proposed terms for an interview, and that the result would be published in their Sunday *Magazine*. They have agreed to submit questions in advance, and to print (though not necessarily in full) my responses as written, with any editorial changes needing my explicit approval. Any introductory comments, prefacing the interview, would also be subject to approval.

Assuming that I would find this acceptable, Jonathan has forwarded their list of questions, though he says that I can reject any that I don't wish to address, and suggest further ones that I do. The list of questions, which are banal, is not extensive, thus allowing answers of some length. They will need it. Had they been framed by one of my A-Level group, I would have returned them for further consideration. I almost did so with this semi-competent journalist, the young woman of no distinction, who has been passed the job by her creepy editor. But I prefer an ignorant interlocutor to a knowing one with an agenda. Someone suggested that I should submit myself to the scrutiny of Ms Lynn Barber, whose columns I adore because she has a merciless eye and accompanying turn of phrase. Why her subjects agree to be eaten alive is a mystery that passeth comprehension.

I considered revising the submitted questions, but demurred because I knew more or less what I wanted to say, and they would give me adequate basis on which to do so. As any politician knows, though few teachers do, it is not necessary to answer a question on the terms on which it is offered: you begin with what you wish to say, and tailor it to resemble an answer.

Jonathan and Lucy agree that it doesn't so much matter what the questions are, it's the answers that are crucial. They are both anxious: he that I may say something libellous, she that I may say something typical: unguarded, oppositional, and self-regarding. I have assured Jonathan that he has nothing to worry about, and Lucy that I will be as careful as I can. She will recognise this as no concession whatsoever. They both insist, or beg, that I will submit my responses to them before I send them to *The Times*. I have not answered this request, because I will not. They think they can manage me? Cleverer people than either of them have tried and failed.

There is no reason to take the questions in order, but I am an orderly person, so started at the beginning:

**Having served your sentence, have you any reason now to reassess the conduct that led to it?**

I didn't have sufficient strength for my conviction, and nothing will put me back together again. I do not regret having helped my wife to die, which was the right thing to do. But it was foolish of me to plead not guilty to murder, in order to stand trial and make my case, since I was not allowed to do so because of a hostile judge and aggressive prosecutor. I could have pleaded guilty to manslaughter, and might have avoided prison. Like Oscar Wilde, I chose to go to prison; like him, I did so in ignorance of the conditions I would encounter; like him, I suffered the consequences of this foolishness, and continue to do so.

*Is your support for the cause of assisted dying strengthened or diminished by your incarceration?*

In the UK we are lagging behind much of the world in our attitudes to this subject. Even (many of) the United States have more humane legislation than poor, hidebound England. If I felt the Church still had any power, I would blame it. But the responsibility rests squarely with those of us – so very many – who are incapable of challenging our cultural and legal norms, and urging change when it is necessary. The reason for this torpor? Poor education. No one is taught to think any more.

*The world has changed enormously since you were incarcerated . . . How much did this matter to you in your confined surroundings?*

Prison walls shrink your world. Most of my fellow inmates cared more about the football results than about climate change. I both envied and admired this. But, for myself, there was little enough to do in prison, and I found myself increasingly interested in current affairs. The brink of extinction is more worrying than the brink of relegation? I'm indifferent to either. The human race was a biological error, and no more deserves to survive than the poor innocent dinosaurs, who made a better fist of things, and did not cause their own demise as a species. We had our chance, we fucked it up.

***What do you regard as the most important single issue of our time?***

Thinking, respecting facts, and arguing properly: cultivating the ability to distinguish an argument from an opinion, and a good argument from a bad one. Everything deplorable and disgusting about the modern world flows from our cultural failure to insist on intellectual standards, which are undercut daily not merely on social media, but in the mainstream media. Everything is now a motto or a slogan, designed to promote a movement. Get Brexit Done! MAGA! Me Too! Black Lives Matter! Trans Women are Women! Right and Left in full accord: reduce an issue to a slogan, something to proclaim and to shout, and then excoriate the non-conformers.

Where is dear William Blake when we most need him? 'The man who never alters his opinion is like standing water, and breeds reptiles of the mind.'

Having got this far, I paused to read my responses, none of which had flowed trippingly. It was a waste of time. My answers felt stale and second-hand, and though designed to provoke, there would be scant pleasure in that. When I wrote my little manifesto in favour of assisted dying it caused something of ... not a storm exactly, but a lot of wind and some drenching rain. I had expected to revel in that, but hated it, especially when the trolls began to threaten Lucy and her family. No sense in repeating the process, and the mistake.

I wrote to the innocent young Mayfly to thank her for her most revealing set of questions, but said that I found no pleasure in answering them, and was withdrawing from our little project. I would have added, 'with regret', but all I felt was relief. When I announced this to Jonathan and to Lucy, they felt it too. I am such a loose cannon that I am most at risk of shooting myself, which is an amusing misuse of this metaphor.

Mayfly replied immediately, to express her regret. Perhaps the suggested format was wrong? Might we do something over the phone, or might I compose and answer my own questions? This was canny of her. I am a man of many words, surely the offer to deploy them as I chose might be tempting? A product of a certain sort of education, and view of the world, I need to make myself heard. Literature, it was once maintained – and I signed on dutifully – is potentially a moral force. Though I have abandoned the belief, the instincts abide, and if books are an unsafe refuge, they are nevertheless an habitual one.

In prison I had plenty of time, I was serving it, to compile a reading list defined by two attributes. First, all of the books would be composed by writers in prison, and second, they might be mined by the unwitting and insufficiently sceptical as a potential source of wisdom, and consolation. This would involve a lot of skimming, because most such books are long-winded and grindingly earnest. I called this project PROSE AND CONS. A few of my fellow inmates thought this was amusing, once I explained it to them.

An expected offshoot of this too worthy effort was that I began to detest most of what I read, because the default position of the literary incarcerated is to seek some wisdom which might transform their misery into philosophical acceptance. Once you see the pattern, it is ubiquitous and supremely boring. My prison diary itself, an occasional form of amusement if not of consolation, soon acquired some of the lifelessness of my sources, and though I was aware of it, I found it impossible to provide an account of my days that didn't reflect and embody their colourless drear. I may have been stripped of my freedom and health, but to be delivered of my prose, formerly so sprightly and lively, was insupportable. I could hardly abide the very person who regularly recorded the tiresome events of a tired life.

The only antidote to this, ironically, involved a secondary

writing project: if I had to wade through the witless drivel of the imprisoned sages, I could quote from them selectively and begin to compile a commonplace book, in which I might subject their fatuities to the disdain that they deserved. Scorn brings out the best of me, emotionally and stylistically, focuses my eye, hones my ear, transports my tongue. As Oscar said in his *De Profundis*, 'One sometimes feels that it is only with a front of brass and a lip of scorn that one can get through the day at all.'

I could not employ such rampant dismissiveness in my ongoing prison diary, much as I might have wished and however obvious the opportunities, for fear that shabby volume might fall into the wrong hands, for we had nothing but wrong hands in HM Prison. Such things are best kept private. Had I satirised the Jocks and Wallies, I would have ended up searching for my nose, whereas my chosen sages were only a danger in that they might bore me to death.

It wasn't long before I began, unexpectedly, to take genuine interest in this reading, and used my diary to record the bits of nonsense with which the few literate convicts have consoled themselves. This habit provided me with one of the few pleasures of my first year in prison, and I contemplated the project of compiling some sort of booklet to send to my friends, perhaps at Christmas. Something finely printed in the private press manner, elegant and superior.

The only problem with this amusing little fantasy was that it would require me to continue reading a large amount of worthily unworthy tripe. I could imagine Suzy laughing sardonically. She'd been a caustic commentator on the Sages of English literature (at which she'd rather excelled as an undergraduate, receiving the top First of her year) proclaiming that Wordsworth, Dickens, George and T. S. Eliot, all that lot – were 'shitslingers', whose portentous words led the unwary astray onto the path of righteousness. I found no reason, perusing the words of the prison-bound worthies, to dispute this judgement.

I could get even with them for that, and perhaps recover some ease in my writing. My head is forever stuffed with words. Words are all I have. I may employ them as mere recording devices, but sometimes they merely want to come out and amuse themselves, to have fun in the word playground, tilt on the seesaw, swing on the swings, twirl round the roundabouts, climb the slides and wee all the way down, in this prelapsarian linguistic Garden of Eden, before the fall into seriousness and moral rectitude.

I retrieved my diary, found the final draft of this little project, typed it out and puckishly sent it to the sensitive girl at *The Times*, saying that it encapsulated most of what I had learned and felt in prison, and that it might interest her readers. Perhaps she might write a brief introduction, explaining the circumstances, before printing my piece?

# DE PROFUNDIS

## A COMMONPLACE BOOK
## OF VARIOUS COMMONPLACES

*'Most of the propositions and questions to be found in philosophical works are not false but nonsensical.' (Ludwig Wittgenstein)*

*'There is no sentiment so noble that it does not stand in need of correction.' (James Darke)*

I have prepared this *jeu d'esprit* as a Christmas or Easter Offering, though I have scant regard for these grisly occasions. Many of my quotations are from Christians, their attitude to adversity mis-informed by the delusion that all will come out for the best.

The citations are from books written by authors in prison, which is often regarded, by those who have never been incarcerated, as a congenial location for contemplation and composition. These few quotations amply demonstrate that whatever happens in one's cell, increased discrimination isn't one of them.

I have thus added a few corrective responses to each entry.

§§§

*'I tremble with pleasure when I think that on the very day of my leaving prison both the laburnum and the lilac will be blooming in the gardens, and . . . the air shall be Arabia for me. To regret one's own experiences is to arrest one's own development. To deny one's own experiences is to put a lie into the lips of one's own life.'*

(Oscar Wilde, *De Profundis*)

\*Oscar's 'poetry' is replete with such lifeless tropes. What he was yearning for, on leaving prison, was not nature but city life, a salon, and an adoring audience. And something to put 'into the lips' – some delicacies, a draught of champagne, and a few dicks.

§§§

*Stone walls do not a prison make,*
*Nor iron bars a cage:*
*Minds innocent and quiet take*
*That for an hermitage.*
(Richard Lovelace, *To Althea, from Prison*)

\*After Lovelace was released, the discerning Althea, worried what marriage to her delusional swain might envisage by way of domestic arrangement, married someone who could distinguish the Tower of London from a manor in Gloucestershire.

§§§

*'Because of my imprisonment, most of the believers here have gained confidence and boldly speak God's message without fear . . .*

*Together as one body, Christ reconciled both groups [Jews and Gentiles] to God by means of his death on the cross, and our hostility toward each other was put to death.'*

(The Apostle Paul, *Letters from Prison*)

\*Typical apostolic fare, overblown, unlikely and unverifiable. Paul, or Saul to use his proper Jewish name, was a crippled ginger dwarf, who needed elephantine opinions to garner attention. The triumph of the little man!

§§§

*'Let valour end my life . . . Speaking much is a sign of vanity, for he that is lavish with words is a niggard in deed.'*

(Sir Walter Raleigh, *History of the World*)

\*Who completed only one of the projected five volumes of his magnum opus, because an axe is more efficient in ending life than valour.

§§§

*'Purification being highly infectious, purification of oneself necessarily leads to the purification of one's surroundings.'*

(Mahatma Gandhi, *An Autobiography: The Story of My Experiments with Truth*)

\*Anyone who's been in prison knows that you don't 'purify' it by 'purifying' yourself. Neither is possible. The only thing that's 'infectious' about this nonsense is that other people might catch it.

§§§

*'To judge from the notions expounded by theologians, one must conclude that God created most men simply with a view to crowding hell.'*

(Marquis de Sade, *Juliette*)

*Consolation through fantasy? Of course, most men are neither imaginative nor energetic enough to go to hell. Nor will they go to heaven, where those with low energy reside. Sade would not have cared where most women go, except down-side up and tied to the bedposts.

§§§

*'Among wise men there is no place at all left for hatred. For just as weakness is a disease of the body, so wickedness is a disease of the mind. And if this is so, since we think of people who are sick in body as deserving sympathy rather than hatred . . .'*

(Boethius, *The Consolations of Philosophy*)

*Bobo's overarching beneficence is insidious. We need hate as much as we do love. Hitler did not need sympathy or pity, he needed to be exterminated, like a roach.

§§§

*'In a real sense all life is inter-related. All men are caught in an inescapable network of mutuality, tied in a single garment of destiny. Whatever affects one directly, affects all indirectly . . .'*

(Martin Luther King, *Letters from Birmingham Jail*)

*Any sentiment that begins 'in a real sense', isn't real and makes no sense. What follows is mush: spurious 'networks' and ill-fitting 'garments'. Pulpit-speak, sloppy and misleading: an exhortation windbag-piping the credulous on their journey to the Broken Promised Land.

§§§

'. . . a man there was, though some did count him mad, the more he cast away the more he had.'

**(John Bunyan, *The Pilgrim's Progress*)**

*Actually, he was mad.

§§§

## FOR SUZY,

### From whom I learned so much:

*All they're doing, all these wise men, is showing how deeply they can penetrate, how rigid are their principles, how large their understanding: dickslingers! The more elegantly and compellingly the wise men present the results of such a quest, the less convincing they are to anyone with a brain, by which I mean a cunt.*

Retrieved, edited, ready for transmission! Though Little Miss Sensitive will find this offensive, and could hardly print it, she would be wrong if she thought it directed particularly at her and her sort. It is for everyone, and will offend most, save those still able to think for themselves.

I did not expect to hear from the Mayfly, not even a hands-on-hips harrumph. I received, instead, a reply from the loathsome Archie, who sent me an email (cc. his editor, Jonathan and Lucy):

*Dear James Darke,*

*I am in receipt of your submission to my colleague Juliette Mayberry, who has passed it on to me for comment. I have read it with some care. You have of course, suffered the many privations of imprisonment, and my enquiries confirm that your health, both physical and mental, has deteriorated, as might well might happen to a man of your age and background. It is only by taking this into account that I am able to*

61

*understand somewhat, if not to forgive, your disgraceful submission to my young colleague, who was dreadfully disturbed to be exposed to such blatant prejudice and misjudgement. Your use of the C-word is disgraceful. That you should express such extravagant contempt for many of the greatest thinkers is more than regrettable. It suggests an impaired capacity for thought and respect for truth, in one who claims that those values are most dear to him.*

*We will not, of course, be publishing your statement. No one would, it's intellectually fatuous, preening and obscene, the stuff of moronic bloggers.*

*I will be asking our editorial board to withdraw our support for the Suzy Moulton Foundation, which I regret. It is a good cause, and you were once a good man.*

*Yours faithfully,*

*Archibald Horniman*

I received this communication at 10.23 in the morning. Having perused it, I began to count. I had reached 123 when a message arrived, not from Lucy but from Jonathan. 'Please send copy of your submission. J.' I did, and started counting again, aware that, such was the quality and depth of my *De Profundis*, that it would take him time to read and to savour properly.

I'd reached 311 when the phone rang.

'James! Jonathan.'

'Indeed.'

'Well, this is rather surprising. You promised you would clear any submission you made with Lucy and me first . . .'

'I did not. You asked me to. I never agreed.'

'In any case what's done is done. I have read your piece quickly, though Lucy hasn't yet, says she's not up to it just now, with the children demanding everything, and home-schooling in progress. So I am talking just for myself, you understand?'

'I do.'

'Well, it's funny, apt and memorable, all those take-downs of the greatest and the goodest. I love thinking of those pompous arses at *The Times* — dreadful newspaper, ghastly people — wetting themselves with indignation. Typical oppositional James Darke stuff. I hope you will now put it in a drawer, and leave it.'

'Well, thank you, I'm glad you caught the spirit of it. But I'm concerned about the threat to withdraw support for the Foundation.'

'They already have!'

'Oh, God, I'm so sorry!'

'They offered us a thousand pounds last year, which we declined because it takes more money than that to qualify as a Corporate Sponsor, which is what they wanted. They haven't invested at all, just given us a few mentions and plugs. Fuck them!'

'Amen! What about Lucy? Will she be upset?'

'Of course, you know that. You're going to get a mouthful, for sure. Not so much because of the Foundation, but because so much of what you say, and imply, is anathema to her. Your way is not hers: you interrogate ideas, all ideas, sceptically and ironically. Lucy doesn't have an ironic bone in her body.'

'You may well say!'

'To tell the truth, James, I admire that in her: scepticism is a useful tool for taking things apart. But you can't build anything with it.'

'I suppose that's true, if you're sufficiently literal. But what you can do is create a cultural atmosphere in which ideas don't run wild, in which each has to be justified ... and if you don't think of that as "building something", then I despair.'

'Sorry to let you down. I see what you mean. I hope you see what I do.'

He sounded weary, and disappointed.

'Please tell Lucy to ring me when she reads it, and perhaps to keep an open mind?'

'I can assure you that her mind is every bit as open as yours! I think you and she need to have a serious talk ...'

'My dear Jonathan, I detest "serious talk", it's so earnest and one-dimensional. The only talks worth having – if any – demand irony and playfulness and a sense that truth emerges imperceptibly only at the edges of things. Anything that announces itself as The Truth is not, and cannot be. Wise men, and stupid ones, if you can even tell the difference, simplify things, and then proclaim them.'

'Well, that's very James Darke-ish, how very agreeable. It is that attitude, you know, that landed you in prison!'

This was a bit much, though I did not say so. What had 'landed' me in prison was, in part, Jonathan's incapacity to mount a proper argument in my defence. With the attendant irony that I neither wanted nor needed him to do so, since I wished to be found guilty. Who could make sense of such things?

'If you say so ...'

'I do! And now you're about to repeat the process, and get yourself, and Lucy, into trouble by blabbing away when you might, in all conscience, stifle yourself. For everyone's sake, but mostly for your own. Why enter the public arena again, and generate yet more hostility?'

'Why? Because for the short time to come I still have a life, and a self, and a voice. And no one seems to appreciate that I am, if apparently egregiously oppositional, having some fun, and amusing myself.'

'I can assure you, James, that Lucy will not be amused!'

'Morally serious people rarely are. Tell her I adore her and send a big kiss. And try to talk her out of this "serious talk" nonsense.'

'Ha! Have a good day, James.'

I went downstairs to the kitchen, broke three eggs into a mixing bowl, added a tiny amount of cream, some salt and pepper, and set them cooking over a low flame in a saucepan on the hob, while I cut two slices of sourdough and popped them in the toaster, ground the coffee beans, then stirred the eggs.

There remained my rejoinder to Archibald Horniman, who had been named after John Betjeman's Oxford teddy bear, and looked the part, a scruffy, dangling affectation. He detested his obvious nickname:

*My Dear Archie,*

*Thank you for your prompt response to my email, it's so lovely to encounter such efficiency in these slovenly days. I am sorry that* The Times *does not wish to avail itself of my musings, which have so upset your sensitive young colleague. I assure you she will get over it, and move on to offences more distressing than mine own.*

*Yours faithfully,*

*James Darke*

Having composed this restrained and elegant missive to the crapulous human teddy, I repaired to Amazon to research a suitable anonymous gift to send in acknowledgement of his supercilious dismissal of my efforts. If anyone is going to do supercilious dismissals round here, it's me.

My search located two strong possibilities: first, a product called Barrel-o-Slime, which 'flows like liquid jelly but is not sticky. You can tear it apart but it will rejoin perfectly. Imagine a liquid that isn't wet!' And second, and equally compelling, 'SHENZHENDAKANG Fake Poop: Realistic Poop Designs, with Fake Turd for Real Laughs, Perfect Gag Gift.'

It's impossible to choose between these perfect make-you-gag gifts. Always err on the side of generosity! I ordered a box of each, and instructed that they be sent, properly gift-wrapped, to Archie's office at *The Times*. He has apparently consorted with and offended so many dubious types, that he won't know which of them is responsible for the parcels. I wouldn't even be on his longlist of suspects.

I included two unsigned cards that read 'Sweets for the sweet' and 'Honey for my honey'.

# Chapter 4

Apparently it's called an 'underlying health condition': which renders one more than likely to fall prey to an itinerant malady or virus. I used to think of this as life itself, having had friends and relations die suddenly and unaccountably. But our governing buffoons have now assigned the label to specific citizens, and according to Lucy's 'HEALTH' file, I am now a certified underlier. Certainly I will be soon enough. This means that I am doubly enjoined not to venture into the treacherous world of contagion except in certain very limited circumstances, such as a visit to a doctor or hospital. As I understand it, this also means that my isolation must be absolute. I hope that's right, because it already is metaphorically, and I'm delighted that our leaders have made it literal. Nobody out, nobody in. Story of my life.

Newly returned from the land of the living dead, I have only the sketchiest of recent health records, and my bumbler of a GP having fallen off his perch, I don't have access to a regular medical practitioner. My firm intention is to keep it that way. I have long regarded my home as a fitting place in which to die, and will require no more assistance in this process than my own final decision that the time has come to move on, or if this suggests some destination, then perhaps I mean move out, or away. No forwarding address. I helped Suzy on her final journey (are vapid travel metaphors inevitable here?) but will require no such for mine, having made adequate plans for a satisfyingly fatal cup of tea, honey, and drugs, and the long goodbye.

Lucy suspects this, of course, how could she not when so much of her endeavour is directed towards helping people in a practical way to make this final decision for themselves? I am the exception to her moral position: the rest of the world can shuffle off this coil whenever and however, but it is my job description to carry on. Her major anxiety, and project, now concerns my 'wellness' – God forgive her the concept or my using it, which I do only ironically – and her computer file is stuffed with recommendations of various medical practitioners who will assist me in 'recovery'. She has taken a policy with BUPA to cover almost any eventuality: there are lists of recommended cardiologists, GPs, screening clinics, colonic irrigation hotspots – and, damn the girl, therapists, nutritionists, and personal trainers, which are apparently not a form of shoe. I am enjoined to begin regular exercise (when it is permissible), to start eating properly, and begged to stop smoking, which would be sufficient to have me reaching for the Montecristos (which she provided!) if I didn't know that a few puffs would make me faint.

Fainting is a new pastime of mine. It began in the first months of prison, when one day I found myself on the floor of our cell with blood on my face, and the floor. I called faintly for help, and one of the screws – I quite liked prison lingo, and was making a glossary – escorted me to the infirmary, holding my arm to keep me upright, a towel pressed to my scalp to staunch the abundant flow.

The nurse was called Singh. I was rather pleased she was an Indian, for I once had Hindu neighbours of impeccable professional provenance, and am rather inclined to prefer a thrusting and ambitious sub-Continental to their demoralised English equivalents.

She stood up as I entered, shook my hand while introducing herself, and guided me to the chair in front of her desk. I looked round and saw nothing. A room. Outside the dirty window was a plot of scraggy grass, not worth looking at.

'Before we begin,' she said, looking at her computer screen, 'please tell me how you wish to be addressed?'

My head was still whirling.

'James?' she asked. 'Or is that too formal? Jim, perhaps?'

I didn't answer. *Dr Darke.* Bowed my head and bled.

'That's a nasty cut,' she said, removing the towel gently, and reaching for some swabs and a bandage. 'Scalp wounds bleed profusely, but there's no need to be alarmed. Tell me how this happened.'

'I don't know. I must have fainted, found myself on the floor . . .'

She looked sceptical. That's a common prison excuse, rarely true.

'Never happened before . . .' Of course it had, recurrently: an attack of vertigo, a stagger, sometimes a faint. None of them had caused significant damage, until now. No sense going into it, making a fuss.

'Let's have a thorough look at you then,' she said. 'Are you feeling sufficiently recovered to stand up? Would you take off your shoes, and step on the scales?'

The scale weighed me at 68.2. Kilos, I presume. I don't believe in them, and have no idea what this signified in stone. The decline of the British Empire accelerated on the day we adopted metric measures.

Next my height, which is diminishing as I age, like the rest of me. I started at 6 feet 1 inch, and have been heading downwards for the last few years. I am now 1.82 somethings.

'Would you roll up your sleeve?'

My arm was soon strangled with a tube, which swelled and swelled as she pushed a bulb. My arm compressed as if constricted by a boa, and I suppressed, just, the urge to scream and tear myself away. Breathed in and out slowly with my eyes closed. Tried not to faint. At last she gave some reverse squeezes and the snake let me go.

She eyed the gauge.

'188 over 90,' she said, as if announcing a cricket score at Lord's.

'Is that good?'

She looked at me steadily.

'What is it normally?'

I shrugged.

'It is high. It might be white coat syndrome . . . that's when the situation in which the blood pressure is taken – as in my office or a hospital – causes it to rise.'

She paused, waiting for a response to this bit of pop psychology, but didn't get one. The only blood-pressure-rising coat syndromes I get are when I meet someone badly dressed.

'Tell me, do you have any unusual symptoms?'

This was sufficient to raise a snort.

'Headaches?'

'Of course.'

'Fatigue, or confusion? Irregular heartbeat? Shortness of breath?'

'Yes.'

'Which?'

'Depends when you ask. Some, all. Depends.'

'What about chest pain?'

'Not a lot.'

'Well,' she said, 'let's address this. These are various symptoms associated with high blood pressure. I will prescribe some tablets to bring it down.'

I shrugged again. I don't want them. If the pressure rose further my heart might attack me, which would be no bad thing, if fatal.

Next I was instructed to unbutton my shirt, and she stethoscoped me front and back as I breathed in and out to order. This went on for longer than seemed necessary, invasive and uncongenial. It brought her too close to me when she did my front, I was looking down at the top of her coiled black hair – she smelled of exotic spices and perfume, with a hint of vegetable samosas – and when she sneaked round the rear I felt exposed and ambushed. Next thing my trousers would come down too.

'You can sit now. Please will you roll up your sleeve, I need to take some blood.'

When she inserted the needle I fainted, again. She bent over me solicitously, raised my head.

'Jim? Jimmy! Are you all right?'

We saw each other regularly over the next few years, as I fainted and wasted, and ignored her injunctions to take better care of myself. How could I do that? In prison? Yes, apparently I could: eat more (!), take daily exercise, perhaps practise yoga or meditation? She had tapes to teach me how to do either, or both.

*In the morning I showered, huddled skeletal and naked, my back turned, an unappetising aspect for even the randiest of buggers. Then I went back to bed, and faced the wall.*

*I cannot read, sometimes I drift off. I want to be unconscious, it's almost as good as dead. When I wake it is time for exercise in the yard. A pick-up football game is in progress, various balls are tossed, people run round in circles. I sit quietly in the hope that one of my chess partners might show up. Mental exercise. My game, never more than adequate, has deteriorated, which makes perfect sense.*

And now Dr Singh is replaced by Dr Lucy. One of the (many) reasons I don't want to talk with her, is that at the first opportunity I will get a telephonic inquisition. Am I smoking? Can I stop drinking, both alcohol and coffee? (I will demand an explanation for the full provisioning of each that greeted me on my arrival!) Do I still use so much salt? That is: can I cease being me? I understand her anxiety, she's pleased, however much I disappoint her, to have me back in the world, and wishes me to tarry awhile. But I regard my health as my own business, and have no plan to 'look after' it, as if it were a child, and I its nanny. Come along, health, let's go for a brisk walk in the park! And don't nag me for an ice lolly.

I want to enjoy what little is left of my life. As I recover my equilibrium I will undoubtedly eat more and better, and will no doubt gain weight, not because that is required, but because I enjoy eating, if the food is right. As for smoking and drinking? Of course. I still have the matured contents of my wine cellar, and no reason to retain the bottles for future use, nor anyone with whom to share the pleasure. Good wine is only to be enjoyed with company that knows what it is drinking. My only friend who fit the category was dear Philip, who could not only distinguish a good argument from a bad one, but a great claret from a good one.

I saw him, for the final time, when he visited two months after my incarceration. He'd sat through much of my trial, and participated in my preparation for testifying, knowing full well that I would ignore his advice. He'd believed entirely in my cause, but not my capacity for promoting it, which was hardly prescient of him. No one did. Not even me.

I was deeply touched that he should wish to visit, which would have been taxing for him in his weakened state. He was now receiving what is called palliative care, which is to say the administration of increasingly potent pain medications, but resisted going into a hospice on the sensible grounds that he didn't wish to be surrounded by dying people in ugly surroundings. He still employed the mildly mysterious middle-aged woman in white, Katya I think she is called, who did for him in many ways, perhaps every way, no one knows, though it is a subject of interest. Our fellow poetry group member, the bad novelist Dorothea Thornton, an inveterate snoop and gossip, claimed to have 'some dope' on the subject, but I made it quite clear that I didn't want to know. She was enough of a dope already.

'Ah, yes, James,' she sniffed, 'of course, you're rather above all this mucky human stuff!' Which was funny, as I've rarely encountered a muckier human than her bawdy and over-upholstered self. She'd made it known to me, following Suzy's death, that she'd like to get to know me more and better, more *deeply*. In her presence I tended to claim, and latterly actually to suffer from, constipation, and retreat to the toilet for a long relief. She began to enquire about this symptom too, as if she'd like to administer some invasive remedy.

Philip had written to ask if he might make this 'final visit', as he wanted to bid me farewell in person. It was certain to be an emotional occasion, and I dreaded it accordingly. We English – by which I mean our sorts of English men, Philip's and mine – are hopeless when burdened by a surfeit of emotion, our usual resources of analysis, urbanity and irony unfit for purpose.

He came into the visiting room slumped in a wheelchair, vastly depleted but with his smile at the ready, pushed by one of the screws. I rose unsteadily to meet him, and bowed to shake his hand. I should of course have held it, and him, embraced him, but an Englishman is never so natural as when he's holding his tongue. However odd a demonstrative foreigner might have found this measured reserve, we knew what it was and meant, and were commensurately moved by the moment. Had he looked closely he would have seen tears in my eyes. He didn't, I blinked them away.

'Dear Philip, it's so good of you to come . . .'

'Thank you. I'm so glad I did.'

There was something of an agreed and prolonged pause, as if we had now said everything worth saying. The screw who had pushed Philip to the table had stood back, and was looking worried, as if the two elderly gentlemen had misplaced their faculties. It was only when I sensed him about to intervene, to offer a glass of water, perhaps, that I allowed myself to continue.

'I won't ask how you are ...'

'I will tell you: I have crossed the line ...'

I was puzzled: it was clear that he was going to shortly enough, but he was still on the living side of it.

'... the quality of life that remains is not worth the price I am paying for it.'

'I often feel that way myself, Philip, I quite understand.'

'You don't. And I very much hope you will not, not for some time yet.'

'Does this mean that you have had enough?'

'On Thursday evening I will die. Easefully, you know I have provided for that. A final bottle of claret, a final solution. Upon the midnight. I would say I am looking forward to it, except that would imply that one can enjoy being dead, which seems, to my way of thinking, quite inconceivable. Even undesirable.'

'I will miss you.'

'You have added interest to my final years, I'm grateful for that.' He laughed weakly. 'Though I can't say that I will miss you too. It's why I'm here.'

This final leave-taking stuff can go on too long. Best draw a line round it. Better to talk about politics, Brexit perhaps, even that. He had been active in the campaign, was a fervent Remainer, and had utter contempt for our Prime Minister and his shrivelled little-Englanders, all of whom he knew and disdained accordingly. We had disagreed on the subject in our few letters. I construct a world in my image. I am a man with sharp edges, I do not invite people in willy-nilly. Countries should be similar. I cannot bear being commanded by Germans and patronised by the French. Anything, even the undoubted debacle to come, is better than that.

I suppressed a shaming impulse to ask what he was reading, as if he were a new acquaintance. Anyway, he'd read his last.

Aware of the retreating flow, he asked, 'Lucy. Is she all right?'

'She'll be fine. She's still angry with everyone.'

'I suppose she will get over it, she's a hardy soul, feisty like her mother must have been.'

'Yes.'

'Do you think she'll forgive Sam?'

'I rather hope so. I do. If I can forgive him why shouldn't she?'

He thought for a brief moment, and paused to rub his nose.

'She won't. It's important to her to have a target for her rage. The fires of wrath need air to flourish, otherwise they burn within, if you see what I mean. It's rather shaming, I sound more like Blake as I get older . . .'

We reminisced feebly about the details of my trial, and shook our heads at the stupidity of the verdict, however much it was the verdict that I deserved, and sought. I was of no use as a moral example if I was innocent. That had seemed persuasive until I understood what I had chosen.

There was nothing to say but goodbye, and that had been said and was best not repeated. Had he been able to stand up he would have, instead he gave a brief nod to the man lounging by the wall, who came over immediately to stand behind the chair.

'May I say travel well, dear Philip?' I said, taking his hand.

'Of course. Goodbye, James. Take care.'

When I was first incarcerated Philip had sent me Boethius' *The Consolations of Philosophy*, a book that he admitted he had not read for some decades, but which had been an early and abiding influence. 'A noble soul,' as he described him, Boethius was one of Philip's touchstones. But it is one thing to read this sage in the comfort of a common room or study, quite another to encounter him in, if I might put it this way, the appropriate surroundings. *The Consolations* was written when its author was in prison. Would it have any impact on one similarly situated, however differently?

After a few weeks had passed, Philip wrote to enquire how I was getting on. Was I finding any of the proffered consolation?

'Scant,' I replied. No lines of ancient wisdom would ameliorate the everyday trials of discomfort and humiliation, the exposure, internal rumblings, the disgusting everyday smells and sights, persons and situations. It was not horrible, it wasn't as important or piercing as that. It was demoralising, undermining, and desperate, and no words of some puffed-up ancient sage were of the slightest consequence. That this had resulted in my ongoing *De Profundis* musings was, I thought, unwise to mention. No one knew anything about that, excepting, I liked to imagine, its dedicatee.

If anything had been firmly and incontrovertibly fixed in Suzy's mind, it was the fatuity of wisdom, as properly adumbrated and understood. This left a final puzzle for her final deliberations. As she lay in bed, in increasingly debilitating discomfort, then worse, Suzy planned her funeral service with the same attentiveness that she used to give to her undergraduate essays. 'No way am I going to let some fucking vicar curate my goodbyes, with his droning Hymns (she thought of them as Hims) and fatuous homilies!' When I observed that this was what she'd signed up for when she insisted we join the small Oxfordshire congregation, and bought a burial plot, she said she'd supposed she could get round the problem when it came to it. And when it came to it, she couldn't.

Having rejected the Hims, she discovered that the few women who had written hymns had produced generic rubbish. Hers? *None of the above,* she decided, asserting at the same time that women are worse at composing poetry than men. She rather enjoyed the fact that this was counter-intuitive: for centuries women had been confined to the domestic arts, and what better way to express oneself than drawing-room verses? But for every Emily Dickinson there were ten Robert Frosts, and even the neurotically emancipated Sylvia Plath and Anne Sexton were hardly a patch on their many male contemporaries.

This was a most unfashionable view, and Suzy loved promulgating it. She was excoriated for writing a harsh review of a new woman poet, in which she put this case, and extended it by claiming that the only 'transcendent geniuses' were men: Homer, Sophocles, Dante, Leonardo, Copernicus, Newton, Galileo, Shakespeare, Goethe, Freud, Marx, Einstein ... all that lot. The monstrous regiment of women armed themselves, fired and blazed for a couple of days, some rejecting her premise, others attempting to find a few girls to go with the brainiest boys. Madame Fucking Curie? Rosalind Who's She Franklin? Suzy guffawed.

Her answer to the problem of her funeral service, like her answer to many of life's problems, was simple: *Fuck it!* After all, it was the Church of England: bland, formula bound, as imaginatively interesting as a senile snail. Let that poor little vicar have his poor little service. I could choose the hymns and readings, it didn't matter.

Instead she turned her mind to her memorial service, which would be much more fun, based on her tastes and customs, much more SUZY! She chose readings from the small group of women writers that she most admired, and for a full week filled her bedroom with melodies from Ella Fitzgerald, Edith Piaf, Billie Holiday and the Supremes. I took refuge in my study, and begged her to keep the volume down, to which she responded that dying people are surely allowed a bit of noisy fun.

Nothing came of it. When you're passing away the thought of a jolly commemoration of your life is appealing, but when the organic realities bite, the lungs clog and the airwaves shut, all that fussing and preening palls, in comparison, say, to the imperative to draw the next breath, and the next.

I sat with her as she died, appalled and silenced. I had forced myself into a biddable willingness to do as required, as asked, as expected. I grimaced and managed as best I could, and could easily have been mistaken for a dutiful loving carer. For all I know, that's what they are like, if you examine them forensically. Needs must. I prepared meals, changed sheets, cleaned here and there and – yes – everywhere, sat and held hands, read from our Kindle, played music, suggested films when she was still interested, and as the time neared, supplied cooling cloths for her forehead, chips of ice to provide a trickle of liquid into her clogged lungs, turned her over, stroked her back, or arm or forehead, whispered that I loved her.

As her attachment to the world waned, as it does with the terminally ill, her attachment to me diminished as well. The more I did, the less well I did it. Nothing was good enough, nothing was adequate. Having been a solution to her many problems, increasingly I was one of them: incompetent, stultified and emotionally barren. In letting go of the world, I reasoned, Suzy had also to let go of me. I understood that, and resented it accordingly.

If she'd lost interest in the idea of a memorial service, which was a relief, I nevertheless conceived the inward project of composing the eulogy that I might have delivered had such an occasion actually taken place. I am a happy and willing public speaker unless my deeper feelings are engaged, though they seldom are. But in speaking of Suzy, not so very long after her death, I feared that the emerging mass of feeling would overwhelm my capacity elegantly to express it.

Eulogies, in any case, are merely packages of overstatements and lies, post-mortem braggadocio, as if a form of branding of the deceased. It's hard not to laugh at the loving, inflated descriptions of the dead delivered tearfully by their friends and relations. *What? Really? You cannot be serious!* The antidote to this was to set myself the project, to allow myself to compose an inward final description of my wife that was not, as it were, recommending her for entry into the kingdom of heaven, but was, merely, if such a thing can be mere, merely true. To construct an account of the travels of Suzy Moulton upon this earth that would be as ruthlessly accurate as her own descriptions of the many characters in her novels, few of whom escaped the evisceration of her wit, and judgement.

Her two early novels – after which she clogged up – deployed a range of characters venial and self-absorbed, of the sort who, were they to enter your drawing room, would make you look for someone else to talk to. Some reviewers thought the books witty and satiric, others found her immature and snarky, a description to which she willingly acceded. For a short period 'like a character in a Suzy Moulton novel' had a currency in literary circles, to delineate a bloated nonentity of a pathetically libidinous kind. An Oxford don, perhaps – Suzy had been propositioned by a few as an undergraduate – or (after the success of her first novel) a publisher. Or a literary agent.

I sat at her bedside, in her moments of restless semi-consciousness, putting together an account of her life, from the precocious and entitled childhood, where she was something of a hellion in her genteel Dorset manse, indulged by an imported Ayah, to her later incarnation at Oxford, a tennis bully and precocious undergraduate. We met in a tutorial at St Anne's, and the relationship developed a trajectory in which she dictated and I followed. The major event of the marriage, perhaps the only one of significance, was the arrival of baby Lucy, a bawling and insistent presence much resented by her mother from the very first moments. She'd never liked babies, and made no exception for her own. She longed for the blithe company of adults: 'I need to get my tits back! And my life!'

She was dangerous, compelling company, this handsome, sardonic, disappointed woman, with her relentless eye and sharp tongue, a great gossip and dismantler of the pretensions of others. This frightened many women, who loathed the easy, but by no means effortless, capacity with which she bewitched their husbands. She had numerous courters and courtiers, and she took advantage of them, while leaving them with the impression that they were taking advantage of her.

I knew this. I reciprocated and retaliated as best I could amongst the mothers of my charges, and affected an urbane acceptance that ours was the way of the world, free of illusion or subterfuge. We did not ask each other where we had been, or with whom. That was easily avoided, until Suzy's last years, when her tennis partner, and lover, Lawrence (Dr Larry) Weinberg became her physician, rather against my advice, and saw her through her final year. As I sat with her in those final weeks he was frequently present, and after a time we all abandoned the pretence that his reasons were medical. There was nothing left for him to do, except to increase her pain medication, sit by her bedside and hold her hand. I shoved over.

When I was interviewed by the police, and later tried, both the arresting officer, a canny and dour Scot, and the Public Prosecutor, a smarmy arsehole, made much of my 'motives' for killing my wife: not only did I inherit her not inconsiderable estate, but I took revenge for her (forensically detailed) affair with Dr Weinberg. Money. Jealousy. Murder.

Suzy let it be known, slyly and cruelly, that he was both an ardent and an imaginative lover, which we both understood to mean that he found parts of her more exciting than I did. I have never, admittedly, been a Kama Sutra-ish type, much less a Lawrentian one, having no desire to root out the secret places of shame. They should stay where they belong, and do what they are formed to do. Believing in the separation of Church and state, and the rituals pertaining to both, I am, I suppose, rather conventional. My few lovers never asked sensual questions of me that I could not answer, nor I, them. But Suzy? Suzy always wanted more, and different, more exciting and better. Wanted Dr Larry, who sat at her side and held her hand. I never left them together in the room, even with her in her withered state, for fear he might decide to do some pre-mortem examination.

By the time I had recovered these memories and associated

feelings, put a shape on them, and constructed some inward eulogy, one thing had become clear. Much as I loved her, I often didn't like my wife very much, perhaps never had, and certainly not then, not at the end. Why would I, as she lay there, entirely withdrawn, treating me so carelessly?

The police, the prosecutor, jury and judge found me guilty, and I was, as charged. Jealous and vengeful. Dr Larry had testified in court with the arrogance of his kind, preened almost, as if anxious to offer the salacious details of his trysts with Suzy. His wife arrived with him every morning, and sat at the back of the courtroom, as if in support of her wayward husband. She had a notebook in her hand, followed his testimony closely, making copious notes. Six months after the trial, she applied for a divorce, using these notes as evidence. I was delighted to read about it, which provided a few shafts of sunlight in my cell. I despised him, and had capitulated cravenly to my own humiliation, which was what I had signed up for in sanctioning a free and easy sexual marriage, which is what Suzy required.

Had I the energy and the self-confidence, I would have given Dr Larry a cup of that fatal tea as well, and left them to it, in bed together to the end.

# Chapter 5

It has been my life's habit to write only for myself. I've always been a compulsive diarist, and the single, slim pleasure of my time in prison lay in the constant reliance on my journal-keeping, however pedestrian the result. Miles the literary hound, knowing this, had dangled the temptation of allowing me to say what I had to say, in my own form and in my own manner: *My Trial and Trials*. But surely not the diary! It isn't sufficiently sprightly, why should it be? Might it be sensible, instead, to consult him about placing my *De Profundis* with the right literary journal? I shall send it to him, he'd be amused.

*De Profundis* is an example of a genre, I suppose you'd call it, that I had slowly reinvented during my incarceration, busily skimming the material written by other inmates over the centuries. In the eighteenth century they called such compositions 'pamphlets', occasional writerly expressions on the topics of the day meant to be cheaply available to as mass an audience as might be arranged. Pamphleteers often addressed themselves to political and religious topics, and it was dangerous to do so. That was the point of it, and them. The writer risked opprobrium and imprisonment for the very sake of the truth as he perceived it.

I soon found myself turning away from the tedium of my diary, the recordings of humiliations and outrages large and small, in favour of an immersion in outrages that were larger, less personal and more egregious: the lunatic topics of the days, the political nonsense, the righteousness of the aggrieved and the convinced, the opinions on both left and right that drowned public discourse and made any right-thinking person wince in outrage. It is increasingly impossible to be a sensible, fair-minded person.

In America, any utterance, however banal, however true, that causes 'outrage' – it doesn't entirely matter who is outraged, as long as they are loud – draws an immediate apology. Apologies are the currency of the times, what you pay for speaking your mind, and they are so similar in form that I suspect a Prefabricated Apology Form must be available on the Internet. It would come in four parts: 1) abject admission of guilt; 2) shame at having insensitively offended and distressed so many; 3) promise to do better, and 4) to re-educate oneself. This form is so obviously rote that the resulting apology, while necessary, is by no means sufficient.

This was the point, of course, of the extension to *Gulliver's Travels* that I had written for Rudy. Gulliver, returned home to London for what I fancifully termed his final voyage, has compelling truths to tell his fellow men: that they are Yahoos, base at tooth and claw, a disgusting and irredeemable species. His adumbration of what seems to him a simple fact, discovered on his Fourth Voyage to the land of the Houyhnhnms, leads to no end of troubles. He is excoriated, attacked, mocked, and mimicked, and sentenced to a term in Newgate Prison. He does not and will not apologise: the point of telling the truth is simply that it is the truth, and – as Captain Gulliver might have said – damn the consequences.

I feel hypocritical saying this, for I had, against my better literary and historical judgement, tacked a spurious happy ending to my tale of Gulliver's final years, in order to assuage Rudy's fears about my fate. This concession, both necessary and humiliating, was one of those sacrifices which require the abandonment of integrity in the service of love. But – this makes me feel better – it is one thing to abandon artistic integrity, and quite another to cede it in the moral arena. I made no secret of the fact that I had assisted Suzy's death, and however much I was attacked for it, never contemplated any sort of apology. Rather the reverse, I welcomed the attacks as an opportunity to reiterate my position. My rejoinder, in the form of what I now think of as my Dog/ Wife essay, was crudely and hastily expressed, under too much pressure, but it adumbrated a position about which I was proud, however much I was urged to reconsider or to recant, if only in the service of my own comfort. Of course I refused, and went willingly to prison. This was unwise, given what I know now, but most days I do not regret it. Wisdom, as I have frequently observed, is a debased currency.

I wrote *De Profundis,* like most of my other compositions, in the 'library' at our prison, a tiny room with a few shelves of books, mostly dog-eared thrillers, many of them missing more pages than not, with a table and four chairs, for those inclined to tarry awhile.

*I dislike reading in my cell, because the likelihood is that I will lie abed with my Kindle and fall asleep, so I spend a lot of time in what I call our bibliothèque, sometimes reading, more frequently writing in my journal or working on my project. Wally, having discovered this, often joins me, and I immediately taught him that libraries are places of solitary contemplation, and silence. To my surprise he both understood and acceded to this concept, his normal garrulousness curtailed by his own work. The quieter he is, the more I like him.*

*He is writing a family memoir, hunched over the table with an exercise book in front of him, manipulating his pen with care, as if it were an explosive device, which of course it is. He scowls as he writes, purses his lips, slows down and leans back in his chair – a perilous undertaking — then returns to his work. No matter how long I stay at the table, he leaves after me, painstakingly filling pages, his face contorted in concentration, each letter emerging as if independent from the last, each studied, steadied, formed, oddly distinguishable from its last itera-tion. None of his individual letters were quite the same, they slanted left or right, changed shape and volume, teetered on the edge of illegibility but never fell off it. His scowl registered the incessant challenge, his hand trembled with the effort, he shook his arm to forestall cramp. It was how an illiterate shot-putter might have assayed writing, it was appalling, and heroic.*

*He asked me if I would 'have a look' at what he is writing, but I advised him — not merely in self-defence — that it is best to write entirely on one's own, and that the showing part comes at the end. I have some doubt about his literary capacity: though he had worked in schools, it was only as a PE teacher. But his scribbling keeps him busy and quiet, so there's a blessing for both of us.*

Wally hopes, though he is bashful about expressing it, that his story 'might interest some folk'. He confuses this not unlikely fact with the further belief that it might be of interest to some publisher. I doubt that very much.

Yet the zeitgeist is blowing his way. In my time, long ago, liter-ary publishers demanded excellence, and literary prizes rewarded it. The former Head of the Booker Prize, a charming gossipy invert named Goff, once told Suzy (who called him Goof) that the judges for the prize were simply enjoined to *pick the best book*. This was decidedly not subjective, but the product of discrimination, deep reading and attentive argument. It did not matter, he main-tained, if the year's shortlist consisted entirely of men, or of women, or indeed of midgets. All they had to do was to excel.

Now it's all change, and what is valued is called 'diversity': publishers seek books that mirror and represent the culture in all its variety of skin tone, persuasion, and perversion. Their lists are scrupulously interrogated: are there enough white/brown/yellow writers, men, women and trans, he/him, she/her, they/them? And if the literary products of this diversity are unabashedly agenda-based, that is a good thing: it rights many wrongs, and recalibrates the culture in a beneficial way! That such writing might be regarded as aesthetically diminished is accepted, if accepted at all, as a price worth paying.

Not for me it isn't, what you gain isn't worth what you lose. There are standards of excellence, and they are arguable but not entirely negotiable. Excellence is colour blind. At Oxford and Cambridge, when you sit your finals, the examiners do not know whose script they are reading. It might be by James or Gillian, Mohammed or Kwame. What matters, simply, is how good it is, and the awarding of marks measures achievement, and that alone. It is neither subjective nor is it culturally relative.

I said none of this to Wally, who wouldn't have understood. In prison I kept my opinions strictly to myself, which wasn't difficult because opinions were dangerous. So I encouraged Wally, and he scribbled away, bit his tongue and pencil, wrote his stories. It made him less angry, he said, which was certainly a good thing.

Word got round, as words do, and Wally's fellows, surprisingly, began to regard me as a sort of walking resource with regard to written discourse. I say 'surprisingly', not because I am not such a resource, which I most assuredly am, but because they seem to trust me enough to appear as regular supplicants, asking for the drafting of a letter to a loved one, advice on reading legal papers, and sometimes guidance on reading anything at all. I was at first averse to this role – who gives a damn? – but it soon occurred to me that I might parlay my modest undertakings into a bargaining chip. I decided to put this squarely to our Warden, who did not like me, and never had, from the first moment we met. He'd been brusque and hostile, took me through the necessary induction, and hustled me on my way. Stunned by the frostiness of his demeanour, I left his office thinking of poor dear Oscar's eviscerating reception at Wandsworth Prison, those many years ago.

'Your sort doesn't last two years here.'

*His sort*, I thought, as I shuffled to my cell. *I'm his sort.*

Yet the Warden could now assist me in one of two ways. First, by arranging transfer to a less inhospitable venue of incarceration; second, if this was not possible, by ameliorating my conditions in this one. It was in his power to give me various privileges, if I earned them. Ameliorations, easements. I wasn't likely to get Cordon Bleu cooking, but a better cell, more privacy and extended privileges if I 'earned' them.

He had been insufficiently sympathetic to recommend my transfer to a more easeful facility, but he soon heard of the role I was playing with my fellow inmates. I made sure of that. When I asked for an appointment to talk with him, he scheduled a meeting two weeks hence.

'Ah, Darke. Yes. What can I do for you?'

'Thank you for agreeing to see me, Warden. I have a request. If I may.'

He nodded as generously as a Roman Emperor at the Circus, and as well-intentioned.

'I am increasingly occupied assisting my fellows with matters of literacy, reading and writing letters for them, helping them to do research in one way or another. There are even a few who wish me to set up a reading group, or a writers' workshop . . .'

'Ah, yes, indeed.'

'And I am not averse to any of these requests, though they now take up much of my time. But I find that the confines of my cell are inadequate for the amount of work I need to do, the reading and drafting and consulting, and I would be so grateful if you could move me to larger quarters. I gather there are cells that are, shall I say, more capacious?'

He paused for a moment, blankly. He rarely met my eyes, as if they were mesmeric and dangerous. Or perhaps he was just off on his spectrum, they're like that, those types, and because they have no understanding of other people's emotions, are often to be found running prisons. And governments.

'Perhaps, Darke, you are under the impression that this is some sort of hotel. And that we offer upgraded rooms to our favoured customers?'

He understood my point exactly.

'Heaven forfend, Warden. I simply need more space to be of more assistance. This does not pertain at The Ritz.'

'I wouldn't know. You may go now, Darke.'

Go? I had nowhere to go, no projects, no hopes or dreams, no prospects intellectual or social. Prison sounds the death knell of going.

Even writing this in my journal flummoxes me, when there is little to report, and so little going on inside me. I am, to be fair, returning slowly to some hollowed-out simulacrum of my former self. At Lucy's – urging, shall I call it? – I am now taking the forbidden daily stroll, I used to call it a constitutional until the pomposity of the phrase slowed me down. I can just manage fifteen minutes to the park, once round the pond, and back again. I do not wear a mask because they restrict both breathing and being, but I am exceptionally adept at social distancing. I don't need a damn pandemic for that.

Lucy is aware that such strolling is strictly *verboten* for the frail at heart, but has encouraged me nonetheless, the beneficial results of such exercise outweighing, in her mind, my chance meeting with a fateful airborne antagonist. My first foray into the wilderness of my West London neighbourhood was sufficiently startling that, I am ashamed to admit, I only got about fifty feet down the road before a severe attack of – I dislike the word 'anxiety', perhaps what I need is something philosophical and literary, shall we say 'existential angst' as per *M*. Sartre, for whom the epithet 'froggy' was doubly applicable – caused me to turn back. As I opened and quickly closed the door, the relief was immediate: in here, just fine; out there, dangerous.

In prison, though we yearned for the freedoms and expanses of everyday life, in time we became habituated to the restrictions of space and range and choice. The world contracts, and your spirit and personality contract commensurately. Take to the outdoors once again, too quickly, and the immediate reaction is to seek the comfort of the restricted and the enclosed. If prison is no longer available, which can be a curiously saddening thought, then home confinement is a substitute.

Within an hour of my departure, which was scheduled for 10.00 a.m. by Controller Lucy, who has set me various schedules which it is easiest to accede to, or at least to pretend to accede to, the phone rang, Alexa having been banished due to lack of use. At first I simply disliked it/her, but once I had bashed my forehead it was imperative that I be invisible, first due to the welt, later the large scab, and after that – the premature removal of scabs being one of my lifetime pleasures – the regular coursing of blood down my cheeks. On some days I looked like a Hindu with one of those red forehead marks, and at others like Jesus *sans* crown of thorns but with plenty of blood.

'So, how did it go?'

'Good morning, my darling. You mean my little walk? It was lovely. So good to get out in the fresh air, if that term isn't now discredited, and have a little stroll, so freeing to the spirit!'

'Oh, Dad! You did go, didn't you?'

'Of course, of course, lovely!'

'Tell me where you went. How long were you out for? How did it feel after all these years?'

'It felt fine. I was out for about half an hour, I had to walk slowly ...'

'What? You usually walk fast?'

'. . . because I got a bit puffed. Sat down once or twice, then carried on.'

'Sat down? Not near anyone, I hope? You know the rules, don't you? You have to . . .'

'Of course I do. But I'm just having a little rest now, so let's talk soon.'

'Tomorrow, please. After your walk.'

Tomorrow? I don't need a damned walk, and I certainly don't need to turn up the volume of my fraught state. *Outdoors. Air. Going for a walk.* The terms threaten as if I were an agoraphobic, undone in the open spaces.

I lied to Lucy the next morning, and the next and next. I'm a rotten fibber, much of it was beaten out of me as a child, and now when I am forced to tell an untruth, my mouth dries, my lips pucker, and my voice shifts to a higher register and slows down. I cower inwardly, and Lucy (like her mother!) can see and hear it. She knows that a full frontal on the topic at hand, or not at hand, only heightens my evasiveness, so she goes through the motions and retreats, thinking of Plans B and C. But for now all I get is the simple query:

'How was your walk?'

And she accepts the simple answer.

'Lovely, thank you.'

We move to safer topics. Am I looking after myself properly? Have I managed to clean the house, all by myself?

Though I evaded walk-talk, I was determined to carry on. Short distances at first, then slightly longer, as they recommend in those manuals about changing your behaviour gradually. To my surprise and dismay, it worked. I hate to think of myself as programmable in such a manner, the fit subject of some therapeutic method, but I found that, if I walked slowly, breathed deeply and – hardest of all – thought positively, then most days I could manage to go a little further, a little less anxiously.

I prefer to think, though, that my stately progress was caused, not by therapeutic twaddle, but by the company and assistance of my beautiful antique walking stick, left in my cupboard with a cheery 'Welcome Home' note from Lucy and Jonathan. It has an exquisite gold-plated knob, decorated with chasing and repoussé, with an intricately etched eighteenth-century dedication at the crown. Below is a beautifully tapered and surprisingly heavy ebony stick, the whole satisfying in the extreme. It is so very beautiful that on first putting it to hand, I needed to pause for a moment to collect myself, and then to try it out in the hallway, finding just the right combination of steps, pressure and release. When I did this in front of the floor-length mirror, my new possession seemed more accessory than implement, not a tool but a theatrical prop.

Oscar, again! He'd frequently been photographed, always holding a cane, for which (unlike me) he had no practical use, just an aesthetic one. He wore it, just like those outsized fur coats and cravats. Something was nagging at my mind, and eventually I found it, from an auction in Scotland in 2009:

*An ivory-handled walking cane once owned by Oscar Wilde, inscribed with the engraving 'O W, C33' – his initials and the cell location Block C, floor three, cell three. It also features the date 16 October 1898 – which would have been Wilde's 44th birthday.*

The cane had been estimated at between £300 and £500, which was nonsense, not because it was too low, but because the silly thing was an obvious forgery, a fabrication foisted upon the gullible. It sold for £7,275.

Could Lucy and Jonathan have known about Oscar's cane? And known, too, that I would greatly prefer an antique example to an ugly modern one? I'm sensitive like that. I rushed upstairs and penned a note to them both, expressing highest praise for their acumen, and thanks for their generosity.

Clutching my stick self-consciously and probably too firmly

(when I returned home my hand was aching) I made my way to the postbox, a few hundred feet down the street, experimenting as I walked with how much pressure was best, and how much tap-tapping I wished to generate. It was going to take practice before I looked elegant, a sauntering boulevardier, an Oscar. But at least it helped me to walk, more or less, in a straight line, instead of weaving my way down the street, drunk with degeneration.

I popped my letter in the box, and carried on to the bus stop, where the whooshes and fumes disgusted and frightened me. Though the newscasters assert that the streets are deserted and that life is 'on hold', I experience the reverse: people driving uncommonly fast because the city thoroughfares are open and unpatrolled, bicyclists who give way to neither man nor beast, walkers who stride and joggers who self-propel as purposefully as if training for the Olympics, checking their stopwatches and monitors as they go, hogging paths and pavements. If there is danger here, it is hardly from touching the wrong surface or breathing the wrong air.

As I walk my head rises imperceptibly, no longer assuming the downward and downcast mien of my days in prison. It is almost animating, peering into the closed shops, at the few pedestrians, and at the occasional vehicle of note, a heart-warming white Porsche Speedster, a vulgar Ferrari Testarossa driven aggressively by an Arab.

Pedestrians on the pavement step aside, not merely out of the current courtesies, but because they have stopped to look at me, a slim elderly gentleman with his elegant stick, so dressed up though with nowhere obvious to go. Catching their eyes, I tip the rim of my hat gently, and wish them a good morning, a salutation that is usually reciprocated. If you get enough bad mornings they somehow morph into the degraded modern simulacrum of good ones, as the forgotten decencies recur.

I stopped at our earnest Pakistani newsagent, who thinks in pennies and is the better for it, bought my copy of *The Times,* and was resuming my stroll when I was approached by a youth hunched into a brackish sweatshirt, his light brown face barely visible under its hood, in filthy jeans and trainers. I felt it unnecessary and possibly provocative to tip my hat, instead nodded in mild salutation and acknowledgement.

He looked me up and down, I could see his eyes scanning the image I presented, easily parsed as: rich, and helpless. He reached into his front pocket.

'Oi, mate?'

I immediately prepared to surrender my wallet, but my walking stick would be another matter. Perhaps I could whack him with it? But I wasn't likely to do so quickly or powerfully, which would only intensify his aggression.

'Yes? Good morning. Can I help you?'

He stood stock-still, pondering my accent and interpreting my words. He took his hand from his pocket, which now held a crumpled cigarette.

'Gotta light?'

Of course I did. I carry my small pack of mini-Montecristos wherever I go, and often have one mid-morning, lit by my – more trouble coming – gold Dunhill lighter.

I could have denied the possession of such, but didn't. I am a fair judge of teenage boys, and though he was outside my normal catchment area, the more I looked at this bedraggled specimen, the less threatening he seemed. Desolate and impecunious, certainly, but not, I thought, not hostile.

'Yes, of course.'

I fished the lighter out of my waistcoat pocket, and he put the injured cigarette to his lips, I snapped the lighter into flame and he leant forward, and inhaled with a sigh.

'Thanks, mate.'

As he turned to move away, I asked him if the cigarette dangling from his lips was, perhaps, his last one.

'Yeah,' he said. 'Be the last for a while.'

'I wonder,' I replied, 'if you might permit me to buy you a pack?'

He looked at me even more steadily, presumably having encountered all too little gratuitous benevolence in his recent life.

'Good of you, yeah, thanks.'

I turned back to the newsagent's.

'What sort do you smoke?'

He coughed and laughed, redolent with what was not quite self-pity, just a realistic expression of his place in the world, or lack of it.

'Whatever.'

I bought a plastic cigarette lighter and twenty Benson & Hedges, drawn perhaps by memories of their former gold packaging, and handed them over. I considered offering him a fiver, but felt, oddly perhaps, that it might be regarded as patronising.

His eyes showed signs of life as they met mine.

'Ta!'

He put the cigarettes in his pocket gently, as if they might fold and disintegrate inside their packet, and walked away quickly. I stood and watched his figure recede, cowering and chilled in the spring air.

I soon sauntered past the greengrocer's bedraggled piles of the produce of the world – mangoes and pomegranates, large bunches of small bananas, lettuces shedding their leaves, fat melons and tiny grapes – which were being perused by a variety of people from a variety of countries, themselves exhausted produce, but to my eye one of the joys of West London.

Soon enough I arrived at the entrance to the park, to seek a bench on which to sit and read the paper. From daybreak to sunset the space is tenanted by myriad noisy children and defecating dogs, though both are capable of each activity, often at the same time. I read the headlines until I felt exhausted, whether by the walk, the prose or the news was unclear, and began tapping my way home, inwardly rendering an account of my progress: two minutes to the postbox, five to the newsagent's, seven to the veggies. Quarter of an hour in all? Add a couple for the boy, ten to the bench, perhaps five minutes' reading time before I was overcome.

And of course the same time to get back home, or (to be strictly accurate) 20 per cent less to get home, on account of enhanced ambling. I opened my door, leant against the wall to catch my breath, propped my elegant proper-upper in the corner of the hallway, walked to the kitchen and filled a glass with cold Vichy water, added a thin slice of lime, and sat at the table to raise my glass in ironic toast to the adventurousness of my spirit. Home again, to warmth, and comfort, and as plenty as any man could want, and more. It made me think of the boy, to wonder where he might have gone, if indeed he had anywhere to go.

I did not inform Lucy about these forays into the not very remote regions of my local terrain, because I knew that nothing is ever enough. Gone for a half-hour walk, have you? Try to go a little further next time, and for longer. Are you walking quickly enough? It's good for your cardios and your vasculars. Remember your social distancing. Did you wear your mask?

No, thanks, none of the above. In any case social distancing has been my life's strategy, and all of a sudden it's fashionable, how marvellous. But I cannot abide the ugly breath-stiflers that I am urged but not required to wear. No one with any sartorial self-respect would be seen in public in such apparel, like a bandit in a grade-B cowboy film. If that is soon required, I will cease to go out at all. Geographically I am by no means an out-person, I much prefer in-, though on reflection the first category fits me more snuggly. *Out*: of prison, of energy, of time, of luck, of sorts. And particularly, of patience. The world into which I have been released disgusts me; even in the four years of my absence from it, human life has deteriorated appallingly. I twiddle my thumbs on a dying planet inhabited by morons, soon to be parched, fried, and starved. I would regard this with more than equanimity were it not for thought of Rudy and Amelie.

My walks provide regularity, fill almost an hour in the long length of a day, and I can discern some return to the minimal fitness of my former self, a renewed capacity to amble without puff and cramp. In prison my days were regulated, and what free time I had could be filled with reading or writing, a touch of wireless perhaps, or some music. Lights on and off, showers, meals, exercise, allowed activities and chapel were at prescribed times, and the days passed one after the other, alike in substance and rhythm. It was easy to regret this, to yearn for the capaciousness of life on the outside, as it was termed. Yet inside correlated cruelly and ironically with my needs and rhythms. School teaching was similar. I no longer teach, and am freed from prison: I can do as I wish, which has a lot to be said against it.

When I return from my daily saunter, having stretched my shanks and read the few interesting bits of the paper, I compose myself, and brew a second flat white, which puts me on the edge of palpitations but not over it. A third would be dangerous and feel fatal, sufficient to send me to bed for the rest of the morning, a result that tempts me. I take the coffee to my study, and tuck myself into my comfy chair to read the *Spectator,* which contains more good writing than thinking, and is more full of indignations, even, than Mr Dickens. By the time I've read a couple of the articles I am fuming at the state of the world, the sheer lunacy of contemporary life, which paradoxically I find soothing, and a catalyst for my own writing. If I do not stoke the fires of discontent, I have nothing with which to warm myself, or indeed to say.

And thus the recurring problem of Lucy. I cannot ring her

after my morning fires are heated, nor can I do so in the evening, when I am likely – my taste for drink now entirely restored – to be more than usually forthcoming. In the afternoon Lucy is engaged looking after Amelie (Rudy looks after himself) and doing what little work she can for the Foundation. So there is, blessedly, no ideal time at which to speak. I suggested that we confine ourselves to texts, to keep in good touch, but that was of course vetoed, and rather hurt her feelings, naturally enough I suppose.

The best time is just after lunch. Jonathan feeds the children, while Lucy retreats to her office to get a bit of peace, which (how odd is this?) includes talking to her father. Our conversations are invariably strained and scripted: the notion that one can talk spontaneously into an inanimate instrument has always been foreign to me. When I listened to, and watched, Suzy yattering away with her daughter for hours on end, it always struck me that she was talking to the instrument that she held in her hand, and not to some invisible interlocutor some hundred miles distant. In this respect I am something of a savage, I suppose, utterly perplexed by the ways of the civilised world, or like one of those poetic Martians who came to our literary earth in the 1980s to observe and to be puzzled. Which was thought rather clever at the time, but the idea was quickly exhausted, having all too little intellectual puff.

'Darling, Lucy! Good afternoon, how's your day been?'

'Don't ask. Have you had your walk?'

'Of course. It was lovely in the park, there were more moorhens than children, it was very peaceful.'

'Good, good. Have you had your lunch? I worry you're not eating properly.'

'Of course. It's one of the highlights of my day. I had some lovely ripe Camembert, fresh French bread, and a few tomatoes ...'

'No wine I hope, you know you ...'

'Of course not. Tell me how Rudy is?'

'Who knows? He hardly talks these days, he's entering the teen-age grunting stage, spends all his time in front of one screen or another. Once he's been fed and watered he's low maintenance.'

'And the little one? And the big one?'

'Both fine, bearing up. Oh, yeah, right? Fucking miserable to tell you the truth . . .'

'Good, good . . . Oh, sorry.'

'There's one thing, though, thank God there's the telly, and loads of good series to watch. Jonathan and Rudy and I are hooked on *Borgen*, did you start it?'

'I keep meaning to. I am watching some French thing about movie stars and their agents. It's a bit obvious, but stylish, some lovely clothes, and I have turned off the distracting subtitles, they're so ugly.'

'I didn't know you could speak French.'

'I can't.'

'Well, must be getting on. I miss you!'

Missing? There's a lot of missing going on. It suits my nature: life is so much easier when you ring-fence love, keep it under control. Lucy struggles to accept this, of course, but has little choice.

'Love you, Dad!'

'And you, my darling, have a good rest of day.'

'Big hugs from us all!'

'You too . . .'

When you are contracted for a daily chat during our Time of No Events, you learn to keep it short. Before each call I make an inward list, which I then jot down because my mentals are not what they used to be, with a few possible topics and questions. *Moorhens, food at lunch, not drinking, the children, reading or telly . . .* Try not to ask questions about feeling or doing, which lead to trouble. Above all, avoid health, cut it off at the root. People who talk about health are unhealthy, and their talk makes them worse. Health-talk is not an *inevitable* consequence of having an elderly body, merely a likely one. I have my worries and concerns, of course – the throbs and missed beats of organic life – but I will not share them. They are mine alone, and it is indescribably vulgar to go on and on about one's entrails and viscera, as if their guarantee hadn't run out years ago. That line of Yeats, about being fastened to a dying animal, provides some solace: if that's what one is as an old man, at least one knows what to do with dying animals, you take them to the vet. If you can find one, or become one yourself, at the last.

Even worse than neurotic health-talk, though, is a new topic, from which Lucy cannot be averted, which is called 'Wellness', a new subdivision of Health, and a term that makes what remains of my hackles to erect. Lucy sends links to various sites run by semi-literate ninnies, who are under the communal fantasy that, somehow, one gets to *choose* whether to be healthy or unhealthy. Change your mind! Change your habits! Change your health! To which I can only reply: Change your genes! (Mine are terrible: none of us lives to eighty.) Hope for good luck!

According to my daughter I am the medical equivalent of a climate change denier. I disbelieve in the science? Eating well, not smoking, and regular exercise don't matter? Unless I am extremely wary, the conversation will soon morph to mindfulness, an idiotic new fashion that makes even Wellness seem relatively reasonable, and pleasingly anodyne.

I remark that I am a veritable paragon of Wellness: do my strolls, have a very occasional cigar, and eat very well indeed. Drink well too: I have not abjured wine during lunch, which is a recurring and not entirely believed fib. The ensuing phone call is made more tolerable if preceded with a glass of Prophet's Rock Pinot Gris, which goes down well at midday, and finished with another.

This has the desired effect of making me sleepy, and by 2.00 p.m. most days I am tucked up in my gorgeous sheets, soon to be happily unconscious, if such a combination is possible, a philosophical conundrum that amuses me as I count my mutton struggling over their fences.

# *Chapter 6*

I do not look up from perusing my copy of *The Times,* for fear of seeing any thing or person that will interrupt my solitude. Urban hermits have to be self-protective, or self-isolating as it is now called, when there are so many more of us. Dogs approach and sniff, children smile aggressively, an occasional adult flicks an inquisitive look or attempts a good morning. So when someone sat on the bench next to me, a most offensive and gratuitous intrusion when there is another bench a few yards away, in flagrant contravention of the new norms, I did not look up. Opened my paper even more comprehensively about my face, double pages spread, and waited for them to register the lack of welcome, and to move on.

'Good morning, you.'

A woman's voice. Recognisable perhaps? It was hard to tell, it has been years since I've spoken to one, save Lucy and Dr Singh. Most of the women I know are dead.

'Is me.'

The tone was hardly that of a stranger, containing a hint of irony and playfulness, teasing perhaps. Reluctantly I allowed my eyes to rise in small increments, taking in the faded jeans next to me, a crudely knitted cardigan in a variety of bright but by no means cordant colours, atop of which sat an orange cotton scarf, adding to the aesthetic offence. I suppose you might have called it flamboyant, if you were sufficiently indiscriminating. I know what I would call it: Bulgarian!

It was her. She.

'Bronya!'

She laughed.

'Is me! I used to say that, didn't I? You remember!'

'Yes. Of course I do.'

She leant over the side of the bench, and came up with a paper bag, and reached her hand in.

'Flat white. Is good!'

I took the paper cup gratefully.

'How kind. Thank you.'

'I bake shortbread too. You still like?'

'Of course.'

She passed me a thick, crumbly biscuit. Burdened now with coffee in one hand, the biscuit the other, a newspaper hovering on my lap, and my stick leaning against the bench between my knees, it would have been impossible to make an escape, which I was longing to do. In my years of knowing her, my amiably intrusive Bulgarian had been a barely adequate cleaner, and later, accompanied by her journalist boyfriend Thomas, had assisted in various ways in the months of my arrest and trial (during which she looked after Rudy). She had morphed from her modest incarnation as a domestic servant into a science tutor for various Bulgarian children, at which she apparently made an adequate living.

Shuffling slightly to the side, her buttocks half off the bench, she turned to look at me closely.

'You lose weight, yes?'

'I presume, Bronya, that Lucy has sent you?'

'No.'

'But then ...'

'Not sent. I am not a parcel. She told me where you would be, and I decided to come to see you. I was worried about you, all these years, and I was so sad when you didn't answer my letters ...'

'To be frank, Bronya, that had nothing to do with you, not personally. I didn't answer anyone's letters. Except Lucy's, sometimes.'

She had the sense not to pursue the topic. I had behaved in character, she knew that, and was by no means so self-engrossed that she thought she might become an exception to my almost universal distaste for my fellow man. Though, to be fair, I didn't dislike Bronya. She was what we used to call a good sort, honest, hard-working and well-intentioned, eager for self-improvement. She could be trusted; like all Eastern Europeans she was excruciatingly literal and sadly incapable of circumlocution or dissimulation, much less irony, and had the accompanying stalwart version of integrity. She could be counted on to say what she meant, and to mean what she said. Worthy, but lacking spark.

'I want ...'

She paused, trying to find words that, while literal and true, would not be rejected summarily.

'I want, please if you will let me, I want to help you.'

A sideways glimpse revealed that her eyes were downcast and her cheeks had reddened.

'That is so kind. But I am getting on very well on my own, and anyway it isn't allowed, is it? Not if it means coming to the house. Even Lucy can't do that.'

'I can.'

'Why is that? I don't understand.'

'I already had it, the disease. It's over now, so I am safe to be with ...'

'You had it? When was that? Was it very bad?'

I thought I felt a shudder, some sort of organic contraction at my side.

'I not talk about it, ever. It was, I don't know right word, maybe is . . . *grim?*'

'I see.'

'You don't. I hope you never will. But it means I could come to see you and maybe help. I can clean still – you will need that!'

'Thanks, but I'm getting on fine.'

'This is impossible. And you will need your laundry doing, and some shopping, and perhaps setting a fire when nights get cold. You do that?'

'No.'

As I said so, the impulse to flee this benevolent inquisition became irresistible, and, having finished both coffee and shortbread, I folded my paper, gathered my stick, and rose.

'Bronya, it has been lovely to see you once again. I hope you will forgive me if I leave now, I find I tire so easily these days . . .'

'Of course.'

She rose and would have shaken my hand had one been available.

'It was good to see you too.'

As I tottered away, supporting myself with my increasingly necessary stick, weaving minimally along the path, I could feel her gaze. I detest becoming an object of interest, and even more so of pity, and the ministrations of the well-meaning, even of my daughter, are unwelcome. I can look after myself. The house may be increasingly dusty, but my laundry and dry cleaning are sent out and returned, my larder and wine cellar are adequately stocked. I am content to wait out my remaining time in solitude, to serve this final sentence.

Of course, the worldwide state of affairs will end, though I hope not too soon, and I will be reunited with my family. This will be a trial, and also, I suppose, something of a relief. But as the days shorten and shadows impinge, family is not a consolation but an additional source of anxiety and of stress, not a solution to the problem of the end of days, but an exacerbation of it.

It was rude to flee from Bronya so precipitately, though so urgent was my need of escape that I was hardly aware of the offence that it would have caused. Polite discourse had been required, enquiries about her current life, and what has befallen her over the last few years. I am minimally interested to know, though not enough to ask. Or, indeed, even to have read one of her letters, which would presumably have told me. The problem, to be direct – and why else do I write all this self-absorbed stuff if not to be so? – is that my reluctance to reintegrate Bronya into my life is because she at one point got close, not perilously but discernibly, to foregrounding herself in my feelings. There was a scene in the kitchen, sometime after Suzy died, of a physical warmth and intensity that could easily have morphed into something intimate.

Not sexual, surely I am past that, never think of it except in happy retrospection, am by no means sure that I could rise to such an occasion, and very sure that I would not wish the humiliation of struggling to do so, perhaps popping blue pills and looking towards the warm south as hopefully as Keats. It was only – can one say only? – a clasping of the hand and an intense proximity that is nature's way of presaging further intimacy to come. Not for me it wasn't. Would it have been, for her? I am hardly a gay Lothario, and she was/is an attractive woman decades younger than me. Do I flatter myself that she was offering, and there for the taking? I drew apart. Would that have distressed her? I have no idea. I didn't know her, she was my cleaner. And even now, after the increasing closeness during the arrest and trial period, I still do not know her. Why would I wish to? This has little to do with her. I have no general antipathy to Eastern Europeans, irritating though they are. I don't need one in my life.

I am solitary. I am not lonely. My life requires no interventions, and Bronya's, in particular, would be unwelcome. She is too well-intentioned, tactile, and willing. I was right to walk away from her entreaty in the park – no, not entreaty, that is both unkind and inaccurate, her kind offer of assistance – and leave things just as they are, and as I like them. From that morning I changed the route of my daily constitutional, and located a less agreeable but adequate direction and resting place to read my paper. I did not meet Bronya again, nor the poor unfortunate youth.

I didn't tell Lucy. (I must count: surely this is the most common sentence in my diaries.) Whatever her protestations to the contrary, Bronya is indeed like a parcel, at least where my daughter is concerned. I can only hope that she isn't scheduled for a new delivery. The recurrent thought that I might soon have to deal with a recurrent Bronya nagged at me. Finally I brought it up with Lucy, who had been cunning enough, which was rather unusual for one who blabs as much as she, not to mention Bronya at all. When she and Bronya make their plans for my improvement, they are discreet enough to qualify for trilbies and trench coats.

It was a few weeks later, and Lucy and I were halfway through our standard conversation, when I abruptly changed the script.

'Oh, I forgot to tell you. Guess who I met in the park the other day?'

'Who? Which other day?'

'Bronya.'

There was a pause, while Lucy put on her big fat liar voice.

'Oh, what a surprise! How was she?'

I'm not good at amateur theatricals. She knew that I knew, and I knew that she did. Why the blather?

'She is fine. As you know. I was a little surprised that you sent her. As you know, I don't wish ...'

'I do!' Lucy said impatiently. 'Of course I bloody know! But that doesn't mean I have to respect every damn one of your self-sabotaging strategies.'

This was rather hurtful. Self-sabotaging has been my life's work, and I'm proud of its results. I hardly have any leftover self to sabotage; so successful have been my efforts that I am now reduced to these black marks on a page. I detest those who go to their groups and therapists to enhance their selves, 'building self-esteem' it is called, when it is the proper job of a mature person to lower theirs, to become more attentively self-critical, to cultivate humility and how and when (as frequently is necessary) to express contrition. 'I am so sorry' is the key phrase in any marriage, much more serviceable than 'I love you, Pooh Bear.'

The self, after all, is a metaphysical proposition about which I have as many doubts as Descartes. I have many selves, a panoply of often conflicting voices and opinions. Myself, in the corroded contemporary sense? I try to pay it and him no mind. In general it is preferable to stifle a self, tear it down and skulk into silence, exile and cunning, where you can't inflict yourself on the unwary, and where any hurt you cause is at least from a safe distance.

I do not say this to Lucy, of course I don't, even one as retracted and oppositional as I knows how to keep silent now and again. You have to pick your moments, and fights. Is Bronya one of them?

'Dear Lucy, whatever you say. But don't I at least retain the right to choose my acquaintances?'

'No. You don't. Not when you are totally incapable of looking after yourself properly, and when I am unable to come to help you. It is the most awful situation, it hurts me all over ...'

'I know. It hurts me too. When I think of you and the children ...'

The ensuing silence was prolonged even by Lucy's standards, which I calibrate on a scale that begins with *short* pause (uncertainty, tactical cogitation), to *medium* pause (incredulity), to *protracted* pause (extreme hurt, sometimes rage). This went on longer, even, than the last of these, perhaps because it was symptomatically all three.

'Oh ... Do you? Really?'

'Of course I do.'

'I see. Tell me this then. When did you last speak with Rudy?'

In response I gave her one of my short pauses (stalling) while I worked out what not to say.

'Let me think. You know, one day is rather like another, I'm not so sure ...'

'I am. It was seventeen days ago. He called you.'

'Ah, yes. I remember. We talked about his schoolwork. And football.'

'You did. I was listening for the full four minutes.'

This was uncommonly meticulous, and commonly aggressive of her. In fact, the call only lasted that long because I did most of the not very much talking. It is hard to get many words out of Rudy's contemporary incarnation. Hormonal self-absorption no doubt, I've seen a lot of it over the years, boys reduced to mute grunting animals, not wild exactly but hardly domesticated, incapable of keeping themselves fed and watered, hence resentfully reliant on the providers of such services.

I am pleased to have fathered a daughter, and only a daughter, though God knows they – she! – can be exceedingly difficult. The fact is that mothers are better at raising daughters, and (I am less sure of this) fathers, sons. Suzy and Lucy, though combative from the very start, were united by a commonality of desire and of interest. Suzy claimed to detest modelling children by gender, but instinctively found herself dressing up with her little girl, playing with scent, make-up and jewels, gossiping about the events at school, in ways that – if I'd had a son – I would hardly have generated, or tolerated.

What would I have done instead? On my extensive experience of boys, as little as possible. Boys are tribal. I would have introduced my son from the earliest age to other sons, and let them get on with bickering and fighting, supporting teams and lacerating enemies. I would have found the results intolerable, whereas I was always touched by tiny Lucy in her dressing-up phase, cheeks rouged and smelling of flowers, trailing a mini-gown with a boa round her neck, decked with a tiny scarlet beret. It melted my heart, a metaphor that suggests nothing but the wrong images. Something that melts only recovers when it returns to ice.

According to Lucy – the conversation soon ended – Rudy was brooding and unhappy in a manner both new and disturbing. It had been going on for the last couple of months. Something was happening to him, presumably at school. I know enough about this to understand that the unhappier a boy is, the less he will talk about it. Queries are met with a shrug, empathy with a 'whatever', which has quickly become one of the most objectionable words in our formerly great language. The humiliations of school life are widespread but usually not fatally undermining. School life is established upon the ubiquity of failure. The vast majority of boys learn daily that they are not clever enough, are insufficiently popular or sporty, have the wrong accent or background, are generally disappointing to their fellows and ultimately to themselves. This prepares them for adulthood, love, marriage, and professional life. But it can be taken too far.

In one of my final years teaching at Winchester a boy from Gabon entered the college. His name was Loic, and though his first language was French, he spoke excellent English. He tried to fit in, ingratiated himself abjectly, fetched and carried, smiled a wonderful smile, asked for nothing, and got less. He was docile, perhaps by nature, and his anxiety to please could in such surroundings be mistaken for a more profound submissiveness. The boys called him Gibby, a familiarity that he initially found endearing until after a long hard time he realised that they weren't saying Gabby, after his homeland, which he would have liked, and which the prevailing drawl suggested. No, it was a diminutive of Gibbon. Not Edward. It could hardly have been more insulting if the boys had thrown bananas.

I tried to intervene, and failed. Loic, quite incapable of defending himself, shrank and withdrew. The boys joked that it might soon come to blows, that'd be just the job. I swore quick vengeance on the worst perpetrators. Without much hope, I consulted our ineffectual headmaster, whose only function and desire was to avoid trouble, and to be left alone to smoke his pipe in his befogged office.

I explained the case to him.

'Yes, yes, Darke, unfortunate indeed. Nothing to be done, best leave it, these things always settle down. Boys will be boys, you know. They will deny it hotly, claim they meant no such monkey-business, and no doubt complain to their parents about being unjustly accused. Next thing I know ...'

Of the many troubles that his school could offer, I was one of the recurring ones. I made no secret of my disdain for his lazy moral withdrawal, and made the point unsubtly by never affording him the title Headmaster, calling him instead by his first name, and not even that, not Anthony, which he tolerated, but Tony, which he loathed.

'You see, Tony, the boy is dreadfully isolated here. He doesn't have English as a first language, and though he speaks well is self-conscious. He is rather sensitive, and is relentlessly taunted and bullied. He has few friends, is freezing cold all of the time, and spends most of his waking hours cooped up in his room with the electric fire on three bars, writing homesick letters to his parents ...'

'What? Not thinking of withdrawing him, are they?'

Nothing animates a headmaster more than loss of income, unless it is loss of face. This would entail both. African students were a modest but increasing revenue stream, and he was keen to keep them cooped up as warmly as chickens.

'I don't know, but I doubt it. He's a plucky chap, he'll tough it out.'

'Good, good. Well, that settles that then, doesn't it?'

He rose from his chair and came round his desk to usher me to the door. I stayed put.

'Unless, Tony, you are prepared to take some action here, I will have to myself. But it would be best coming from you, the highest authority.'

He looked modestly pleased, and perhaps surprised, to hear this.

'What exactly do you suggest?'

'Have the boys in ...' I handed him a sheet of paper with seven names on it. '... and read the riot act.'

Our head hadn't read a riot act since studying the Tolpuddle martyrs, against whom all of his instincts were directed. He certainly wasn't going to start another potentially bloody confrontation now, not on his watch.

'You deal with it, Darke. It's your role, not mine. But do be ...'

I stood up to leave, and turned my back on him.

'I certainly will, Tony. You can count on it.'

Why he didn't reprimand, or even dismiss, me was a mystery. I suppose he disliked a fuss – and there would have been one – even more than he disliked me.

The boys that I questioned and reprimanded were unanimous in praise of their own behaviour, and claimed an overweening affection for their attractive African schoolmate. Appalled that I should have misconstrued their intentions, and misunderstood their accents, one or two threatened to bring the matter up 'at home'. To my mind and ear, the bullying abated somewhat, though bullying is so insidious that it cannot be tracked and traced like a virus. Not that we are very good at that. Loic ducked and dived, got his place and second at Cambridge, returned home and soon became minister of this and latterly of that. As did many of the English schoolmates who had bullied him.

I tried to learn from this experience. Racism is universal, either covert or palpable, and is obviously built into the human genome. It is *natural*. We, who are prone to the fatuous belief that what is natural is good, tend to resist this truth. But it's a fact: humans, like many other animals, do not like difference, especially palpable and ineradicable difference, it frightens us, this instantiation of other-ness, and is perceived as a danger. Racism may be ameliorated but will never be erased. When Lucy was three, she embarrassed me profoundly, at the local newsagent's, when she stared at a Black man who entered the shop, and enquired loudly, and innocently, why he was so dirty? I hustled her out, and tried to explain.

When Suzy once did a British Council trip to Kenya, the small school children peered at her, giggling and pointing, and whispered *mzungu!* A white person. It wasn't hostile, nor was it friendly. It was the kind of response they might have made if a hippo had come to speak to them. *Not one of us.* It's universal. But 'Gibby' was a vile name for a Black person. And to poor Gibby himself? We were equally alien, equally other, though being in the minority he would hardly have made a point of this. After he returned to Libreville, he sent a letter to express his gratitude for my support. I wrote to thank him for saying so, but did not otherwise engage except to wish him well. The last thing he needs is a former white master to whom to feel grateful.

Racism, though, is only an instance. Boys latch on to other differences just as fiercely. When a boy is bullied at school because he is weak or poor at sports, weedy or fat, slow at lessons or dyslexic, ugly, crippled, or merely small of member, the results are permanently imprinted, a source of lifetime humiliation. Bullying is universal too.

And so? What was happening to Rudy? Unhappy boys will retreat and retract, do not minimise so much as deny, always in a telltale half-whisper, a monotone, sotto voce. Nothing. There's nothing wrong. Turn away, shrug. Whatever. And this happens, of course, in the optimum situation in which you can sit down together, get as physically close as is allowed, and meet the eye, if it is offered. But now, in our socially distant Alexa world, there is no way forward in such a situation. Rudy is gone, for now. There's no need for Lucy to be so anxious, things will sort themselves out.

Even in the case of poor Loic, they eventually did, once he starred in that year's performance of *Measure for Measure,* where neither his sex nor his Blackness prevented him from making a passable, slightly coquettish Isabella with a French accent. The boys loved her.

I told this story to Lucy, in the hope that it might reassure her. I never learn. It did not. Lucy likes action, and wants counsel not of patience, but about what to do. The head at Rudy's school is apparently a humane man, easily approached and sympathetic, and she had informed him of her worries, and he subsequently had a fireside chat with Rudy. Nothing came of it. It never does. We live in a world in which most of us believe that there are problems, and then there are solutions. You just have to match them up. It rarely comes out as hoped.

Boys are problem machines. If they aren't bullying or being bullied, they are in love or out of it, in the football team or out of that, miserable because their skin is pitted with acne, or cannot comprehend solid geometry or conjugate Latin verbs. Their world is peril, nothing but, and it is astonishing that boys survive it so comprehensively. Most of them. Occasionally one gets lost for ever, or tops himself, which causes a new generation of mothers anxiously to find out what their boy's problem is, and then attempt to solve it. Fathers know better, and know better, too, than to say so.

I sympathised and commiserated with poor distraught Lucy over the phone, and concocted a plan, which could be summed up in the unprepossessing suggestion that I write to Rudy. What good would that do? None, probably, though I assuredly did not say so, but it would open what is stupidly called a 'line of communication'. If his oral discourse was gruntish, Rudy could be surprisingly articulate and forthcoming when writing. Talking to someone was too close, humiliating.

When writing, your relationship is not with a person but a

piece of paper, and with the subsequent marks you make. If he was willing, of course, to allow me even this mitigated entry into his life. I'd have to work my way in, gain his trust, make him lower some barriers. There is no profit in a straightforward *Tell me what's been upsetting you*. No. You have to offer something unexpected, and might not be reflexively shrugged off. It was a technique that had worked for me before, though more often it failed.

*Dear Rudy,*

*Forgive me writing, if writing ever needs forgiveness, but as you will have observed I am not an Alexa person, and your mother's suggestion of Zooming caused me to feel nauseous. As you don't seem entirely comfortable on such screens and devices either, we just stutter and fail to start. You and I have been dearly close all your life – give or take my four years of absence – and I am so anxious to resume our closeness.*

*I am a word person, and (if I may say so) you are too. Many of our cherished, closest moments have come when we shared stories, first when I read to you as a little boy, and later when I wrote that extension of Gulliver, which I modestly regard as one of the proudest moments of my life, both intellectually and emotionally. I loved sitting by your bedside while you snuggled under the sheets, demanding more. I thought of this often in prison, and it comforted me.*

*What I wish to know, and it is easier to ask this way, is what are you reading just now? I remember you love Blake, which fills me with admiration and joy, but tell me what else has excited you? And, even more pressingly, do you write at all? I don't mean school essays, which are inevitably a dead form because you can't allow them to become real, but writing privately, just for yourself? If you do, or even if you don't, but might, would you consider writing something for me, as I once did for you? Anything at all, poetry, fiction, non-fiction, fantasy, whatever, so long as it is real, because real writing comes from the unimpeded heart, and is so satisfying, when you learn to open yourself to yourself.*

*Is this making any sense? I worry that my mind may be as doddery*

*now as my body, but (to be frank) it isn't, not yet. And it's all yours. Try
something out on me, give me what used to be called An Offering. I'd
be so thrilled and grateful.*

*My very best and biggest love. I miss you literally (to use that
fashionably over-used word) more than I can say.*

*Grandpa*

A bit schoolmastery, no doubt he will instinctively resist such an
assignment, but the best I could do. What next? Nothing. I'm
good at that, have always been unthrustingly patient; a by-product
of my time in prison is that I can wait and wait with the worst of
them. Rudy will either answer, or he will not, that is up to him,
and I will not prompt him. Nor will I tell his mother what I have
written, or she will quiz me and monitor Rudy, or perhaps it is the
other way round. Lucy is a subverter of the subtle, has not the
patience or indeed the wit to allow an emotional process to play
itself out. Rereading that sentence makes me ashamed. I sound
like Sam, only more pseudo-Wise, counselling.

I will forget about Rudy. For now. My intervention, welcome
or not, may marginally affect his mental state, but mental states are
quite good at righting themselves by themselves, if you leave them
alone. They are difficult to improve, easy to exacerbate. When Suzy
was depressed, following the publication of her second novel, she
went into therapy with some quacking Austrian woman, under
whose care she descended more deeply into gloom and self-
fixation. She was, fortunately, bright and sceptical enough to see
this, paid off her therapist and shut her down, and recovered slowly
by working in a second-hand bookshop, which only shows how
low she had fallen.

I was surprised to get a response from Rudy within a few days,
and opened the envelope to discover, to my astonishment, the
following:

*When The Gampster settled into his new surroundings, he found that he quite liked it. He had his own room, just like Captain Gulliver had his own stable, and the food was simple and plentiful. Not oats and fresh water, more like porridge and milk. It was enough for The Gampster to keep up his strength. This was not easy, but when you are a famous traveller you have many adventures and meet many rough types. But this was a different sort of adventure. After a while he was not so strong and became ill. He was frightened because travelling is supposed to give you freedom and he had lost his. He was locked up. He was so far from his home that after a while he forgot all about it.*

No explanation was offered. Just these few words, clearly a continuation of the story that Rudy sent me four years ago, and to which I had not responded. I was embarrassed by it then, it was not child-like but childish, a regression that could only be explained by shock and denial. His grandfather was in prison. How does one assimilate or cope with that? The first example was sad, and made me want to cry in mortification, though whether for him, or myself, or both of us, was unclear.

Only a few months previous we sat together in the evenings, newly incarnate as characters in my little Swiftian story. And now I was The Gampster, and Rudy was … what? Was that the point, what was not yet revealed, that Rudy was … something … what … something other, or else, not the author of this simple sad tale, but its invisible or unrevealed protagonist. The Rudester? It hardly bore thinking about, but I did, to no avail. From such impoverished roots, what could possibly flourish?

What this meant − about which I had no idea − was less important than what it initiated and presaged. I am uncertain whether what Rudy has sent was written when he was eight, and kept in a file, or written now, but in his former voice. This matters, though I am not entirely clear how or why. My task, having asked him for something, is to accept what is offered. Some sort of admonition, I suspect. I wrote back, not quite immediately, I let enough time pass that it would not seem that I was shocked, or worse, disappointed. I was both, but I think I have enough confidence in my clever grandson to give him his head, and mine.

*Dear Rudy,*
 *I am most grateful for this, and very interested indeed. More please!*
 *Best love,*
 *Grandpa*

I considered adding 'aka The Gampster', but rejected it quickly enough. No sense encouraging that, because if Rudy follows up on the story, it will surely lead to something other, and different. And probably more disturbing.

The major effect of Rudy's missive is that I feel under attack: his intention, whether conscious or otherwise (not a distinction that much convinces me) seems hostile. A payback. Much deserved. I ought to feel pleased that I have elicited this response, and (however disguised) this strength of feeling. Suzy's Austrian quacker claimed to like it when Suzy attacked her, called it negative transference. Which was rubbish: the only negative transference in psychotherapy is from the client's bank account to the therapist's. And here I am, sufficiently defensive and uneasy, to be thinking the kind of nonsense thoughts that would make SamWise brim and fizzle with excitement. Please God he doesn't interest himself in Rudy's mental state, that would be a disaster. But he's unlikely to notice it. Lucky him.

# PART TWO

# *Oppositions*

There lives no man who at some period has not been tormented
by an earnest desire to tantalise a listener by circumlocution.

Edgar Allan Poe, 'The Imp of the Perverse'

# Chapter 7

I am more than usually bored. I have abandoned my daily stroll (too dull, increasingly puff-puff), and detest what is offered in the media as either news or entertainment. Am not likely to watch some boxed-set adventure located in a very cold place with subtitles. Televised sport is repellent. Magazines irritate me, novels go on and on and end up nowhere. I sit, nap, smoke, and drink, and listen to wonderful music, an art (unlike literature) which not only bears but constantly rewards repeated attachment. I can listen to the late Beethoven string quartets every day, they never wear out, they are still deepening and expanding after my forty years of immersion in them, when they are not on the CD player they are playing in my head. Literature cannot do this, it is (comparatively) thin: I would kill myself before I consented to reread *Middlemarch* every month.

Sitting in my chair, the music in the air, I dream of what once was, and later have nightmares about what will be. I fill my time learning new recipes, often from Mr Otto Lenghi, and was often in a state of exasperation trying to source the myriad obscure constituents (dried barberries, pomegranate molasses, black garlic, rose harissa …) until I realised that they were for sale on Otto's website. Talk about cunning Israelis! When these ingredients became freely (ha!) available, I could spend hours compiling an amusing ethnic meal for one. Or more, really, as it's advisable to have leftovers. After all, that's what I live on.

I drink Peter Mertes Gewürztraminer, which is good with most of Otto's recipes, and meditate on my new scheme, and laugh. I have at last conceived a project worthy of wasting my declining powers on, which will furnish my final days with sufficient amusement to chuckle me into the grave. My topic will allow me re-entry into the world of Indignations, only this time they will not be those of Dickens, C., but of Darke, J. Unlike Mr Dickens's, my harrumphy expostulations will not be leavened by sentimentality, or undermined by whimsy. Mine are not quite the real thing, they are a parody of it, and constitute a different genre, which I am inventing. Not Indignations, but Oppositions, a terrain in which I feel increasingly at home. They keep me awake at night, composing and giggling, when I'm tossing myself about, unwoken.

I will not write, I will compose, a novel, which is an absurd thought, as I have neither a novelist's imagination nor facility, as Suzy often reminded me. Apparently I don't see things clearly, which heaven forfend I might, and have no ear for voices other than my own, which seems both fair and desirable. Distinctly *not* a novelist, which is ironically perfect because what I am going to write is not a novel, but a pastiche of a novel, which will suit me much better. Of what sort of novel? The contemporary sort, which I do not read, but which I often read about: reviews, mentions, interviews, articles.

Such novels are decidedly not written by Mr Barnes or Mr McEwan, who are probably still scribbling away, though no one notices or cares. These contemporary fictions are sanctifications of the lives of the dispossessed, written by a new *brand* of novelist, whose topic is the wretched of the Earth, who poignantly live a long way from England. The characters in an English novel are miserable because they live in Hampstead, those from diverse authors, because they do not.

I already understand the formula, it's hardly subtle. Stick to the agenda! Abjectify the characters but make them brave. Set the tale somewhere poor and obscure, which English readers will be so ignorant about that they will accept any details as verisimilitude. A small African country, perhaps. Best if it is unnamed, that way nobody can spot the implausibilities. Foreground a sensitive protagonist, preferably a woman, struggling against impossible trials. Add her heroic mother and judgemental mother-in-law, two intimate female friends, a worthless husband and a bevy of feral children with names no one can pronounce or remember. Supply a few teeth-clenching scenes of sexual violence and armed conflict, throw in a drought, sprinkle with locusts, and starve a few thousand nameless and meaningless ciphers to provide skeletal authenticity.

I will need to invent a suitably diverse and ethnified background for myself as the writer, and perhaps supply an author picture: use tanning lotion as necessary, the browner the better. Have wild hair. Wear shabby ethnic dress in a bright tribal fabric, add some colourful pebbles on a rope. Maybe even grow a beard, which makes it clear the author is VarySexual: him/her/it/us. Adopt a name with a middle syllable, that's very diverse: Ashar Kum Qwat, Kwami Bil Tong. Then invent a pseudonymous background: perhaps an injured child-soldier, followed by a period of recuperation, and a Creative Writing degree with Distinction from the University of Khartoum. I cannot resist this latter location, because it is the site of the greatest of all dirty limericks:

> A pansy who lived in Khartoum
> Took a lesbian up to his room.
> They argued all night
> Over who had the right
> To do what, and with which, and to whom.

I will offer this dubious CV as a puzzle on a plate to any young commissioning editor sufficiently sceptical to write to ask the university to confirm the award of this degree. Not one will do so, modern publishers are both lazy and credulous. Why would this exciting new novelist have any need to falsify their credentials, which are writ large on every page, and in the capacious heart that penned them!

Am I going to do this, actually do all that transvestite browning, do that myself? It's an enchanting fantasy, but beyond my powers, I'm no thespian, and however you paint me, am clearly not a young African writer, much less one that either is or identifies as a woman, these being, to the diverse mind, much the same thing, plus or minus a few bits of plumbing.

Suzy would have loved this, she was mad about dressing up, and had Humphrey Bogart as an alter ego. But me? I can imagine my new text and incarnation, but surely being it/him/she/they is beyond my powers. I will need the help of an out-of-work actor (they all are) who might be enjoined to secrecy, dressed up, and given a few bob to help pay the rent. As an added incentive, I might offer to share my evening Israeli feast. Would such an impostor come in the midst of our virus, when forbidden entry into other abodes? Of course he would: he's an actor.

If I manage to compose my text, and it's not asking much, it's the sort of rubbish that Mills & Boon writers can produce multiple times a year, it will be amusing to submit the result to publishers. It ticks all the boxes! Right demographic, right setting, right characters, wretched as nuts, with a compelling moral agenda and a story that will tear at your heart and haunt your dreams. A story that needs to be told!

Perhaps that's stated too earnestly, too easily scorned and rejected? To make such a point you have to approach from the side, or better yet sneak up from the rear, puckered and dangerous. Perhaps I could write a second fiction, in which an impoverished elderly English novelist, unable to live on his declining royalties, has to sell his Hampstead flat to a thrusting young ethnic writer of indeterminate gender, recently shortlisted for a Big Prize. Could I steal the title *The Shock of the New*? There's no copyright on titles, I could just as easily call it *Things Fall Apart* or *Heart of Darkness.*

Oh, dear. First I conceive an amusing, solitary *jeu d'esprit,* next thing I am teasing publishers with the result, then contemplating a campaign (however ironised) against the bullying by the new generation, in favour of the received wisdom of the old, which is ironic given that I am no campaigner, and distrust wisdom as much as I do diversity. And then I am planning another novel?

*Hee haw!* as John Wayne used to say. Suzy adored him, when he perched on his horse with his rump weaving seductively in the air, hollering and shooting his gun. *Hold on! Round 'em up one at a time, cowboy!* The very thought of this project spiralling out of imaginative control under the influence of a few glasses of wine makes me inordinately . . . I was going to write 'happy', but I've forgotten what that feels like, and it's an unworthy goal. 'Engaged', perhaps? No, that's wrong. I'll settle for 'happy'. I'm happy to do that.

One thing at a time. The danger will be me, my views and my voice. Am I capable of moderating or self-expunging? My invention, my new voice and authorial persona, have to be simple and declarative. The prose has to fit, and be fitting, plain as plainsong. The simple heart speaks its simple truths, it is not literary, indeed the heart cannot write at all, only the mind can do that. Every subtlety, every unnecessary punctuation mark, will be an offence against authenticity. Keep it simple to make it deep. But to the rightly attuned ear, will it still be readable as parody? Will some look to the horse, some at its shit? As I say this, I know I am once again racing ahead, rein myself in (steady, old boy!) and begin to compose self and story.

The happiness has vanished, I feel anxious and alone. When I was writing my *Gulliver* I had an ally, a listener, an enthusiastic supporter.

Of course, Rudy can hardly play that role with the new fiction. What provisional title might I give it? Let me settle for present purposes on *A Simple Story*, which I can replace later with something more diverse. Not *In Darkest Africa*, though that'd be fun. Nor *Black Lives Matter*, tempting though that may be. We live in a post-satiric age. Too many sacred cows and not enough beefburgers.

Might Miles see the fun of this? He has a puckish nature, adores fronting, centring and entering, or did when he was up to it, and is at the end of his career, with nothing to lose. And of course, if he hops on board, he is the perfect person for the ensuing drama, can send out the proposal for the novel with his warm commendation, and see which publishers bite. And in the end, when all is revealed, it will be he who is bitten. By me: a pleasure long contemplated, and cunningly delayed.

I wrote to him accordingly, setting out the tentative nature of my little plot, asking if he might be interested? And got an immediate response:

*My Dear James,*

*How lovely it is to hear from you, and to find you – I had feared otherwise – in such good spirits. All of us in this lock-up are bored, fretful and however much we Zoom about, basically underemployed emotionally and intellectually. I can hardly read any more, though thank God I no longer need or even wish to. I have sold the agency, though it will keep my esteemed name, and I now appear as some sort of fatuous eminence très grise, go to parties and chat up women whom I have neither the hope nor the capacity of seducing. It was only the fucking that kept me at it. Now I'm thoroughly sick of the literary world, bored by literature itself, and spend my time slouched in front of the telly watching* Carry On *films, drinking my way through my cellar.*

*So your impish project comes at both a bad time – my present lassitude and irritability – and a good one: I'm bored and underemployed, and nothing is amusing any more. The literary world has been hijacked by zealots and proselytisers, and the idea of having fun, much less oppositional fun, is now* verboten *to the point of death by a thousand tweets, which is called cancellation, though it most assuredly is not. My new* mot *is that the collective noun for authors is A Diversity, which amuses the unfaithful.*

*If I were to show your proposal – and I promise I will not – to one of my younger colleagues they would be horrified, censorious, and wet their knickers with indignation, which is a waste of wetted knickers. They are an earnest militia, and you will be attacking them on all fronts, and rears too. They will be offended, scream and thrash about, and then wish to punish you, but not in a fun way.*

*Which is to say, I like it! But – you will have sensed this coming – I cannot help in any way, even be implicated in the hoax. It would do harm to the agency that bears my name, my poor little chicks would be mortally offended, and our few publisher clients would treat us even more shabbily than they do now.*

*Warm regards, and good luck,*

*Miles*

I carry on, carrying on. It passes the time. I'm rather enjoying it.

The air is dark with dust. I sniff and look upwards hoping for some sign of rain. I tell the children that Allah will provide, but their bellies are never full. They play fitfully and argue. In the village the sun beats down at midday, and all is still. There is never enough time. Now I prepare the *nsima*. Later I will fetch water.

It's a start, perhaps a bit forced and provisional. To the diverse modern ear it will, I hope, sound convincing, to a sophisticated one, a mere compilation of the usual tropes: weather, poverty, anxiety, family . . . What our French baker calls 'local crullers'.

Which gives me pause, I'm hungry, it's time to make something complicated for my dinner. Then I will do just enough research to fill in a few blanks under my African skies. There's no need for me to finish the fiction, thank God. If I provide an opening section and a short specimen chapter or two, that will be sufficient to send round the publishers, together with some misinformation about its author.

Lucy wants to make an appointment for me at one of those Harley Street clinics, which are apparently still functioning, because a private doctor's love of money is unceasing, and a neurotic's desire for medical attention is eternal. I will grudgingly accede to the script, but I don't want to be examined by an avaricious stranger, and since my former ineffectual GP is no more (not that he was ever much) I get to choose his replacement. But I don't know any doctors. I hardly know anyone. When I was at Merton there was a very bright chap reading medicine who has apparently set up a successful practice in Oxford. I can remember his constantly averted florid face and hunched walk – he was called Bashful by his peers, after one of the seven dwarfs, but his proper name escapes me, nothing that some judicious googling can't solve.

Hutchinson, Dr Robert, Beaumont Street Surgery. I email him to describe what (Lucy says) I need, and suggest we set up an appointment, without mentioning our former acquaintance. With any luck he will be too busy, fail to remember me fondly, or perhaps have closed up shop. But I received a charming reply, praising the work of the Suzy Moulton Foundation, for which he thinks I am responsible, and suggesting a date two weeks hence. I am already in a state of heightened anxiety about this.

I will, Lucy insists, need to wear a mask, and she has posted several that she purchased on the Internet, which she thinks will amuse me. All are brutally ugly instantiations of Penguin covers, and when I tried one on in front of the mirror I cringed:

# THE PLAGUE
# ALBERT CAMUS

I wore this on a quick trip to the newsagent's, and no one noticed it, not understanding the joke, or insufficiently interested by it. Most will not have heard of Camus, French existentialists being extinct.

I dread going to this doctor, in retrospect a bad choice. Surely it is better to be poked by a stranger than an acquaintance, however former. Loathing the thought as I do, I am still less intimidated by the prospect than I am by Lucy's increasingly strident insistence that I *look after myself properly.* Following our meeting in the park, Bronya told her that I was looking 'very thin, pale and very poorly, and could hardly walk'. Together they have determined that I need Help. I am informed this is no longer up to me.

It's an idiotic intrusion. I don't want Help, and I won't agree to receiving it. But short of refusing to answer Lucy's calls, I cannot put her off. *Relentless* hardly captures the tenor of it, which if I resist will morph into *ferocious,* and then escalate. I will go to the damn doctor. My first consultation is scheduled to take an hour, which will be followed by an assault and battery of invasive tests.

The last time I was in a private clinic was when Suzy was first diagnosed with her cancer, and became a patient – much against my will – of her Dr Larry. She resisted my pleas in favour of some other quack, saying that hers was already comprehensively aware of her organic functions, and hence the right man for the job. His offices were on Wimpole Street, which he had chosen with typical Jewish anxiety about being the right man in the right place, adjudging it a tonier location for his office than Harley Street, which is peopled entirely by more than usually greedy doctors and their fatly veiled Arabian hypochondriacs.

If anyone were to read this journal, which is more than unlikely, they would observe with some distaste that I am frank about many things: my organic functions, internal processes and oppositional feelings, my few likes and many dislikes, the trials and humiliations of increasing debility. Journals are useful friends, the pages someone you can commune with, without feedback or opposition. That is why sensitive teenage girls are often portrayed as writing each entry starting 'Dear Diary'. Someone to talk to, frankly and unabashedly. Also why their mothers always have a peek, recoil, and worry about what to do next. You can't address a problem you are not allowed to know about.

Even I, though, have my boundaries and limits, and my frankness is not open-ended, though I myself have been, all too recently. I will not record the details of my visits to the no-longer Bashful, the garrulous Dr Hutchinson, nor the subsequent humiliation of my many tests and examinations at the John Radcliffe Hospital, which if they did not exactly locate me amongst the terminally ill, almost caused me to be so. I was chagrined that they allowed me to enter the premises, amidst the respirators, the gasping and the dying. It frightened Lucy: perhaps I was terminally ill? But it was merely a case of an old Oxford connection, which allowed me early admission, as if I were some sort of precocious scholarship boy, rather than an enfeebled old one.

When I was a child, more or less Rudy's (former) age of about eight, I was an assiduous gatherer of little-known facts, a category that has now disappeared. For my ninth birthday a new copy of *The Guinness Book of Records* arrived in the school post, with a card from my mother, and on other occasions I received books about geography, nature, history and art, and sometimes (the only ones sent by my father) sport. The most exciting of these presents arrived when I was ten, and consisted of a full set of the *Encyclopædia Britannica,* a second-hand edition published a few decades previously. Enough facts to make Mr Gradgrind swoon! I conceived the project of reading it from A to Z, after which I would know everything. I got a little way past Anchovy, an uninteresting, tiny fish, when I gave up and started skimming. I never got to the Bs.

Nowadays, of course, nothing is little-known, everything is

available to a googler, though whether the results are trustworthy is not listed on the tin. So I try to learn things, when I can, from reliable sources. Such as the nurse who performed an echocardiogram on my poor quivering self, anointed my chest with lubricants, and pressed some gadget against it while I lay on my left side learning my new facts the hard way. The incessant whooshing sound emanating from the machine, that was from me, was my blood circulating as my heart pumped it. I found this terrifyingly close to the very mystery of being, and its awful contingencies. Stop the whoosh, stop the person. I was quivering so piteously that the kindly nurse ceased for a moment to enquire if I needed a rest, or a drink of water? What I needed was a fistful of Valium.

When at last I was wiped down with an oily rag, the nurse told me a little-known (to me) fact, which I wish I had not learned. I don't like it. I don't like any facts about inner organs, except those of beasts and fowls. The fact was this: the human heart beats about 100,000 times a day. Not more or less, that's the oddity, you'd suppose some chaps are fast beaters and others slow, but it's almost as regular as clockwork. Mine, I was told, beats 100,030 times a day, which is well within the 'margin of error', which I hope refers to the statistics and not the heart. I was about as pleased to learn this as I would be to witness the growth of a tumour, or the effect on the lungs of our new virus.

The body ought to keep its secrets where they belong, inside not out. When I go to bed, since learning my new fact, I can hardly restrain myself from counting, then multiplying to see if I am on course. 100,000 a day is 4,166 beats an hour, or 69.4 a minute. So, speaking roughly, and the heart is not an approximate organ, it's almost as good as a Rolex, that comes to more or less a beat a second. It is impossible not to count, and horrifying to do so. Some anxious idiots take their pulse constantly; some of them even have machines on their necks or wrists to do the job for them. I've seen them in the streets, and am as repulsed as if the culprits were publicly masturbating.

A further little-known fact: humans are the cardiacal equivalents of chickens. A chicken lives on average some fifteen years, if it can avoid being consumed, and its heart beats so quickly that on its elderly demise, it has pumped some 2 billion times. So has mine. It's no wonder we elderly folks call each other 'my old chicken'.

I was given a few pages of results involving my blood and many organs, prescribed a panoply of new medicines, and a suggested revision of my eating, smoking and exercising habits. I did not read any of this, though I took the pills, being doubly in fear of my internal processes and my external daughter's admonitions. She demanded the data of my various examinations, but I have some residual pride, and demurred. I'd done what she asked. I would not talk about it further. It's my damn life, I heard myself saying firmly to her, only to be greeted by a snort of disapproval, and disbelief. Apparently I have claim on some of it, but so does she, and so does Rudy. Amelie doesn't care if I live or die.

To my surprise, I kept so firmly to my refusal to elaborate or to engage that Lucy dropped her hectoring, merely to enquire every day if I have eaten and walked well, and taken my pills. She has even stopped enquiring about my internal blockages, bowels and arteries alike. Not much she can do about them, is there? I regard her withdrawal from the Health front as a victory, and am proud of myself for having, at last, stood my ground. Writing this, I am amused at how naive I am. Lucy? Withdrawing? Accepting defeat?

One summer day, as the air freshened and our government began to allow more citizenly intercourse and discourse, my doorbell rang. I didn't answer it, because on looking out through my 180-degree brass-door-viewer-peephole-glass-lens, I could see trouble on the doorstep. Two troubles. I retreated slowly backwards down the hallway, and tiptoed into the sitting room, suppressing a desire to cower behind the sofa. Even the repeated visits of the police, some four years ago, had not filled me with such dread. In fact, I'd rather enjoyed them, played the fop and dandy, mocked, ironised, and ended in prison.

I could hear my mobile ringing upstairs, but ignored it. Perhaps they would think I had gone out for a stroll, and would go away? They did not. Kept ringing for a time, then walked off together and returned ten minutes later with paper cups of takeaway coffee which they sipped companionably while ringing the doorbell incessantly. They both knew that constant noise, however muted as my doorbell is, makes me crazier even than unfortunate human contact. By the time the bell had chimed for the sixty-seventh time, I opened the door, a feigned look of surprise on my face as I rubbed my eyes.

'Oh, my dears! What a treat! I'm sorry to be slow answering the door, I was fast asleep.'

Neither bothered to challenge this palpable fib. Lucy looked at me hard and steadily, as if I were a specimen under a microscope: no tousle, no crumple, no scratchy eye residue. Her eyes, blank and insistent, met mine, studied my face, and made their way forensically downwards, interrogating my parts and limbs, with special attention to my hands, before settling on my slippers, as if she could see through them to the bony bits below.

They removed their masks, came into the hallway and headed briskly for the kitchen.

'We need to talk!' said Lucy.

'Me too!' said Bronya.

Not me. I followed, docile but not yet defeated.

'Can I make you some more coffee?' I asked.

No, I could not.

'What about a biscuit then? I've made some delicious Otto Lenghi treats, I often have them with my coffee in the mornings.'

'Sit down and stop babbling!' said Lucy.

Bronya didn't say 'Me too!' but nodded her agreement at the suggestion, or command.

Ever biddable, I waited like a naughty schoolboy about to be reprimanded. That was a script that I could accede to, and play a part in, because the metaphor only took one so far. These were not my headmaster, they had no punishments to mete out. Could not administer six of the best, call in my parents, or rusticate me for a term. If there was any master present, surely it was me.

If Lucy had brought a gavel, she would have struck the kitchen table with it.

'The time has come . . .' she began.

'To talk of many things!' I intoned happily.

Having a limited range of whimsical reference, Lucy looked puzzled, though she could hardly have disagreed with what I said. Perhaps it was the way I said it?

'"The Walrus and the Carpenter"! Marvellous, I read it to you when you were little!

> *'Of shoes—and ships—and sealing-wax—*
> *Of cabbages—and kings—*
> *And why the sea is boiling hot—*
> *And whether pigs have wings . . .'*

'They fucking don't!' said Lucy, provoked, as I had intended.

Bronya looked bemused, and interested. Perhaps I might recite the whole to her, as she clearly didn't know the poem. It would deepen her understanding of the foundational verities of the English character. I was about to suggest this when Lucy thumped her metaphoric gavel and literal hand.

'This!' said Lucy, inexactly but firmly. 'This is an example of what we need to address . . .'

The 'we' was purely rhetorical, though I began to suspect that if it was plural, I wasn't included, and Bronya was. How might that be? I was, alas, about to find out, unless I could summon one of my faints. I held my breath and leant slightly to the side. Lucy looked at me with some alarm and more disdain. I soon righted myself and nodded in mock attention.

'You don't answer the doorbell, respond to texts or emails, can hardly bring yourself to speak on the phone. You evade your family. Your health is terrible and getting worse, you can barely toddle about. From the look of you, I doubt you are eating properly. You smoke too much, you drink too much, and you hardly go out.'

She read my silence as confirmation of her diagnosis.

'You take your pills?'

'I do.'

'Good. But that's not enough, I'm sorry to say …' (She wasn't.) 'I'm so sorry, this happens when a parent gets old and infirm, families have to face the facts. That time has come. I'm afraid you are no longer capable of looking after yourself.'

I said nothing, and was soon presented with a long list of what else was wrong, and what would soon be done about it …

The children are hungry, but they are strong and lithe. They carry, clean, do the washing and grind the corn flour, go to school without complaint and study their lessons in the evening. They live and play together in the dirt, it burnishes them. The local *mzungu* children are pasty and become filthy when they stray outdoors. Their mothers scold them shrilly. 'Come out of there this instant!' they demand, waggling their ugly pink fingers.

'Dad! Dad! Are you listening to a word I say?'

'Of course, darling!'

'Oh, you are, right? Tell me what I just said.'

'Never mind that. I will tell you what *I* say. I am very touched and grateful that you have come, both of you, and that you care for me so deeply. I do not take this for granted. But my answer is still no.'

Lucy looked surprised to hear this. I'd apparently been lost in reverie. Had I any idea what I was saying no to?

Schoolteachers learn this trick, and use it constantly. Set the class a lesson, make sure their heads are down, then lean back, ostentatiously peruse a magazine, and dream of a better life. At the same time, keep monitoring behaviour, noting who is slacking, who whispering together, observing the passed notes and sly glances, the comics open under the desks. It's one of the few treats of classroom life, to emerge from one's apparent stupor, just before the class ends, to accuse and to admonish the culprits.

'It is so kind of you, Bronya, to make this suggestion, which I assume will disrupt your life. But I do not need a housekeeper, even one who would be as generous and efficient as you ...'

Not to mention invasive, blunt, and irritating. When she was my weekly cleaner, those few hours a week were quite sufficient, partly because she was an intruder, but also, I must admit, because I was getting fonder of her. I introduced her to Dickens, whom she both admired and disdained, and we talked of many things. She was a quick study, confident in her own opinions. A science graduate from Sofia, she had failed to find a job in the UK, and was not too proud to do cleaning work. From her meagre income she sent money to her aged parents, while living in a bedsit in outer London. She was fond of me, and sorry for me in my grief.

Of course I fired her, informed her agency that I no longer had need of her excellent services. But that was not the end of Bronya, who is almost Lucy's equal in tenacity: the two of them teamed up. Lucy was already keeping a close eye on me, during that year of mourning, and enlisted Bronya's assistance, cut her a key to my front door, and waited for her to make some approach. When she let herself in and sneaked up the stairs, she frightened me to near cardiac arrest.

This does too, right now, this new approach. My rejection of a live-in servant has been expected, and a compromise was soon kitchen-tabled. Bronya will come in 'regularly' to do the cleaning and laundry, get the shopping and deliver the dry cleaning, and do some cooking if I wish, which I certainly do not. I am not a dumplings-and-cabbagey sort of person.

We try to thrash out what 'regularly' will entail, but it is clear that it will mean – as Lewis Carroll said of his portmanteau words – whatever they want it to mean. Carroll added that when he made a word work so hard he always paid it extra, a stipulation that will no doubt apply to Bronya, though payment will most certainly not be by me. As my permission is not required regarding Bronya's forthcoming appearances, I shall neither pay for nor welcome them. This bit of grudging meanness was all I could salvage by way of self-assertion, but it felt good nonetheless.

# Chapter 8

To my astonishment, horror, and modest delight, it goes on. It seems to be developing a will of its own.

The only problem child is my first. There are seven of them now, the youngest is almost two and she craves milk and attention. I no longer have enough of either. Their father goes away with bad men in the day and returns demanding food, and sometimes more. The children flock to him, he is jolly when he is drunk, except when he gets angry. He cannot concentrate because parts of his mind have been left in the battles and streets. He likes to tease, he refers to the children by numbers rather than their names. I think sometimes he cannot remember which is which. He resented choosing each name, which we do in a way which is not casual, like the *mzungu*. They think a name is a garment, you choose one and put it on. James, Charles, Sarah, Rose.

For us names are natures. Our first child was a son, who bawled day and night for months. He naturally was called Mavuto, but his father couldn't bear to say this, and called him ONE. Not Number One, just ONE. Our second child was weeks overdue before making his appearance. He is named Chabwera, which means Arrived at Last. That one was easy. His father called him TWO. And so it went. I objected, but the children like this, and do it too.

'Mayi! SIX is eating my *nsima!*'

'You shut up, FOUR!'

Banbo is constantly in conflict with ONE, who resents his drunken unwillingness to support his family. He brings in little money, he does little work. Often he does not come home when the sun sets. No one asks where he spends the night, though I and my dear parents know, and know better than to ask. It will come to no good.

Mother says he must not be blamed. He has seen too much and suffered too much, been wounded in his body and his soul. Like an animal, he eats and drinks and makes love, but otherwise slouches in the shade of the baobab. Mother spends her time nursing Father, who lies in the back of the hut, murmuring and drinking sips of water. His spirit is full of life and wishes to remain in this world. But his bones are ready to make their escape. I urge the children to sit with him for a few minutes, to fan his face so the flies do not settle. He likes to hold their little hands, but they fidget and soon run off.

Painting by numbers. Google a few bits about this or that. Throw in the usual references to poverty, race, family discord. Range from life to death in a single bound. Shun complexity, introspection, intelligence. Is what remains simplistic? Or archetypal? Could anyone take this seriously? Unlike my Swiftian exercise, which engaged my heart and mind, this is just a little test, a provocation. It will probably come to nothing, I'm not facile enough to produce an adequate pastiche, not of this material.

It's hardly necessary to consult an agent, I will do it myself. Because when the hoax rolls out, and if by any unlikely chance it works and fools somebody, then I want the credit. All of it. It's my idea, my production, my vendetta against the received nonsense of the day. That'll woke them up. I think that's the new expression.

When Suzy sent the proposal for her second novel, it was a lengthy and wearying process because in those days young writers understood that books must be offered to one agent or publisher at a time. Their rejection letters – Suzy had a lot of them – ran strictly to form. First a paragraph of thanks, and of praise, sometimes fulsome. Paragraph two began with 'But', and went on to reject the submission, sometimes without giving reasons ('is not right for our list'), occasionally engaging with the text, and why it isn't, quite, well . . . good enough. There was then a final short paragraph, or perhaps it might be part of the 'Yours sincerely' bit, wishing the author good luck.

I will of course submit my Simple Story to many publishers at the same time, and collect their rejections into a little folder, edit them, and perhaps publish that. It would be more amusing, and certainly more revealing, than my African so-called novel. It could be a companion pamphlet to my *De Profundis*.

If necessary I can self-publish, apparently there's no longer a stigma attached to this. I'd need a name for my press. What larks! The Opposition Press? Diversity House? There used to be a Fuck You Press in New York that published a poem titled 'The Platonic Blow', a sloppy job by W. H. Auden. Perhaps I could resurrect that imprint.

I'll need a pseudonym as well. I am more likely to catch the spirit of the times and tempt an unwitting agent or publisher with my novel, if I am (more or less, to a degree, in my own special way) a woman. VarySexual, not merely non-binary, but non-trinary: She/her/he/him/us/it. Her name? *Mayeso Ndipo Wakuda*: in Chichewa this translates as *Test from God and Dark*. A dozen roses to the winner if anyone twigs.

The sensitive young editors will surely respond to this hybrid gendered person. *Very* cool! They have the agency to support whatever submission they fancy, so long as it is sufficiently diverse. Trans is hot at the moment, they are women, most certainly not defined or limited by having a uterus and vagina, which are no longer necessary to femalehoodery. Unless you might want to have a baby, in which case they are distinctly useful.

Whoa! Rushing ahead again, trying to do too much too quickly. Grandmother used to say, when I ran about like crazy, 'Wild horses couldn't stop him!' The reason for this plethora of fantasy plans and jolly japes is that I am, how odd, how peculiar, it is almost as unexpected as being happy, a description I resisted until its sheer accuracy overwhelmed me ... that I am, at this one and very time, *excited*. It's as surprising as an erection, as I remember them, but lasts longer and is more satisfying.

And exhausting. I will go upstairs, take some Armagnac and Valium, and sleep away the afternoon. That will provide some test of whether this ... excitement ... still resides in my mind and informs my spirit, in which case having come out of Africa, I will return to it. In truth? I rather hope I will, suspect I will. I intend to.

On awaking, though, and I suppose this is a sign of some residual moral seriousness that I cannot expunge, I found myself thinking not of my hot huddle of Africans, but of my grandson. Who has not responded to my last letter, nor added to his cryptic reincarnation of the dreaded Gampster, a word that my fingers find hard to peck, and my mind to accommodate. Might that be part of the purpose of his re-emergence? Though I had promised myself that I would leave the next move to Rudy, it was becoming increasingly clear that there was no next move. Except in the sense that he had apparently moved on.

That is his right. A point that I made to Lucy from the start, and recurrently to myself over these intervening weeks. I have confidence in his underlying seriousness, balance and goodness. Rudy has no need to prove this by writing once again. But, as I have remarked *ad nauseam,* if there is something to be said for such wisdom, there is more to be said against it: once established in the mind it descends and degrades into insincerity and moral rote. Wisdom retreats into homily.

I wrote again to Rudy. A proper note on best-quality paper, addressed the envelope 'R. Parkin, Esq.' I think that might amuse him, but then again I don't know him, not any more. I adored him, then, but the then Rudy is gone, and so is the now Rudy, unless I manage to find him. Rereading this clumsy and emotionally laden sentence I think I can see what it means, and what I am trying to say. It makes me more than sad, rereading my note before stuffing the envelope, pasting the stamp and tottering to the postbox.

*My Dear Rudy,*

*I rather suspected that I would hear no more of The Gampster, that figure having absented himself for these long years, though I was touched to hear from him again. I believe I know what you are trying to say.*

*May I make a suggestion, which I hope you will not find foolish of me? When I was away, I often thought of the two of us celebrating your eight-and-a-half-year-old birthday at Browns in Oxford, sharing a hot fudge sundae. I so loved that. I can still taste it.*

*Browns is of course still closed, but might we once again meet over an ice-cream, perhaps at the café in St James's Park, and have a chat? I think I know what we need to talk about, or what I need to. The fact that you have said so little is because it is I who need to do the saying.*

*May I? I would be so grateful.*

*Much love,*

*Grandad*

*This Sunday? Say at 2.00?*

Apprised by her son of this new plan, Lucy was quick to respond, having no inner portcullis that she can draw between thinking something and immediately expressing it. She sent a text:

Winner of the Gold Cup for Acuity in Child Psychology: Darke, James. For conceiving the project of treating a surly almost thirteen-year-old as if he were eight, and taking him for an ice-cream.

145

Silly old fool that I am, everyone stays the same age. He probably drinks beer by now, and smokes stuff. I am not up to this sort of thing, I'm an arse.

Two days later I had an elegant italic script note from Rudy saying that he would meet me there. Not effusive, exactly. Halfway, I suppose, a halfway house of ice-cream, of which I am once again the Emperor. I will smoke a big cigar. It will make me sick. I am sick.

And tired. Of everything. I had the fantasy – hope never dies in my poor struggling heart, however I try to stifle it – that on my return home I would at last encounter a problem-free life, and could ease myself into retirement and senility. It works at a material level: enough money, sufficient luxury, a house that suits me. But that is as nothing compared to the emotional level. It never stops. If I must have an emotional life, couldn't it be simple, and straightforward?

In the night I awoke and sleep was irrecoverable. Better to get up, pour an Armagnac, and retreat to my study. The thought of my forthcoming meeting with Rudy, the ritual sharing of ice-cream, makes me so anxious that I try to banish it from consciousness. I wish I were not me, not here, not now.

The children are curious, and lurk by the entrance and stare in at his bed. The *mzungu* call it a deathbed, as if life ended entirely upon it. To us, this is where eternal life begins.

The flies have taken possession of his face, his soul is readying itself for transportation to paradise. Mother sits with him to wet his lips with water, his breathing is irregular. Soon he will have departed, and all of us will feel relief, and joy at his passing into eternal union with the Compassionate, the Merciful. We have dug a grave at the burial ground, prepared the sheets, and have water ready to be heated for the cleansing of the body.

In the afternoon our esteemed Sing'anga came to visit, and ordered me to brew bush tea and mix it with palm sugar. When it was ready he left it to cool for a few minutes, and added some herbs that he took from a sachet in the pocket of his robes. Sitting by the bedside he fed the liquid gently into Agogo's lips, which seemed to smile in gratitude. After ten minutes it was all gone, and Sing'anga stood up.

'He will sleep now,' he said.

He declined tea himself, though we pressed him, but accepted a small gift, which he will put in his charity fund, to assist the poor, the miserable, and the dying.

That's enough, though my mind races and my fingers twitch with anticipation of the next phrase or image, as my poor characters struggle to come into life. But I am due at the café at 2.00, so order Driver for 1.30. This will get me to the park at 1.45, as there is no traffic these days, no one has anywhere to go, nothing as pressing as an ice-cream appointment. I will sit on a bench and compose myself.

When I reached the café there was no sight of Rudy, so I plonked myself down wearily on a bench, even the walk from the roadway left me short of puff. Dr Bashful (I have reinstated his name, he was more agreeable when he talked less) says this is caused by my heart condition, and it would help with my breathlessness if I exacerbated it by walking quickly. This feels counter-intuitive to me. Walk more, be even more puffed, get the heart rate up! I have spent my life trying to keep it down, it's too late to change my ways, dispositions, or desires. If one afternoon my weary generative organ were quietly to cease its ministrations I would be relieved of the great burden of being, the onerous task of being me.

In my notebook I have time to write for a few minutes.

The children mass round the graveside as the shrouded body is laid gently in its final resting place. We sing our praises quietly, then louder, wishing a speedy and happy transit to eternal happiness in the gardens of delight. Mama Agoga weeps silently. It was she who covered his body with the shroud, composed his face and eyelids tenderly, and placed his hands together in eternal supplication. Their union, she says, was happy, and death will not end it. Soon she will rejoin her beloved. Until then, they are still as one. Her grandchildren come up, one by one, to hug and to comfort her as she weeps.

I am beginning, which rather alarms me, to take some interest in this emerging story, which is threatening to escape from jolly japery. It seems I cannot write something without taking it seriously. But what 'it' is this? Is it still a hoax? It surely cannot be anything approaching a serious attempt at an exotic, diverse, fiction. I don't know anything, anything at all, about my subject. I'm just flipping words about, like pancakes.

'Hello. I hope I'm not disturbing you.'

The well-spoken young man in front of me stood back on his heels, awaiting my response, which was slow coming. It was Rudy, was it, surely it was, was him? It seemed unlikely. Tall and lanky, his voice now at that transitional moment between adulthood and childhood, pitched lower but uneasily so, it was most remarkable for having shed any vestiges either of his father's drear Northern inflections, or the Oxfordshire burr of his infant schooldays. He sounded as I had always wished him to sound.

And looked, how? The curious, sad answer, is that he looked typical of so many well-brought-up children, in that he didn't appear much different from a badly-brought-up one. Just as his mother is indistinguishable from your low-born slattern. The habit of dressing well is well-nigh extinct. Rudy was appallingly attired in a pair of blue jeans that were faded and torn in various places, and even more shamelessly in a Sheffield United jersey that bore the stains of a hundred (mis)matches. To be fair, it was only this garment that allowed me confidently to locate him as my grandson, so thoroughly changed was he.

He'd gained perhaps six inches and three stone, had a healthy glow on cheeks that seemed to have been shaved, and his face had filled out and formed into incipient manhood. His hair seemed modelled on Boris Johnson's, only messy. It was easier to locate in his visage an image of the man that he would become than the child that he had been.

All of this figuring out and taking in took a few seconds, no more.

I rose, and cradled him in my arms.

'Grandpa! We're not supposed to hug! Social distancing!' I could feel him trying to free himself gently from my arms, but I didn't let go. Acceding, he slowly and gently then firmly put his arms around me, and we remained for some seconds in imperfect, intimate proximity. We stood apart, a little awkwardly, and I looked at him again. It was indisputably my grandson, but it was not, as I had understood the term, and the person, and the name, *Rudy*. It was someone else, someone other. What had he to do with me, and I with him? Why, oh why, oh me, why would I have invited him out for this regressive treat?

He detached himself gently, stood back and laughed.

'I'm gagging for that ice-cream,' he said. 'Shall we wander over?'

I picked up my parcel from the bench.

'Me too! Let's!'

We soon returned to the bench and sat side by side licking and murmuring with pleasure. What a capital idea, to conceive this ceremony. Everyone is a sucker for ice-cream, even of the degraded English park variety. It brings people together. Even grandfathers and their newly re-acquired grandsons. The further pleasure was that, as we sat at the bench slurping and wiping our lips, we were not looking at each other directly, which is in my opinion the best way to handle an emotionally tricky situation. Don't meet their eyes, or have them meet yours, lest they flash, or water.

Thirteen, he'd be thirteen in a few months, the age at which boys came to my schools. It's a tender time for them. Looking at him I thought I recognised the type. When I was a schoolmaster I maintained that there were seven sorts of schoolboys, and like William Empson's seven types of ambiguity, they were both well- and ill-defined. There were the bullies and the bullied, the swots and the hearties, the socially adaptable and the homesick. The seventh category was a canister into which I shoved the unclassifiables, a clear indication that I was talking nonsense.

But if Rudy was partly swot and partly not hearty exactly, but sporty, if being a fencer counts as sporty, actually it's sort of nerdy, he was a good example of the inalienable truth that if boys will be boys, they are distinctly different.

'Darling Rudy ...' I paused for a moment. 'When an adult talks to a schoolboy and doesn't quite know what to say, they always ask about school ...'

'Please don't. I wouldn't answer.'

'Instead, please, please, let me listen. You talk. There's something on your mind ...'

He was silent as he took two extra-long licks of his ice-cream.

'... in my heart, I'd say.'

Useful things, these ice-creams. I applied myself to mine assiduously. Wiped my nose with my handkerchief, folded it into a square and replaced it in my pocket.

'Will you tell me? What it is?'

'You don't know, do you?'

'Tell me, please.'

'It's obvious. You went away ...'

'... of course I did. I'm sorry. But going to prison was ...'

He put his non-ice-cream hand into the air abruptly.

'You went away. From me.'

'Rudy, dear . . .' I turned to face him. He was looking out at the pond and would not meet my eye. 'Surely you know how much I love you!'

He shook his head.

'I don't.'

'But surely . . .'

'I don't because you don't. You didn't. You went away for four years, didn't answer my poor little letters, sent love to me through Mummy, sent money for my birthdays. Not even a card. Wouldn't even allow me . . .' He wiped his eyes with his sleeve.

I wiped mine with my creamy hanky.

'I am so sorry . . .'

'If you loved me you'd do something about it. Love is doing stuff, like walking the dog . . .'

I began to frame an uneasy answer that would have begun by observing the inappropriateness of the analogy, but he continued. He'd had a long time to work out what he needed to say, and how to say it. He wanted to get it right. My job was to listen.

'When I was eight I loved you so much. And you loved me. Read to me, even wrote that story for me. It was about us. And when you went away I tried to write one for you, and . . . I was only eight but . . .'

'Dear Rudy, I'm so, so, sorry!'

'Are you? You loved me when I was eight. And now I'm a different person.'

'Of course.'

'And the sad thing is that you're not the same person either. But in a bad way. You used to love me . . .'

'Darling . . .' I reached to take his hand, but he pulled away.

'Mummy says that when somebody really needs you, you run away.'

'Do I?'

151

'Of course. Think how you treat her!'

'I won't ask you what you mean, but . . .'

'Both of us adore you. You know, you're like our hero. But the feeling only goes one way.'

'Rudy. Darling Rudy. I am so proud that you can say this, which is so hurtful because it is so true. Thank you . . .'

We dried our eyes again.

'I am not a very good man. You're right, I have failed you. It's true!'

He nodded but did not look up.

'Will you please give me another chance? To show love rather than just declaring it?'

'Yes. And to Mummy too. She cries every time after she speaks with you.'

Was it possible that Lucy put him up to this, wrote the script, set the play in motion? I toyed with the idea ungenerously, and rejected it. Lucy is not subtle enough, if she has something to say she's a full-frontal sort of girl. Isn't she? But according to Rudy she has been suffering, from me, from my behaviour, and said little by way of remonstration. Allowed me to get on with, or get away with, my apparent mistreatment of her, suffered on the phone, and grieved after ringing off.

'I will. I promise.'

We finished our ice-creams, and dried our eyes. I had brought some wet wipes with me, and took out the packet, pulled one out and cleaned my hands properly. Passed it to a quizzical Rudy, who did so as well. As we did, one of the many dogs who were walking their owners round the path stopped and approached me in a manner that might be called friendly. A fetching ball of white fluff, not so much an animal as an animated toy from Hamleys, stopped by my side, and looked up. I suppressed a surprising instinct to give its head a little scritch. Its owner looked pleased that we'd formed an unhostile connection.

'Mavis likes you,' she said. 'He doesn't usually like strangers.'

I didn't ask the obvious question. It's London, after all. I took another wet wipe from the packet to clean my hand in case the aborted scritch left some trace. Taking the carrier bag from my side, I said, 'I have a little present for you,' and took out the two books. As I began to hand them over, Rudy said, 'How did you know?'

'Well,' I said, 'I know you are so fond of Blake, and this is the first edition of Gilchrist's *Life of Blake*. It was published in 1863, and it was the first biography of him.'

'I remember,' said Rudy, taking the two volumes into his hands gently, running his fingers over the brown cloth and beautiful gilt figuration on the covers, the three angels, and the image of Blake's head and shoulders, with creeping floral surrounds.

'When I was little, and Mummy and I were in your house and sometimes if you went out, I would go into your study and take these books – these are the ones, aren't they? – off your shelf, ever so carefully. I had to stand on tiptoes. And then I would just sit in your chair with them on my lap, and feel the covers and sigh because they were so beautiful. And sometimes I'd take one of those other books, you know the ones with all the illustrations?'

'Yes, the Trianon Press facsimiles.'

'And I would sit and try to read a little of them. You know, about the chimney sweep and the lamb and the tiger? But mostly I'd look at the pictures. I tried to work them out. Sometimes the characters looked like statues and sometimes like angels ...'

'It's true. I often wonder whether Blake actually drew very well ...'

'He did! I love them!'

'But Rudy, this is so wonderful. Why did you never tell me? We could have had such fun reading together!'

'I was too frightened.'

'Frightened? Why?'

'That you'd think I'd get the books dirty, or tear a page, or put them back in the wrong place. I was only little, but I was ever so careful.'

I was chagrined to hear this. Am I so fastidious and judgemental?

'Well,' I said, 'I hope I can make amends with this gift, which is properly yours now, not mine. I would have inscribed it for you, but that would be a desecration, so I've included a simple note.'

He took it out.

'For dear Rudy. "In my book to take delight." Much love, as always, Grandpa.'

He looked at the page for a very long time. It said what he needed it to say, and did what he needed it to do. He stood up.

'Give me another hug!' he said. 'A big one!'

I did, though this time it was me who was retracted. I'd had my quotient of intimacy, which made me feel satisfied, if slightly bloated and flatulent. The effect of the ice-cream perhaps.

I withdrew gently. I hope he didn't notice.

# Chapter 9

When I was summoned by Alexa, the picture showed Lucy with Amelie seated shyly on her lap. She and I have not met since her infancy, and she is quite rightly rather frightened by the solemn scarecrow that occasionally appears on the screen. To date she has hung off to the side, clutching Lucy's garments, saying a few halting words until she is allowed to go and play, or whatever a four-year-old does offstage.

'Hello, Amelie. How are you today?'

What does one say to a shy little one? I was never much good, even, with my own, and I lived with her. Amelie peered at the screen, anxious to put her thumb in her mouth. It would have got there had her mother not taken her hand, as if affectionately. Yet Lucy sucked hers at the same age, and of course she doesn't now. I don't know why parents make a fuss of it, save to rescue themselves from an atavistic desire to suck their own thumbs. I quite understand the impulse, I smoke my cigars, a more wholesome substitution than that favoured by dear Oscar.

Amelie turned her face to the side.

'Hello, Ganpa,' she whispered.

'Did you like the present I sent you?' This was surely the occasion for the phone call, the modern equivalent of the more elegant thank-you note. Do four-year-olds compose such, with a little help from their parents? It would be nice to think so.

'Yes! Thank you, Ganpa!' She reached into her lap and brought up the stuffed super-fluffy white dog that I'd ordered online. A bichon frise, they are called, and this one is quite lifelike, if that isn't a stupid description, which it is.

She was holding it up to the screen with both hands. It obscured her face entirely, creating a comical image.

'Isn't it cute, darling? Have you given it a name?'

'Yes.' She put the dog back into her lap.

'Good. Will you tell me what it is?'

'Mavis! Rudy told me.'

'How lovely. And it is so nice to talk to you.'

Lucy soon decanted her daughter from her lap, and the little one was out of the frame but not out of my mind. I rarely talk with her, but am getting almost fond of our truncated visits. It's rather a strain, children are a foreign land to me, but needs must.

'Rudy's just going out, but says he'll see you for lunch on Saturday.'

'Of course, I'm looking forward to it.'

'So is he. He doesn't tell me much about it, what do you do? Do you go out?'

'Out? Of course not. We stay in and play . . .'

'Play? What do you mean?'

'Sometimes we read to each other. Other times I read and Rudy draws . . .'

'You mean those funny little animals with leaves and flowers?'

'Sometimes, yes. He's rather good, he's got some natural facility . . .'

'Amelie loves them! Sometimes Rudy draws a lot of tigers and lambs with a pencil on a piece of paper, and then Amelie colours them in.'

'He loves that too.' I didn't add that one of our little projects was to design a simple fabric with animal images from Blake in red, yellow and green, and have it printed and made up into a garment. You can do this online. Rudy wants to order a dress and some pyjamas to give to Amelie for her next birthday.

We began work on this little project, while I suppressed a shadow identification with a classroom Arts and Crafts teacher, decked in sandals and beard, sincere, enthusiastic and moronic. As soon as I could without Rudy remarking my distaste, I moved us on to something more interesting.

'And the other thing we do is try to learn about food.'

'You mean cooking?'

'Not yet. I'm just introducing him to different kinds of tastes and dishes.'

'I don't understand. He has a very limited, what do you call it? Repertoire? He thinks pizza is a food group, loves chips with everything. Fish fingers, sausages, beefburgers, he'd eat at McDonald's every day if we let him.' His father, who had a palate more limited even than that, subsisted on Northern grub of the most proletarian sort, mushy everything, and encouraged Rudy from his earliest age to eat nothing but pap. Fast baby food.

I didn't want to go into this with Lucy, who wouldn't have understood, and quizzed me. I demurred, it was too complicated. When old folks are full of complex feeling, and need to talk about love, they babble about food.

Rudy ate what he has been given for his whole life, at home and at school. He is ignorant about food, extends occasionally to what the dreaded SamWise calls a Chinky nosh-up, at which he will eat spare ribs and chop suey. An occasional Indian of onion bhaji and chicken korma. That's it, the suburban range of sophisticated international fare.

Every week he and I order something new and interesting – chosen by Rudy from a variety of takeaway menus – and have it delivered by Uber Eats. The idea is to have an adventure, and we both accept that not all travels come out well. I make sure the fridge is stocked with a fail-safe meal of cheese and cold meats, and that there is a fresh baguette, in case his taste buds do not accommodate the newest food experiment. But I have been surprised, and he is rather proud, that he tries and usually enjoys everything we order, takes notes and rates each dish out of ten. Last week it was bao buns with grilled pork (10) and Japanese slaw (7), before that Cambodian sweet and sour soup (6) with prawn rolls (9), and prior to that Peruvian barbecued chicken (10) with coriander sauce (2). We discuss each dish, and he likes improving his descriptive categories and vocabulary, as if learning a foreign language, which in his home it certainly is.

There is a concomitant risk, of course. I am sending home, week after week, an increasingly discriminating eater, who then survives on a subsistence diet of sausages and baked beans. I told him about the food in prison, and how remarkable, and how odd, it was to come home to a world bursting with flavour.

'Do you mean, Grandpa, that I should think of home cooking as, like, prison?'

'I couldn't possibly say that, but ...'

'I could! And I do!'

'Never you mind. I know what we'll do.'

'What? When?'

'Hang on, you'll see soon enough.'

On my next call with Lucy, we avoided the subject of food, largely because she didn't know it was on the table. What most pleased her, of course, was the dramatic improvement in Rudy's mood, and behaviour.

'He's back to himself now, better really. I'm so thrilled. Clever you, you worked it out ...'

'All by myself, you mean?'

'Surprised me!'

'And me! We're having such productive afternoons. Now he is working on a story – I told him never to mention it to anyone ...'

'You mean me!'

'I do. Sorry, I shouldn't have! When you write you need to let the process play itself out before you show the results to anyone, else you get unduly influenced, and lose your voice. You know I used to do Creative Writing groups at school? The major rule was: finish the piece, *then* read it aloud to the group. Then comes the best part, revising. Writing is rewriting, if you do it seriously.'

'He will, he's like that.'

'My reason for ringing is not to talk to the kids, but to you. I have a great idea, and want to try it out on you.'

'Ooooh, a great idea! Goody, I never had one of those.'

'Be careful, Lucy. You know what?'

'What?'

'Nobody likes a smart arse.'

'Quite right! Got a lot of friends, have you?'

'Touché. Want to hear my idea or don't you?'

'Longing to.'

'I want to take us all on a family holiday.'

I heard an intake of breath and a soft whooshing sound.

'You do? But what's the occasion? None of us have a birthday coming up.'

'Not an occasion, an opportunity. While we're still allowed, before we're locked up again.'

'Down, locked down.'

'Same thing. Never mind. I thought we could rent a pleasant house, maybe by the sea ...'

There was a silence that had none of Lucy's usual pausal qualities, as if she were suppressing a gasp rather than readying an expostulation. We'd not had such a family outing since well before she was married, as the idea of spending much time with her Sam was unappealing. He was preferable in small quantities, not because he improved that way, but because they were small. We had a few days a year in London over Christmas, and by the end they made purgatory seem a Relais & Châteaux hotel.

'Dad? Hello? This is you, right? Do you actually have anywhere in mind?'

'Let's look together. There are a lot of rental sites on the Internet, and I've browsed a bit – the Landmark Trust ones are promising – and a few of them still have vacancies at the moment. I can send you links, but it's better if you just surf and see what you can find.'

I'd located a couple of beautiful Georgian homes, one in Devon and one in Cornwall, that would be perfect, if available. Secluded, large gardens, heated swimming pools, one with a tennis court. Double bedrooms for me, Lucy and Jonathan, a single for Rudy, and maybe for Amelie if she's not intimidated by sleeping alone in a strange room. And another room for Bronya. She could help out with the kids, do some babysitting and shopping, generally pitch in. Both houses have Internet, so she can Zoom.

But it would be better, alas, but nevertheless preferable, if Lucy and Jonathan located a desirable holiday let themselves, otherwise the vac would be entirely *mine*, start to finish: my idea, my choice of house, my money. Whereas if they find the house, honours are shared, if not exactly equally. It's a better gestalt, as SamWise puts it. Thank God he's been replaced by the amiable Jonathan, though I wish him no harm, and, to be fair, I rather miss piercing him with the occasional dismissive witticism, though even that pleasure is mitigated by the fact that he never noticed when ironically targeted. Northerners are like that. So too are Bulgarians, but I try not to be dismissive to Bronya, who is much kinder, more capable and agreeable than Lucy's ex. Cleverer, too.

'Well, Dad, this is a surprise. Can I talk to Jonathan, and maybe come back to you about dates? Is there any particular time you're thinking of?'

'Lucy! All time is the same. I'm as free as a bird.'

'Thanks, Dad. I'll get back to you.'

Bird. Gilded cage. Nice prison, lovely and secure as in a poem by Yeats. Safer there than on the brink of extinction, here.

The thought of the impending family holiday is daunting, as what seems a great idea can turn out to be disaster, can't it? Examples abound. Even in my prime, if I ever had one, even when I was younger, I was an unenthusiastic, crotchety traveller, the sort who brings his own provisions of bottled water, newspapers and magazines, tobacco, and loo paper. Suzy would have stuffed a few bits in a canvas bag, headed for Heathrow, and caught a plane to any destination that appealed at that very moment. She once convinced me – I was still young, and more than usually biddable – that it would be 'freeing' if we did this together.

Our agreement being that we'd get any aeroplane that took off an hour after our arrival at the Heathrow terminal, we had a choice between Marrakesh and Budapest. Suzy chose unwisely, and we headed south with one small bag each, containing a change of clothes and our toiletries, arguing constantly in our crimped economy seats. When we arrived at the hideous African airport, the tourist booth booked us 'the most luxurious' hotel they could offer, sent us somewhere nondescript, and no doubt pocketed a huge kickback. In our three-star accommodation in a corner of the souk, we ratcheted up the discord for three days, until I insisted that we go home, or at least that I did. If I didn't change my clothes they'd not only stick to me, they would fumify our entire house.

It is a horrible city, beloved of beatniks and other degenerates, its disgusting markets stuffed with garish tat, the invasive smells of boiling animal skins, hashish and a variety of spices, many of them not what they claimed to be, the sweaty, crowded alleyways crushed with tourists, importuning merchants, canvassers for restaurants and other earthly delights, and children variously on the make. The air was so thick that it clogged my lungs until I felt in danger of drowning. Outside the souk, snake charmers, acrobats and beggars besieged us in the square, pickpockets too. I clutched my wallet in my front trouser pocket, and insisted Suzy wound her handbag strap twice round her neck, so that if anyone tried to grab it, she'd be a trifle choked but the bag would be safe.

Following that hideous experience, we always travelled first class, which I can afford and just about tolerate, and if Suzy wanted 'an adventure', she organised it with 'a friend' (I didn't enquire) and left me to the genuine holiday feeling of being alone in my own house. People from round the world have their hols in London, it's a place to come to, not to leave. I am of the Johnsonian persuasion: I never tire of London, and do not wish to be elsewhere. Anyone who is tired of London is tired of life? Perhaps that wasn't subtle enough. I am thoroughly tired of life, but still grateful for my native ground.

Leaving it, even for a luxurious holiday – if Lucy and Jonathan stint on the choice I will have to subtly upgrade them – already makes me anxious. I will of course bring my computer and writing materials, CDs and their player, and must confirm there is a room that can be dedicated only to music. And reading too, by which I mean newspapers and not books. If I want to read something good, I will write it. Who said that? Disraeli, was it? I sometimes mix him up with Gladstone, I'm bored by hairy Victorian worthies, the only difference I can remember is that one of them was Jewish. The Israeli, before his time.

I will bring some basics: wine, Vichy water, smoked oysters, foie gras and caviar, boxes of proper cracked-pepper crispbreads. None of the vacationers will eat much of the above, with the possible exception of Rudy. I presume that Devon and Cornwall are now habitable, and have local merchants for provisioning families with fish fingers and sausages, oven fries, pizza, soft drinks, and ice-cream. I will confirm this well in advance.

*A family holiday.* Images from 1950s films fill my mind: caravans and charabancs at the seaside, ill-matched and worse-dressed Cornish-pasty couples, their ungovernable snotty children and noisome dogs, rusty barbeques of sausages and frankfurters, tins of beef and beer, squalor and squabbling, knobbly sandy knees, buckets, spades. Ugliness, mayhem. The English at play.

What have I done?

The depressing thing about our newly installed window of plague easement, allowing lowering of restrictions until they are inevitably re-imposed, is that it makes it difficult to resist invitations, or issuing them. Social distancing suited me wonderfully, it's what I have always done, much to the regret of some near and dear – now that it is required I luxuriate in it. No more. Lucy and the family are already scheduled, but not quite yet. Apparently we shall soon be regarded as a bubble. Various playful deconstructions of this airy metaphor occur, but none settles, and they pop in mid-air. Amelie is excited by the literal prospect, and certain to be disappointed. I considered ordering a jar of kiddie bubble soap and a blower thingy, but soon forgot about it, and I had no desire to reanimate the impulse. Icky bubble residue will coat the furniture, even my clothes, and though Lucy will assure me that one cannot feel or see it, I can, and will. I'm sensitive that way: others fear the invisible germ that flies in the night, I, the invisible residue.

Next thing I know, Miles will propose a drink, or lunch, here, there or somewhere, to discuss what he has irritatingly – I wish I'd thought of it first – labelled my little projectile. I have not, of course I haven't, revealed the details of my faux-African narrative to him, though he wheedles and begs to be shown bits of it. I have no idea why it appeals to him. Is he setting me up in some way? That's unlikely. I have no perch from which to fall, save the ultimate. But of course the opposite pertains. Revenge, served chilly. I drop the projectile into the diverse publishing ranks, make sure it implodes, and is uncovered as a hoax of no very great wit or merit, morally disgusting to the righteous brigade. And if Miles eventually came on board, and colluded, what then?

The more I reflect on it, what then is *not a lot*. Though Miles is not as low in the pecking order of literary being as I, he is nevertheless retired from agenting and the concomitant harassment of young women, in which activities he is no longer sufficiently thrusting. So what if he has encouraged, or merely endorsed, a politically incorrect hoax? The joke will go down well at the Garrick, if it ever reopens, and the old white men of publishing, what few of them survive, will mutter, *Good for you*, off the record, as if anything said to Miles ever could be.

It was a flavourful moral and psychological conundrum, unworthy of the adjective Elizabethan, but at least suggesting it. Jealousy, revenge, schemes and ploys, disingenuous conversations saying the one thing but suggesting the other, conceit of the moral if not the linguistic variety. *Amour impropre*. Who's fucking who, or whom?

Wally asked if there was anyone to whom he could send his homely manuscript, but of course I said I knew no such people. Agents and publishers are bombarded by unpublishable guff – I'm about to send some of my own – and are imperiously ungrateful. Wally's story was overburdened by worthiness, and had surely been told multiple times in the past few years. His poor hopeful parents had sailed to England in the 1950s, wanting to make something of their lives and those of their children, willing to work and work to make that happen. They were greeted by landlady signs refusing rooms to Blacks and Irish, made desperate, homeless, and impecunious. Father, long gone. Mother worked to the bones. Two sisters, a nurse and a cleaner. Three brothers, one in prison, one a school custodian, and Wally the success of the family, until he wasn't.

A common story of common folk. I knew nothing of It, and though Wally was keen to fill in my abundant blanks, they were there for a reason. His world, not mine. His was a poignant story, but it was an indifferently narrated one. Touching, perhaps. But not a good book. It was, even after my blue-pencilling, naive, ill-expressed, over-emotive, angry but not under control. An effusion, semi-literate, hardly worth the cost of binding and paper. My only creative contribution, of which I was rather proud, was the title: *Windrush to Judgement*. Publishing is such a thin and fashion-ridden business that catchy titles sell books. Consider *Eats, Shoots and Leaves* by Mrs Truss. Had it been entitled *Mrs Truss's Rules of Grammar*, it would have sold six copies. Actually, I would have been one of the buyers. As it was, I was given three of the cute-titled one for Christmas, like everyone else in England.

Suzy loathed it. Gave the copies that she was gifted to Oxfam, with rude notes scrawled within to offend the twee neighbourhood spinsters who might purchase them. Anything that adumbrated rules and suggested proper deportment, linguistic or social, made her curl with contempt. She would, I suspect, have admired Wally's book, considered as a form of folk art, simple and authentic. I did not share her taste for the primitive, a category into which I was happy to jettison poor Wally's manuscript. And Wally himself.

He was released from prison some months before I, and gave me one of those scrunching hugs on his departure, promising to write.

'Wally! You know I don't answer letters!'

But it would do him good, he said, just to feel that we were in touch. I did not respond that he would be, but that I most certainly would not. A letter arrived every few weeks, detailing his appeal against his deportation order. I sent him a few bob to defray his legal expenses, but lost track of him after that. I have no idea if the process is still ongoing, Home Office procedures make Jarndyce v Jarndyce seem expeditious, but Wally's assault of the officer in charge of his case made it certain that he would be deported once and for all. I found it hard to understand why he hadn't been shipped out immediately.

My banished and near-forgotten Black man has now been replaced by a whole tribe of them, as my pseudonymous hoax would have it, save for the fact that when I returned to the page in my VarySexual guise, nothing much happened. It should have been easy enough, I had put nothing of myself in the narrative, and had no need to make it anything other than risible, though writing rubbish is curiously difficult when my instincts are to write as well as I am able. Isn't there a Henry James story about a brilliant but impoverished writer who decides to write a potboiler just to make some money, only to find that his publisher ruefully regarded it as yet another masterpiece? I feel ashamed to make such an analogy. I only mean to say that one writes as one writes, and is whom one is, and I am not an indifferent pasticheur of the lives of very other others. I'm not bad enough for the job.

My poor pseudo-Africans, I should toss them back into the emptiness from which they have only partially emerged. After all, they are mere enactments and incarnations, made up of my distaste for what the world, and the literary world, has become. So what? Why do I give a hoot, surely I'm too old and jaded, too world-weary and exhausted, to go on hooting? My time is served, my time is up. Rat's alley calls my bones.

Let *The Times* Mayflies and Archies carry on in their clenched righteousness, it has, after all, nothing to do with me. Throw them away, and out. Goodbye, African stooges? They should go, as all that we are and have done and will do, into the darkness, the universal scrap heap of destiny, the black hole? Oh, black, black, black, we all go into the black.

I'm rather enjoying my day.

# Chapter 10

Lucy and Jonathan have failed. Predictably the victims of their own virtue, they felt that it would be spoiled and imprudent to be profligate with my money, and hence have forwarded a suggested list of inexpensive rental cottages for our family holiday. I detest such hovels, which are the pinched dark dwellings of former peasants and labourers stuffed together round an inglenook, the narrow windows increasing the gloom, the rafters grazing the scalp, the bedrooms cramped with incest, the privies foul and replete with contagion. Such cottages are now the second homes of sentimental Londoners, who think them charming.

I have booked, instead, a Surrey manse named Goddards, designed by Ned Lutyens, with a Gertrude Jekyll garden, and pleasing local associations with E. M. Forster. Lutyens is a bit oaky and cutesy for my taste, his dwellings lack generosity of light and height, but the children will be amused by the indoor skittles alley and the croquet lawn, and I have confirmed that there are adequate gastropubs (horrible term) and restaurants nearby, with gardens in which to eat. The local market town of Dorking is not entirely disagreeable, and the house is sufficiently close to London to make the journey there and back less than purgatorial.

Jonathan has suggested that they pick me up in his squat Lexus, which 'has plenty of room for us all', but I will make my own way with Driver. On family holidays it is essential to establish one's distance and boundaries from the very start, lest one be overwhelmed by needy attachment. I have assigned myself the entire West Wing, with both a master bedroom and a further one next door as my study and music room, the bathroom opposite designated as my very own. There are two others that will be sufficient for the five of them. There's still plenty of space, and though the Landmark Trust in its stuffy way does not supply a television for the children, there is Wi-Fi, and they (yes, both of them) have iPads with which to amuse themselves.

I have begun packing early, to make sure nothing is omitted, lest I need return home for my lotions, soaps, creams, medicaments, and unguents. I fill two large suitcases, having unwisely chosen to book our holiday domicile for a full week. I am uncertain what has caused this unusual largesse (and optimism), save that, somehow, a three- or four-day break is hardly worth the preparation and travel time.

We will not dress for supper, so I will need only six full changes of clothes. Rudy will help me to set up my computer, for the keeping of this journal will be a welcome daily task, allowing me (further) withdrawal and the recurrent right of fair, uncensored comment on the daily events. Catharsis, as it is wrongly termed. I will need, surely, something or other to read. I have abjured fiction almost entirely, though I'm still amused by Plum, and have a weak spot for the prose of Evelyn Waugh. Perhaps I might reread *Decline and Fall*, much the best of his novels. I cannot abide the dolorous *Brideshead*, and suffered with Suzy through its adaptation on the telly, with a host of mincing actors making sensitive faces, all dressed up with nowhere to go. The costumery wasn't incidental, it was the point of the whole thing, which was more attentive to the dresses and suits, the coats, hats, and cravats than to the persons cloaked within them. Critics thought it 'stylish', to my mind a clear indication that they had nothing favourable to say. I thought it hogwash, and in the middle of the second episode, I flounced out scornfully but with dignity.

I will bring some cookbooks, not by Mr Lenghi, who is too demanding and certainly too sophisticated for the troops, but a couple of Nigel Slaters will be useful. Rudy and I will cook the evening meals, breakfast and lunch being what Lucy calls 'grazing time'. I suppose we might have lunch out some of the time, though the socially distanced melee in the gardens of the local pubs will be noisome, the service slow and the food as ordinary as the people: there's nothing more disagreeable to the senses than a braying Surrey matron, her hooray husband in a panama, and their entitled brats.

Lucy has decreed that we are to arrive in stages: first she and her family, in order to set things up, inhabit bedrooms and unpack; at 5.18 Bronya will arrive at Dorking station, and be picked up by Jonathan; Driver will deliver me at 7.30 for drinks and dinner, by which time Amelie will (or should) be asleep. Rudy has reassured me that something suitable will soon be on the table. This thoughtful plan was conceived to save me any aggravation or stress, but actually it is designed to do that for the rest of them, who fear my premature presence may make it difficult to settle in, and down. If this were comment, I would regard it as fair.

By the time they arrive, my orders of provisions and drink will have been delivered to Goddards. Lucy will bring boxes and bags of their normal family fare, though there is ample shopping locally. Rudy and I can go out in the mornings to buy foodstuffs for our dinner, and spend the afternoon cooking. In preparation he has been studying recipes, and is already sophisticated enough to reject Nigella and Jamie, and says he is 'almost over' Nigel Slater, which I think premature. But ambition in cooking as in all things is to be commended, and he has been astute enough to 'discover' Elizabeth David, and is keen to do some classical French cooking. That suits me, and the others will not baulk at a *boeuf Bourguignon* or *coq au vin,* safely described as beef stew and chicken stew. Rudy, who is inclined to worry and to plan ahead, assures me that there are local sources of organic meat and produce, and crucially of baby carrots and shallots.

When Suzy and I, knowing it to be ill-advised, once went on a family holiday with her parents, we limited it to a long weekend, brought an au pair to look after Lucy, then aged eight and inclined to cause trouble. Her grandparents disapproved of her carriage, dress, manners, and vocabulary. She scorned them both. It was, as Grandma, Lady Moulton, feared and predicted, a recipe for disaster, solved only by giving the au pair an extra few quid to take Lucy out in the morning and not, strictly not, to return until suppertime. Her bag filled with chocolates and money, she was allowed every liberty to spoil and to mollify Lucy, who loved it. From which I learned my lessons: family holidays are fraught, and a certain amount of strategic planning and expenditure can ameliorate the problem.

Ameliorate! I do not know Amelie well enough by either contact or even reputation to know if she is likely to be a trial, but I assume she is. Such small ones (I have googled them) are ambulatory incarnations of original sin: relentlessly self-referring, imperiously demanding. They make toilet jokes. They cry constantly. They need handling with the same care as other small wild animals, and are about as gratifying as baby chimps, only with less ingratiating smiles. Thus our need of Bronya, who has been a figure in Amelie's life since she was tiny, and who lights up in the presence of BonBon, a name which Bronya thinks is sweet, but which makes my ears wilt.

Driver picked me up at 5.30, because the passage to Surrey will take that much longer in what Americans call 'rush hour', an inappropriate term in London, when the roads are clogged at all times, and it is impossible to rush. As we made our interminable way through the ugly sprawl of South London, a route that he regards as preferable to the M25 at such a time, my phone rang. I fished about my many pockets fruitlessly until the ringing stopped. I soon found it in my overcoat on the seat beside me. It was Lucy. I rang her back.

She sounded harried, of course.

'Dad, Dad! Is that you?' There were enough background noises to suggest an outbreak of hostilities on an international stage. Amelie was bawling, Rudy was shouting about something, Jonathan was pacifying loudly.

'Yes. Did you call?'

'It's Bronya. She just rang, she missed her train. She was at the station and couldn't talk. But the thing is this . . .'

'What?'

'The next available train arrives just past seven, so could you come by way of Dorking and pick her up at the station?'

'Of course. We will see you for dinner.'

I rang off. Going to Goddards by way of Dorking is not quite like going to the Lebanon by way of Bulgaria, but it was hardly a direct route. I instructed Driver, who took the news with his usual sangfroid, and was sufficiently well-trained not, even, to say, 'Yes, sir.' He merely rerouted his internal navigator, and carried on. I sank back into my seat to read *The Times*, and to dream of happier ones, memories of which are increasingly difficult to locate. Indeed, all memories are increasingly difficult to locate, a sign and benefit of old age: you can't *recherche* your *temps perdu* – they wouldn't be *perdu* if you could remember them – so you live in a spotless present, and if you are sufficiently attentive, there will be no one to stain it. By going on holiday with you perhaps.

It had been some time since I'd been through South London, many years indeed since I'd been through anywhere except hell. I soon put down my paper and gazed out of the windows. Brixton grated aesthetically compared to my Georgian-terraced environs, but it was awash with life, a sign of the partial release from social internment. Here were the peoples of the world cloaked in their many colours and skins, going steadily about their business, some smiling, some glum, same as anywhere else. No, not the same. When I saunter through my West London streets, though there are Asian newsagents and greengrocers, and occasional perambulating brown professionals, there is a sameness in the air, which feels flat and stale. English air. As I look out the car window I see wonderfully colourful fabrics mixing green, red and orange on fat African women, smooth-skinned men in Arab robes, sleek girls wrapped in shimmering sarees, West Indians with visored hats on backwards, their luxuriant hair spilling over the sides.

It's an adjustment, not merely to one of my class and nature, but to someone just released from prison, in which difference posed a threat. Here it feels safe, at least from the back of my Mercedes. Within five minutes I saw restaurants from eleven countries, with the diverse masses diverting themselves modestly, eating outside and serving within. People congregated at tables in the street and outside pubs, all these lives, nattering and mattering in spite of this plague, the cold shoulder of Brexit, the animus against the inade-quately documented West Indians.

We are become a disgusting country, unworthy to house our immigrants, who settle for little and give a lot. And I, a Leaver, on my way to pick up my Bulgarian cleaner? I felt a flush of remorse. I thought of Wally, now deported, I suppose rightly, his lack of documentation exacerbated by his lack of restraint, however understandable, indeed admirable. I had a simple letter from him a few weeks ago, postmarked Kingston, to announce that some publisher or other – local, no doubt – was going to bring his book out. Wally's family history was a moral fable, all too neatly inserted into the current political spectrum, as yet another egregious example of the filthy residue of colonialism and arrogance. I sent him a card of congratulations and good wishes.

We pulled up outside Dorking station at eleven minutes past

the hour, I instructed Driver to wait for me in the no-parking zone directly in front, and set off to the arrival area. Standing beside the gate where the incoming passengers queue wearily to insert their tickets, I gazed down the platform as the 7.14 pulled into the station, rather surprisingly on time. It shuddered to a halt, waited for a few moments to settle its nerves, and opened its doors to release the few passengers, fewer of whom had the required face covering. Four carriages forward to my left, I thought I could spot the figure of Bronya, wearing a dark grey puffy jacket and black trousers, struggling to pull a heavy suitcase and carrying a large shopping bag. She stopped to remove her mask, shook her head until her hair twirled, and took a deep breath, squinting up towards where the evening sun ought to be. Failing to locate it, perhaps because she was wearing dark sunglasses, she plodded onwards without looking forward, where she would have seen my welcoming face. She looked like a refugee arriving on some foreign shore, anxious and exhausted.

Though tempted to call her name, I waited for her to come clumsily through the turnstile, looking left and right as she did. Lucy had told her I would be at the station, but the safe assumption would be that I'd wait outside. With a look not so much of relief as of surprise she caught my eye. Which caused, I could see, something of a problem. Bronya neither calls me by my first name, as I have suggested but which she regards as impertinent, nor does she offer the title of Mr or more formally Dr Darke, which would be inappropriate. I am a man with no name, and she greeted me accordingly.

'Hello!' she cried, meeting my eye. 'Is good you pick me up!'

I hurried over to take her bag, but she wouldn't let go of the handle.

'You maybe take this,' she said, offering me a canvas bag filled with various supermarket items.

Since her Toe-mass departed to Bulgaria to look after his

parents, her English has reverted to its Eastern European pidgin locutions. She'd made an effort, under his constant tutelage, to correct her grammatical mistakes, to make her language both more exact and more colloquial, about which she was proud, but which I rather regretted. I preferred her in her native state, untutored like Eliza Doolittle, an innocent East-Ender before the dreadful intervention of the sadistic Henry Higgins. Not to mention the tone-deaf George Bernard Shaw, whose rendering of cockney needed as much improvement as Eliza's delivery of it.

I liked her language just as it was, and is once again. While I had previously tried to help her with her English, now her Bronya-isms made me smile, and warm to her.

'Let me take the other bag, please!'

'No! Is heavy, I pull! Which way we go?'

We made our way through the exit door into the no-parking zone, where Driver was waiting placidly as a traffic warden deposited her ticket under his windscreen wipers. He exited the car to take Bronya's suitcase and my carrier bag, opened the boot to deposit them, closed it, walked to the front of the car to pocket the parking citation, and opened the rear door.

'Perhaps you'd like to sit on this side, miss,' he said. 'There's plenty of leg room.' I excused this voluble outburst, as it was not directed at me, and was welcoming towards my guest, who slid gratefully into the unaccustomed comfort of the rear seat. He closed the door, and came round to my side, opened the door, but said nothing. Bronya watched this with some interest, as I settled down in my corner.

'It's not long from here,' I said, 'we should be in time for dinner.'

She didn't say anything for the rest of the journey, slumped against her door and peered out of the window. She looked thoroughly exhausted. For a moment I tried studying her face with the Suzy eye: a light mushroom pallor, thinly overlaid with make-up with faint streaks running downwards. Lipstick, mild pink, smudged. Hair falling wispily over her ears, when usually it was held back behind them.

When we were young, perhaps in a restaurant, Suzy would set me tasks, insisting that I describe one diner or another. I looked carefully, an activity uncommon and uncongenial, and reported my findings proudly. She would sniff: 'Try harder! You're not exactly Sherlock Holmes!' Though she regarded Holmes's fancy displays of epistemological erudition as showy, and false, she nevertheless recommended him as a role model. I was that hopeless.

I didn't initiate any discussion with Bronya, which would clearly not have been welcome, to ask her what was so obviously – even to my eye – the matter. There's nothing more irritating than the reiterated question – Lucy asks it constantly, screwing up her features and anatomising me – 'Are you all right?' Bronya wasn't. I didn't ask why she'd missed her train, why she looked so forsaken, why she had abandoned her usual good cheer. This is what good breeding teaches one. If she had anything to say, it could wait until she had some food and drink inside her.

We arrived – who says there is no Providence that shapes our ends? – at exactly 7.30 as Driver pulled into the parking space at the side of Goddards. I'd phoned ahead, and Lucy and the family were all outside waiting as we disembarked, like the household staff greeting the arrival of the owners of a stately home. As we alighted, I felt a spasm of graciousness, and leant forward to embrace Rudy, Amelie having headed straight for Bronya's knees. Behind them Lucy and Jonathan smiled broadly, and ushered Driver and our suitcases and provisions into the house. Having turned down a cup of tea, he nodded to me in suitably restrained and deferential manner as he got back into the Mercedes, and backed slowly out of the drive.

As soon as we had entered the kitchen, Lucy took Bronya's arm proprietorially.

'Can I have a word?' she asked.

Carrying her bags, Bronya followed Lucy into the passage, and they were not seen again for twenty minutes, while Jonathan and I opened a bottle of Chablis, filled our glasses, and settled down in the comfy chairs in the drawing room. It was typical of the middle-England aesthetic of the Landmark Trust, 'shabby genteel', a fashionable and stupid aesthetic non-category. All their properties are as one, as if decorated by an aged auntie of declining powers both physical and financial. There was no need to remark the particulars, which was a relief as I was still exhausted from noting Bronya's. Save observing that, on her return, they had altered. Her face was clear, hair in place, and she had abandoned the slump and the sunglasses. Her eyes looked red and swollen, some sort of seasonal hay fever perhaps.

She embraced Jonathan, then turned to me.

'So sorry I am bad company! Lucy has fixed up!'

I rose to pour her a drink.

'Bronya dear, you are not required to be good company. We are delighted that you're here.'

She tipped the glass and swallowed half the contents.

'Is good, thank you.'

She paused for a moment, emptied her glass but did not sit down. On the floor Amelie was looking at a little screen, Rudy was setting the table for dinner, which he insisted had to be in the formal dining room, which had a table large enough for sixteen. It was Lutyens cosy: low-timbered ceiling, a small-mullioned window covered with thin, inappropriately patterned blue-and-yellow curtains, an innocuously tasteful picture on the wall next to it, bland runners on both sides of the table. Nothing to offend a reader of the *Daily Telegraph*. Suzy would have mocked it relentlessly, but she is not here, not any more, and I rather approved of the unostentatious comfort.

Rudy had brought some candles and candle holders, insistent that our first night together be a special event, and placed them round our end of the table. He'd made a casserole in advance, which was in the oven, and had informed us that 'dinner will be served' at 8.00.

It gave Bronya time to collect herself.

'I am so sorry. Is rude of me, but I was so upset ...' She looked over at Lucy, who nodded encouragingly.

'Lucy says I should share. I am not sure, maybe is best ... Toe-mass called me this afternoon. You know, from Sofia? He says is going to stay there, it is home. He says it is my home too, that UK not want us any more. Toe-mass says I must come home, to be with him, and with our families. In Bulgaria we say, "Every frog should stay in own puddle"!'

No one interjected, though I could feel a frisson of impending loss. She continued haltingly, and I could predict some damage to her newly restored features.

'Toe-mass is right. Is fact, he loves me, and I love him ... but I am not going. My life now is here, you are my friends, I have my work. If I am frog, UK is puddle!'

Lucy stood to give her a hug, and Bronya rested her head on her shoulder. In a moment she would start sobbing. Even Amelie looked up, sensing some drama, at which point Rudy, proudly oblivious, opened the door to announce, 'Dinner is served!'

He'd set the table with all of us huddled at the top, but it didn't matter. The lights were low, the candles lit, and he'd arranged a vase of pink tulips at our end, which was set with Landmark Trust blue-and-white china, and simple wine glasses. The bottle of *Vieux Télégraphe* 2016 that I'd provided had been opened, to get some air, which we all needed rather more than it did.

'Grandpa, you're at the head. Bronya can sit on your right and Jonathan on your left. Then Mummy can be next to Jonathan – I'm sorry it works out that way, I couldn't help it – then I can sit on the other side of Bronya, and Amelie can do her own thing ...'

Bronya had in those few moments recovered herself adequately.

'Is wonderful,' she said. 'I did not know you could do so many things!'

'I hope it'll be all right,' said Rudy, 'I might've overcooked the French beans. I'm not used to cooking for so many people. Sit down, all of you, and I'll serve up.'

As he retreated to the kitchen, dressed fetchingly in a little blue-and-white apron, Lucy looked at me and shrugged.

'I gather we have you to thank,' she said. 'He's been planning this for days. He's trying to look cool, but he's so excited!'

'Not at all, not at all. This was his idea, start to finish. He's been practising his French cooking, and coming along nicely.'

'I hope is not frog's legs!' said Bronya.

Lucy reached across to stroke her hand.

'I know it's hard. I'm sorry to hear about you and Thomas, he's a really good bloke.'

'Is giving up so much. We still love each other. My parents, they are old now. If I go to see them, I probably not allowed back to UK. Perhaps I never see them again? Is selfish!'

'Bronya, dear,' I found myself surprised to be saying, 'perhaps you might think of us as your English family?'

Bronya rubbed her eyes, wiped her hands on her napkin, and looked at me with a mixture of pleasure, that I should offer such intimacy, and puzzlement, that I had. What did this actually entail? Was it merely gestural, the product of a moment's ham-fisted sympathy disguised as good breeding? Though she was close friends with Jonathan and Lucy, and the children treated her with familiar ease, we were paying her to be on holiday with us, as we had paid her to be a cleaner. *Mind the gap!* as London Underground counsels. Or every frog to its own puddle, as they say in Sofia. A nice meeting of cultures on the baleful subject of class.

Lucy was quick to solve the problem.

'We already do! The children think of you as their auntie, and you're like the sister I never had. I told you that, didn't I?'

Bronya snuffled, *Yes.*

The emotion was about to slop into the casserole, and I soon put a stop to it.

'Well, then, Bronya. That's settled, except for one thing . . .'

She looked up inquisitively.

'I'm not going to be your adoptive father!'

It got a laugh, things calmed down. But the question of where this left me, and my relations to Bronya, was unclear. Not that it mattered.

'Family is most important thing. I Zoom with parents, long time Sundays. It makes me happy to see them, and so sad. I will tell them about what you have said, they will understand. Be pleased, grateful too.'

So now I have in-laws in Bulgaria. The world's my puddle, until I croak. (Note to self: restraint! This sort of thing can be overdone.)

Rudy's French beans were not overcooked. His *boeuf Bourguignon* was slightly under-seasoned, but better than passable – he looked across at me as we ate, and I gave a nod of approbation – and he'd purchased some lovely *pots au chocolat* for pudding. Amelie, who'd only picked at her supper, and was getting cranky, ate two, and cheered up. One was Bronya's.

Once Amelie had scooped the chocolate into her face, Bronya scooped her up too, to take to bed. She might have gathered me as well, so exhausting had been the day, but I remained to start clearing the table, until admonished by Lucy, and reminded that it was past my bedtime too.

'In the morning, Dad, I'd be glad if we could have a little chat. Bronya can organise the kids, and Jonathan has plenty to be getting on with . . .'

'Of course,' I said. 'What about?'

'You get up to bed now, we can talk over coffee. Try to have a bit of a lie-in, you look tired.'

★   ★   ★

I trudged upstairs to my wing, far from the madding crowd. My suitcases were next to the wardrobe. I sat on the bed, restraining myself from plopping down to sleep, from which I would surely wake in the early hours, confused and disordered.

Unpack, put personal bits in the chest of drawers, hang shirts and trousers in the wardrobe. Get out toiletries and medicaments, put some in the WC and some on the bedside table. Place my *Decline and Fall* – is there something percipient and spooky about my choice of this title? – by my bedside. Go to the room next door to plug in my computer. And then, to my surprise, I found myself booting it up, getting out my mouse and mat, and opening my Journal file. It had been a surprising day, best to get it down.

Amelie was blowing soap bubbles, then chasing them on the breeze as Bronya looked on benignly. Rudy was peeling the vegetables for supper, Jonathan was in the sitting room phoning his office. It was impossible to avoid Lucy, though I tried, had stayed in my room well beyond the accepted lie-in hours, sneaked out for a stroll down the lane. Prolonged that as long as I could and returned to find Lucy seated at the kitchen table, some printed pages laid before her.

'You've been avoiding me, right?'

'I suppose.'

'But you don't even know why, do you?'

'Tone, I can tell by your tone . . .'

'Want to know?'

'No.'

'It's this.' She picked up a three-page printout, and I recognised the figuration of my *De Profundis*. I had hoped, and rather begun to assume, that she had forgotten all about it, because months had passed since I discussed it with Jonathan, who had of course warned me – as if he needed to! – that Lucy would find it objectionable.

'I'd forgotten to read this. Or avoided it, I suppose that is more accurate. Jonathan gave me a heads-up, and I thought why upset myself? But when you suggested this time together, the least I could do was to read it, since you're obviously so proud of it ...'

Bait. Did not rise. Lurked in the deep water and wind amongst the reeds.

'I'm not surprised *The Times* rejected it. What can you have been thinking?'

If you can brandish three pages of paper, she brandished away. Shook them as if they had insects between the leaves, set them down on the table.

'So! This is your legacy, is it? What you wanted to be known and remembered for?'

'Frankly, darling, I'm still thinking of publication. Some sort of pamphlet perhaps, elegant and restrained ...'

'Restrained! It's appalling. Why would you do such a thing? You have moral authority! You stood for something, you went to prison for it! And now you're a compulsive contrarian, with views on a variety of subjects about which you know absolutely nothing! Just say no to whatever, whenever!'

'Ah, darling Lucy. "Without contraries is no progression!"'

'What's that mean when it's at home?'

'It's William Blake. It means that "opposition is true friendship".'

'This means you've made some friends? Rubbish! It doesn't mean anything. It's crap!'

Lucy has always overestimated my powers and importance. I have no reputation to protect, nor any messages by which I wish to be remembered. I like having a bit of elegant wordy-fun, and my Oscariana certainly supplied me with some, and might well find a tiny audience to smirk along. The question of where they might be found had stopped the project in its tracks, just as my *Do You Love Your Dog More Than Your Wife?* failed to catch anyone's attention, except for people who wished to vilify me. I have no 'moral authority' to cede.

'Anyway, what do you mean by "legacy"? Suddenly I'm Winston Churchill?'

She stood up, walked over to the sink, filled a glass with water and drank it. Filled another and offered it to me brusquely, as if it contained vinegar. To show my mettle, I drank it.

'Don't you see? Do I have to spell it out? These are your words, your attitudes, your beliefs. Have you gone totally bananas? If you print them they are out there, you can't recall them, but others will.'

'You overestimate my importance ...'

'Do I? To your *grandchildren*? Are these the sentiments you want them to remember you by? Their inheritance from their scornful grandfather, who could not approach the greatest and best men without throwing shit at them! Martin Luther King! Gandhi! For fuck's sake, what can you be thinking?'

Right, quite right, abjectly acknowledged if only inwardly. What can I have been thinking in sharing my thinking like this?

'You're right, Lucy. I'm sorry.' I was not.

'I'm trying to understand. You were desolate, seeking consolation. Not finding it. I can understand this is a symptom of desperation, like some post-traumatic stress indicator, not some sort of supercilious philosophy. You're not yourself ...'

'Never was.'

'I don't understand. What do you mean?'

'Nothing, I mean nothing.'

It would have been fatuous, frustrating, impossible to explain. Those prison words, and that attitude, were soul-sincere, the mockery implacable. Now I am out if not about, do the words fade and diminish? Not at all. They stand as testimony to what I learned in my cell: that there is no consolation, and that anything posing as such is tosh. *Shitslingers:* the self-appointed wise men are nothing but inflated reservoirs of ordurous nonsense, transmitted as black marks on the page. The best response is to throw the shit back at them. A hard truth, learned the hard way through hard hardship, and not to be abandoned. Nor to be shared? Foolish deluded solipsistic me. To think only of the inwardness of such things, not the outwardness. Rudy. Amelie, one day. Lucy too. Do I care? I did a moment ago, but it has passed like a nomadic moment of indigestion.

How do I make sense of this life of mine, now that it is ending, is over? What does it matter what I do, or think, say privately or in print? What does it matter, any of it, or all? If I were a proper writer I would just carry on as the impulse takes me, welcome and allow the inward integrity of the words, but I'm not ruthless enough. Have not the courage to write the words and face the consequences. To say without expecting favour: *I write like this because I am like this* ... If Lucy wished to sit in judgement, that'd be up to her, she'd relish the indignation. Rudy and Amelie won't care. Ornery old coot, grandpa that was.

I'll print the fucking pamphlet. Twenty-five copies, elegantly typeset. If there is no one to whom to send it, so what? It will make it real, and will give pleasure to its best and perhaps only audience.

When I finish this journal I am finished. Or perhaps it's the other way round? Does this give me reason to carry on with it, as if writing were some guaranteed way to prolong one's life? Unlike any form of art its beginning is arbitrary, and it has neither middle nor end, save those dictated by lack of interest or lack of capacity. It finishes when I get Bored or Dead. It has incidents aplenty, but of course no plot, just the sustaining skein of my preoccupations. It is my nature writ large and long.

I think of it as my legacy. Which is doubly absurd, of course. I do not leave it to anyone, God forbid. I will destroy the notebooks and delete the text before I die. My legacy? The resulting silence that I leave to Lucy and my grandchildren, rather than this extended dyspeptic scroll, this long unscrolling book of the soon-dead. I leave them a few memories of an uncomfortable old scarecrow. And, perhaps, an occasional pamphlet.

I long to write better, to catch the moments as they pass, to supply the small canister of soapy liquid and to gently puff the floating bubbles to chase gaily and to pop. Amelie once called me Pops, she had it from some show on telly. When I admonished her, she cried. Why is spermatic history the determinant of one's name, why does it lay a claim, a definition and obligation? Because I am biologically father or grandfather, why am I linguistically branded Dad, Grandpa? Pops! We don't call our siblings Sister or Brother. I am James. That is my name. It is still my name when one of my generations is Dadding or Grand-Dadding me half to death. I loathe it, I have no sense of being such a person. James, that's who I am. It seems simple to me. But it isn't, not even to Wally or to Bronya.

When Lucy was two, Suzy and I introduced ourselves to her by our first names, we never had the Mama and Dada cutesy stage, but once the small one mastered our pronunciation sufficiently to be understood by others, the others objected. *James? Suzy?* That is quite wrong. Suzy's parents were adamant about it, and increasing numbers of Lucy's friends and their parents deemed it *pas comme il faut*, remarked upon it repeatedly, and instructed Lucy otherwise, as if admonishing her for sucking her thumb. You stop that right now! By the time she was four we were Dad and Mummy, like the rest, like them all.

I will Grandpa myself accordingly. Read, write and cook with Rudy, which is increasingly agreeable, and attempt some inroads on the fragile wispy consciousness of Amelie, who regards me as a clear and present danger, and recurrently embeds in her mother's skirts in my presence. I will read to her, some carefully chosen texts. So much that is written for children is tosh, and a lot of it worse than that, like the awful C. S. Lewis and Mr Tolkien, those ghastly biblio-paedophiles taking little children to bed with stories to seduce them into spiritual submission. Great children's literature requires chatty and beguiling animals, Pooh Bear and Ratty, a caterpillar and a walrus, Tittlemice and Puddle-Ducks. Innocent and simple, as children most certainly are not.

The modern answer to this dearth of children's books, I am informed, is Mr Dahl, which Lucy announces with pursed lips. Amelie loves his less demanding books, as Lucy did when she was a child, though she is now inclined to disapprove of the author. He was not, she informs me, a nice chap. It is said that he abandoned his poor wife after she was disabled by a stroke, and was (like so many of his generation) a thoroughgoing racist and anti-Semite, and was prepared to say so publicly. There's a sort of integrity in that. But he was a writer not a moral exemplar, children adore his stories. They don't care if they are peopled by racial stereotypes or disparaging images of women. They're fun.

I enticed Amelie from clinging to her mother, offering various treats until I had her comfy on my lap, and we made our way through one book after another.

'I have more?'

'Later, darling, we have plenty of time.'

After Amelie toddled off to blow some bubbles in the garden with Bronya, Lucy served a pot of tea with some shortbread. She looked troubled.

'Darling Lucy, is something the matter?'

'I know it's stupid of me, I was so enjoying you bonding with Amelie, but I couldn't help thinking what a responsibility it is ...'

'I'm not sure I follow ...'

'... raising a little one. Trying to plant the right seeds, you know, foster the right values.'

'Well, that's as maybe. I always believed that ...'

'Take reading, for example. I am prepared to give in with regard to Roald Dahl. But it's going to get much harder in a few years. Next thing I know she'll want to read those books about the boy wizard!'

'Oh, my dear! A fate too awful to contemplate, all that guff and mush, it sounds dreadful!'

'I don't mean the books, they're fine with me. Bit boring, but harmless. I mean her, she's dangerous! Have you read her comments about trans women?'

'What do you take me for? Of course not.'

'She insists that biological sex is primary, and that only gender is negotiable. This makes the trans community more than angry, and promotes the cultural bias against trans women ... It's pure and simple hate speech! Our local bookshop won't stock her books!'

'I beg your pardon ...?'

'They won't, they say it is promoting ...'

'I don't give a damn about your bookshop. Did you just say "hate speech"?'

'Absolutely.'

'*Hate* speech! As a description of an opinion freely and rationally expressed, open to debate? You've lived a sheltered life, or perhaps you have no historical imagination! You call that a form of hatred? *String up the Black bastards! Gas the Jews! That* is hate speech, those are hate *crimes!* You should be thoroughly ashamed to think and to talk like that!'

'Well, Dad, we'll have to agree to disagree on this one. The fact is, you're wrong! You've been left behind! Why not open your bottle of wine, sit back and stew in your juices, and leave the modern world to the modern people!'

Lucy has often infuriated me, but rarely has she made me so ashamed. The difference between us – between me and my dear daughter, with whom nothing should be unsayable, but with whom, increasingly, so much is – is not about opinion but about being, about how to be in the world. I am of an intellectual generation and culture that valued discourse, however heated, which respected the opposing point of view, and regarded it as essential that opposition be accepted, encouraged and codified in our practices, whose concept of diversity was to respect different opinions as well as races. Lucy is no such.

And now I read that the ubiquitous feminist Dr Greer has been refused permission to speak at some university, however Welsh. Her crime? She maintains that trans women are not women. Her lecture has been cancelled, and so has she. I find this utterly bemusing. How did these trans persons – I've never met or seen one – get to the head of the discriminated-against queue? Do they suffer more than midgets, spastics and cripples, the brain-damaged, the autistic, the schizophrenic, the palpably impaired, whose problems make those of a boy who wishes he were a girl seem trivial? A dwarf cannot 'identify' as a tall person. But a boy wants to identify as a girl? Fair enough. Who cares? Why is this, all of a sudden, one of the pressing moral topics of the day, sufficient to send universities and schools into turmoil, legislators and religious leaders into paroxysms of confusion, and families – like mine! – into discord?

The trans lobby has been vociferous and intemperate in its attacks, which only goes to prove the point that even Dr Greer might have been reticent to make: this behaviour is so aggressive, violent, and domineering that it is clear that it is a *masculine* phenomenon. The real men in this whole ludicrous genre debate are the trans but not transformed 'women', *who are still men*. This is obvious when you see how they behave: the aggression, the bullying, the gangs who shout and demonstrate. Who are still and inalienably testosterone-driven trades unionists: Jobs for the boys!

You need more than a scalpel and a few hormone injections to de-mannify a man, you can't make maleness go away. *Trans women are men*. They were born as men, and however much they have adjusted their privates and their dresses, they continue to behave in ways that few women could produce, stomach or countenance.

No one is shouting, 'Trans men are men!' Not because a quick fumble under the skirt will provide under-the-counter evidence, but because the demeanour of the unrepresented new gender is intractably feminine, gentle, and unaggressive. They want to be left to get on with their lives, not to shout about them. *Trans men are men*. Sex is like that. Gender, I gather, is up for grabs. It's apparently merely a matter of choice.

My daughter, in the name of her progressive inclusive ideology, agrees with the intemperate judgements on her opponents. She has her fashionable opinions and I have my increasingly unfashionable ones. Am I to conclude that at best we can tiptoe round each other respectfully, and then agree to disagree? That's obvious and perhaps needful, but it's wrong, as Lucy is both obvious and wrong. Therefore I am subtle and right? Do I have to sign up for this conclusion, thus blatantly? Of course I do. At least I have the sense not to say so to my daughter, who would regard my beliefs as so extreme and so disgusting that she would have genuine doubts – which she would have to overcome, of course – about whether I should continue to be allowed entry into her life and house, as if I were a noisome Trump supporter.

After we'd left Goddards and arrived at our respective homes, we left the topic hanging between us, as if from a tree in Mississippi.

# PART THREE

# *Black Loves Matter*

'The goal is oblivion. I have arrived early.'

Jorge Luis Borges, 'Fifteen Coins'

# Chapter 11

Staring at the screen, I composed myself for another, still surprising return to Africa, my fictive folk having miraculously survived my renunciation. The project had flooded the banks of its original course, and the resulting wetland didn't lead anywhere obvious, which is what happens when you choose an inappropriate metaphor. Simpler to say that whatever I was now doing wasn't, quite, what I had intended. This might have been a source of frustration, but what I felt was release, as if it was now only composing that mattered, not the tomfoolery.

Does my story still have to be bad? It is, consciously or not. I have no idea what I am writing about. I suppose the imagination can be like that. Stephen Crane composed *The Red Badge of Courage* at a comfortable distance from the relevant sanguinary experiences. But I'm not a highly imaginative ignoramus, merely an exhausted former schoolmaster, and for every William Golding scribbling away in a corner of the common room, there are ten thousand dreary pedants who can barely compose their school reports.

The question is not quality, but cunningly administered quantity. Can I produce something that the sensitive editorial girls will be thrilled, and fooled, by? Should my protagonist thus be a young woman? Perhaps ONE should be female, she could make her escape to the big city, and become a famous this or that? Or

– better idea! Yes! – should ONE turn out to be a trans person, that way you get both a female and a male protagonist rolled up in *one*. Not he, not she, *they*! What larks! I'm beginning to catch on to this new sexual nomenclature.

Ongoing checklist of topical tropes for typical dopes: *trans Women are Women*? Tick! *Black Lives Matter?* Tick! Two down, what's left? *Me Too?* I could have my trans person sexually assaulted somewhere down the line, as it were. Tick! Is the result sufficiently *Feminist?* Silly me: if ONE is now a woman, the resulting story, overflowing with empathy and understanding, becomes a feminist tract. Tick off the -isms, satisfy the -ists! Tick! But is there adequate *Diversity*? Might I need, how ironic is this, to introduce some white people to broaden the palette? Or might some yellow ones do? Or if Black lives matter SO much, maybe that's as diverse as needs be, if you're a white person.

The political is personal. Most of the passionate advocates of these movements are those directly served by them. The crow wishes everything was black; the owl that everything was white. Trans mottos for trans People! Black Lives for Black People! Me Too for Women People! All this virtue flouting and signalling is motivated by personal gain. Most virtue is. Christians recommend good behaviour not because it is right, but because it pays so well.

If you interviewed these motto-ists about international starvation, the spread of Covid and malaria, or the plight of the world's desolate refugees, they would purse their lips but close their purses. They are more concerned with their supposed personal rights than their social responsibilities. What do all their Indignations come down to? The Politics of ME!

There's profit in these observations if I can find a way to employ, and to exploit them, to produce a literary cocktail of the liqueurs du jour, heady, exotic, eminently quaffable. Yum! Can I have another? Its tipsy readers will stay up all night drinking, fully woke with righteousness, tweeting their delight. As long as I can avoid subtlety, irony, fine-phrase making, any signs of literary finesse, it's irresistible. Aside from the fact that it's utterly banal. Or might that be yet another of its virtues?

'I brought you this. Is all right?'

Bronya had entered silently, as if afraid to disturb my concentration, carrying a flat white in a china cup and saucer, and a plate of shortbreads. She makes both almost perfectly.

She set them down on the left-hand side of my desk, and began to leave the room.

'Thank you, Bronya!'

'I'm sorry to disturb. Writers need to concentrate and be alone.'

'Bronya! Whatever gave you the idea I am a writer? I'm no such thing.'

She looked puzzled. Looked at my screen, and the stacked journals on the table next to my armchair.

'I don't understand,' she said slowly. 'Why not writer? Is what you do. Every day.'

'Let me explain. To me "writer", like "artist" or "composer", is a term of respect, it honours someone whose work is of a high standard. But the world is full of people who paint hideous pictures, or compose trivial verses. These people do not deserve the title "artist" or "poet", they are just hobbyists, amusing themselves. Their work is not worth taking seriously, though they take it seriously themselves. Too seriously!'

Bronya had shuffled to the side of the desk and was looking at the screen. I suppressed an urge to turn the machine off, but would have lost my work.

'I think I understand,' she said. 'But I do not believe you are ... what do you say? ... an amateur in such a way. Like "local artist", is that right? I think your writing will be worth reading by many people. Is that what counts? I wish I could read some of what you write ...'

'You'd hate it,' I said. 'It's just me scribbling away and amusing myself.'

'. . . but I will be guessing one thing?'

'What's that?'

'That it is good! But now,' she said, turning and walking towards the door, 'I make some lunch. Maybe *salade niçoise*, you like that!'

I have taught her how to make one, it's not difficult. None of your Otto fancification here. Just excellent ingredients, perfectly combined, the key to all great, not cooking, but eating. Sushi-quality tuna, lightly seared. Free range organic eggs with orange yolks, Jersey royals, lamb's lettuce, French beans, paper-thin slices of red onion, proper anchovies not tinned ones, and particularly the right oily olives: Black OLives Matter! Be sparing with quartered tomatoes, which can be insistent and acidic, even heirloom ones. Add a dressing that substitutes lemon juice for vinegar, vintage extra virgin olive oil, Dijon mustard and crushed fresh garlic. Salt, pepper. Plate the ingredients gently or they get bruised, but don't 'assemble' them, it's only a damn salad. I don't wish to feel ashamed about deconstructing and devouring a work of art.

'I'd love that, thanks. Shall I come down at one?'

'Whenever. Perhaps you need to write more! I have plenty to do.' She closed the door, as she went off to do whatever might be, other than composing my salad. Household chores, perhaps, or helping to organise my accounts and obligations.

In the afternoon she will do her Zoom tutorials sitting at the table in Suzy's old bedroom. Bronya was at first reluctant to intrude into this private, laden space, but I assured her that it would be good for both her and for the room to reanimate and, if I may be allowed an ugly word, to re-purpose it. It would be used as a guestroom if I had any guests. It is still inhabited by recurrent memories of Suzy's last days, which I do not wish to forget, but I want them to sit, companionably, with newer, happier times.

I gazed at the screen once again, but Bronya's intervention had interrupted the desire, the mood, the flow necessary for composition. I was entirely out of Africa, my people, their landscapes and habitats receding by the moment, until there was nothing left but me, the not-writer: James Darke, compulsive journal-keeper and pasticheur. I sat in my armchair, and risked lighting a small Montecristo, even though it was only 10.30. I turned it in the flame until it was evenly afire, blew on it gently, drew the incomparable first inhalation, and held it in my mouth. Exhaled, and floated a delightful smoke ring, like an itinerant halo only more desirable.

In a few minutes I felt better, not at all light-headed, and returned to my keyboard to write some more. It's what I do.

Of the children, only ONE misses his grandfather. Agogo taught him to hunt and to trap, took him to the lake to fish for chambo, put his arm round his skinny shoulders when the boy was anxious.

Death is over for now. It will return. It is like a drought or a sandstorm. I miss Father, every day he is gone as every day he is still present in my heart and my mind. My tears continue to fall. I console myself with the eternal verities.

Oh, God, whoever You cause to die, cause him to die with faith.

I shall see him once again, comfort him as he shall comfort me. I instruct ONE, but he does not listen, is forever lost in his dreams.

When the little ones are restless they flock to their older brother, begging for one of his dressed-up stories.

'Please, ONE! Just one story, just one!'

'I do not know any stories,' he tells them, 'but I have a friend who does!' Then he disappears for a few minutes and returns dressed as a woman, with skirts and false hair, and bosoms made of rags stuffed under his top. Often he paints his face. He introduces himself as the storyteller. The children sit round his/her feet, but he/she would not begin until they were absolutely still. There was a hush of anticipation.

I do not know how ONE can do this, neither his father nor I am gifted in such ways. But ONE! Week by week he spins story after story about the Life of Little One, as his hero is called. Or sometimes his heroine. Little One's Adventures at the Lake, Little One Encounters a Fierce Beast, Little One Gets Lost in the Big City.

More! More! The children shout and beg. He rises and bows, promising more but not today, withdraws and returns a few minutes later as ONE. He says he remembers nothing of his muse, she is a spirit who overcomes him, and is more real than he is.

The salad is on the table, with a chilled glass of Marcel Richaud rosé. Better than *nsima* and dirty water.

'Bronya, dear, won't you come and join me?'

I always have to ask, and she often finds a way to demur. Lucy says that she is trying to *respect my boundaries*, being under the impression that they are at once impenetrable and fragile, which Lucy says describes me perfectly.

'Thanks, no. I hope you enjoy. I have tutorial in a few minutes.'

She schedules these Zooms to avoid too much intimacy, even of the culinary sort. But in the mornings when she arrives, I make coffee, and she buys croissants at the French bakery. She leaves late in the afternoon, though on Wednesdays we share a light supper over which one need not tarry either in the preparation or the eating. An *omelette aux fines herbes* perhaps, a reverse-seared fillet steak or grilled wild salmon. Since she has re-entered my life I have parted company with Mr Lenghi, and I don't miss him one tiny bit. If I fancy one of his elaborate mish-moshes, I can order it from his Notting Hill restaurant, and Uber Eats will bring it to my door. I usually have a glass of wine over lunch, and two or three at supper, but Bronya abstains. She likes a drink, but not with me. I'm not sure why, though I am grateful for it.

I have no idea what my politics are any more, save for an aversion to almost everything and everybody, so I remain a metaphorical

Brexiteer. Or I would be if it weren't for Bronya. I wonder if she might be deported?

ONE told his stories once a week, though his growing audience begged for more. 'It is not up to me,' said ONE solemnly, 'I am only visited by my dear storyteller on the morning of a Saturday. She has many others to tell her stories to. It's not just you!'

On the following Saturday morning, after the chores were done, a small crowd gathered: now the elder two children joined as well, together with a number of the younger children from the village. By the time the assembled crowd sat in the dirt and quietened down, I could count sixteen children. When ONE disappeared and soon reappeared in his costume, his audience giggled in delight.

ONE bowed to the crowd, a prolonged and elegant gesture, before seating himself on a stool.

'Today,' he/she would begin, 'I have a most exciting story to tell! Little One Gets Lost, and doesn't know where she is, or how to find her way home. It is very frightening!' ONE hunched forwards, his eyes bright, clasping a hand to his bosoms lest they shift place.

A laugh sounded from the rear of his audience. One of the older village boys, who had arrived at the last moment, intrigued by the unusual spectacle, was standing with his hands on his hips, shouting.

'Freak! Homosexual!' I hurried from our hut to shoo the bully away, and he skulked off, sneering. But the magic was broken, ONE disappeared, and the little ones dispersed slowly and solemnly in their shock and disappointment, uncertain of what had happened.

ONE was not seen again for two days.

Where'd he go? Do I need him back in the village? Not a lot more to say. Might it be better to remove him to the (unnamed) City, lay him out in the urban sprawl? Not adventures, misadventures. Pile on the suffering. Some abuse, some despair. People love that. It sells.

I must compose my covering email, introducing 'myself' and my submission, acknowledging humbly that I know nothing of how such things are done. Make up a cover story, never tell the truth, the truth is too easily verified, whereas a good lie has legs that can run and run. Think of all those 'doctors' operating away in London hospitals, their records and transcripts entirely fraudulent, their only backgrounds in carpentry or plumbing. They probably get better results.

Miles told me of a famous New York literary agent called, most appropriately, Wily, who is apparently nicknamed Jackal. *Coyote* might be better. Thinking I might write to him, I looked him up only to learn that he is far too grand to accept unsolicited submissions. Other agents do, but not many. These days you need an agent to get an agent, and the possibility of infinite regress beckons. I approach a few in the hope, and naive expectation, that one of them will be sufficiently intrigued by my cunning cover letter that they will read the attached narrative.

Of course, no agent in their right mind would countenance such a risible project. Unless their mind is very right indeed, *right on*, ticking all the contemporary boxes.

'Bronya, what is this?'

I picked up the wrapped package from the top of the bookshelf under my window, without looking at the label, and showed it to her. I have lost interest in random entries through my door, either persons or parcels. Occasionally, if I have ordered something, I will notice its arrival, and sometimes not. A jar of truffles, nicely be-packaged, sat on the kitchen bench for a week until I thought to open it. But this one rang no bells.

'I told you. Last week, maybe one before that. You said put in study.'

My mind receives a lot of information and stores almost none of it, memory being (as Sherlock Holmes asserted) a small attic in which only essential material should be placed. Most days I'm lucky to remember who I am, and what I should be doing. For the rest I make lists: shopping, medications, Lucy reminders, journal entries of interest ...

'Go on then! Open!'

I had no interest in the damned thing, but it was easier to try to tear it open than to explain why I didn't wish to. I fear Bronya is beginning to find me biddable, and trading upon it. Since coming into her own, or, more accurately my own, she is just as anxious to please, only these days she chooses how to do it. Did I prefer her when she was simply my cleaner? Certainly. Life was simpler and easier then. Sharply defined boundaries.

I struggled to remove the outward plastic covering from the courier firm, only to find a well-taped cardboard package inside. I looked at it in a hostile manner, as if the very force of my enmity might make it reveal its contents.

'Let me do it!'

Bronya disappeared for a moment to return with scissors and a Stanley knife. In a remarkably short time, a book popped out, which she perused with some interest, before handing it over.

I looked at it blankly. It had some coloured folk in a black-and-white photographic montage on the front cover, above which was the title in black: *WINDRUSH TO JUDGEMENT*. Below the photo was the author's name, George Headley Wallace.

'Nothing to do with me,' I said, not recognising the name but wincing at the appropriation of my title. I suppose it was inevitable, not all that clever, really. Handing the invasive object to Bronya I said, 'You can have it if you'd like, otherwise throw it away.'

She took it from my hand.

'Looks interesting. I read maybe when I have time.'

'Whatever.'

I repaired to my desk and to the regular task of recording what

I can remember of my ever decreasing span, my life a shrinking bridge over a shrunken river. Delete metaphor.

'Coffee?' Bronya asked, as she walked away.

'Lovely, yes, please.'

When she returned fifteen minutes later she was carrying our Georgian walnut tray with two flat whites, some shortbreads on a blue-and-white Chinese plate, and the book, which looked ugly and inappropriate in its genteel setting.

'Thank you, Bronya. I rather wish you'd leave that book somewhere else.'

'But, you wait, you! Look at this!'

She came to the side of my desk carrying the book, which she opened to the title page. There was an ugly pen-and-ink scrawl on it. I gazed in surprise, in wonderment. I'd recognise that hand anywhere. Wally!

'Is for you, I cannot read.'

I perused the inscription. I can decipher Wally's hand, I'd had enough practice when I read the final version of his text all those months ago, and made my corrections and suggestions.

> *Dear James Darke,*
> *THANKS TO YOU!*
> *With gratitude and respect.*
> *From your friend,*
> *Wally*

I'll be damned! I looked at the bottom of the page: published by Hodder Headline! He'd played the zeitgeist demographic, and won. I leafed through the book for a few minutes, sipping my coffee. The text was not entirely as I remembered, nor should it have been, for a competent editor had clearly been at work. The result, while hardly immortal prose, read smoothly enough, fit for purpose. The material presumably rewarded the simplicity of its telling.

On the inner back flap was an author photograph, with Wally dressed in a brightly coloured shirt against a tropical background, some blowsy palm trees, blue skies and sea, but not a holiday snap. He didn't have the requisite Say Cheese smile, looked seriously at the camera, as if to say, *You may send me away but I am who I am and I see what I see.*

'Look at back! Acknowledgements!'

In which there was a paragraph explaining the inception of the book, exaggerating the role that I had played in encouraging and shaping the narrative when we were both in prison. I suppose this should have made me proud, but instead I was embarrassed and a trifle irritated, at this unwonted and uninvited invasion of my privacy. I wish he hadn't done it. At the very least he should have asked.

Next thing I know some damned journalist might put one and one together, and think there's an interesting story here! But of course, the book will neither sell nor get reviewed. It was no doubt produced to top up the Diversity Quota of its publisher, and will languish with the rest of such stuff, unread and unloved.

This conclusion, though, was hardly supported by the quotations on the rear of the jacket, in which various luminaries said what an important and moving story this was. I looked them up: a senior member of the Labour Party, two Black authors and one white one, and someone from the United Nations. Worthy puffery, publisher's guff, perhaps, but impressive to an innocent eye.

'You want it now, yes?'

'No. I've already read it.'

Bronya looked a little disappointed, but took it away. I felt relieved, it would have been uncomfortable in my study, were I to place it alphabetically amongst my books, just before (God help me) my P. G. Wodehouses and Oscar Wildes, it would have stuck out dreadfully. I have honed my W's carefully, the wolves have departed: snitbag Virginia is long gone, along with fancy-pants Tom and interminable Thomas. Wally wouldn't fit, he'd be as uncomfortable in such company as I would be putting him in it, not because he is Black (though I have very few books by ethnic writers) but because he is of the wrong class and quality for my shelves, which are a continuing reflection of where I came from and how I have defined myself.

'Dad!'

'Darling Lucy, how lovely to ...'

'Have you got a minute?'

'I'm just finishing lunch, can I ring you back?'

'You won't. Just put it aside, I have some odd news!'

'Do tell.'

'Have you seen the paper this morning? The *Observer*?'

'No, I don't read it. I could pick it up later, after my little nap.'

'Forget your nap! Go get it now, right after we hang up!'

'Why? Has our leader been assassinated? That'd be worth hurrying myself up for.'

'Very funny. No, there's a review of your friend George's book in it. And it mentions you! I didn't know anything about this. You never said. Apparently you were his mentor in prison ...'

'I was not. And he's called Wally, not George.'

'Whatever. If I was you I'd go out and get a copy. You should read it, it's a bit ...'

I will work out for myself what it's a bit of, so cut her off.

'I'll ring you later.'

I hurried out to buy the paper, resisted the urge to open it in the street, tucked it under my arm and fast-ambled home to read it over a glass of wine. Two glasses, as it turned out, and rising.

*This is a remarkable story. Two stories, in fact. The first, a harrowing history of the author and his family, is of the dispossession of the Jamaican immigrants of the 1950s, and their appalling treatment on arrival in the UK (No Blacks!) up to the present day, in which they and their descendants have been dispossessed of their rightful place in the land of their choice. Imported on ships like the Windrush, which recall the slavers of old, they were required to do the menial work previously reserved for the Paddies (No Irish!). Since the dreaded Theresa May was Home Secretary, recent years have seen thousands of former West Indians, many of them actually born in the UK, brutally interrogated about their rightful place, and asked to provide documentation about their English domicile so detailed that it would make Theresa herself weep in dismay.*

There were three more paragraphs, similar in cutesy tone and marginal literacy. The review then segued to the so-called second story, about 'George' (the impertinence of it!) and James (ditto!). Two incarcerated criminals: one guilty of aggravated assault, the other of murder, both of us fundamentally sympathetic. Wally had been intolerably provoked, and retaliated; I had provided a compelling moral argument for my action. A graphic account described the brutal punch on the nose, and Suzy's fatal cocktail of honeyed tea and drugs.

These sympathetic felons got together in their cramped and miserable surrounds and (the implication was clear, how else could an ill-educated Black man produce such a book?) *collaborated*. We had done no such thing. Wally conceived and wrote his memoir. I encouraged a bit and edited a little, and he typically overstated my input and my generosity.

It was a risible review, though I felt a rush of pleasure for dear Wally, justice come round at last, if too late to save his English life, sufficient to establish him in it. It would be interesting to see how Story 1 developed, if the book caught on, and he was interviewed and allowed to tell his tale of woe. Might sufficient explanation and contrition on his part exonerate what might properly be regarded as a crime of passion? He'd served his time. Might he appeal, or re-appeal, the deportation against which he (we) had fought so unsuccessfully?

Sherlock Holmes would have fired up his meerschaum and announced a two-pipe problem, sat, puffed, and cogitated. Aside from his unique knowledge of different sorts of soil and ash, he wasn't actually very clever, which was why he needed Watson: sixty watts burns bright in the intellectual twilight. I'm smarter than him, when I put my mind to it.

If I smoked two Montecristos, though, I'd be quite unable to solve any problem other than how to rise from my chair. Would one cigar and one bottle of wine be an adequate substitute? I consulted my inner Sherlock. He didn't care.

Let's get it orderly, and clear:

**The facts:**
Wally's Book is out.
I am outed.
I will be bearded in one way or another.
**My response:**
Ignore? This would be reported, and scorned. 'Dr Darke is unavailable for comment ...'
Resist? Even more so: 'Dr Darke is unwilling to comment ...'
**Hence, my action:**
Issue a Statement? Give an Interview? Make an Appearance?

While I smoked and hid beneath the (only sometimes metaphorical) bedclothes, I was torn between flight (which I'm good at) and fight (last time I tried that I ended up in prison). When I was fruitlessly campaigning for assisted dying, my guide and comrade was poor deluded Hamlet, who (like me) had problems bumping off a relative. A perfectly reasonable task, if you're up to it, but neither of us was. Like Hamlet, I think too much, do too little, and am occasionally a trifle wonky.

# Chapter 12

More reviews of Wally's book are coming in, full of admiration of a mildly patronising variety. He doesn't need my help, he's already had it. At this point I'm not the news story, but a subject of a possible feature article of the risible English sort, we love crude differences and contrasts of class and race. The title-wallahs would have a ball with us:

*The Black and White Minstrel Show and Tell!*
*The Odd Couple: Mates and Inmates!*

What to do? Write to Wally? There was a return address on the screeds he'd sent me, which I had neither read properly nor answered, but of course I had thrown them away. Send an email? No address either. Send a letter c/o his publisher? Just as soon toss it in the rubbish.

As I was puffing (yes, a second, but small cigar) and quaffing my glass of Palmaz Louise Riesling, lolling in my comfy chair, the answer to my problem rang me on the phone.

'Miles!'

'James! Well, you've been a busy boy! Congratulations!'

I couldn't tell, quite, if he was teasing. I don't know him nearly as well as Suzy did.

'Yes. Thank you. But I could do with a favour …'

'Anything! Just ask.'

'I want to get in touch with George, you know, Wally – I'm not sure how to respond to all of this, or if I need to at all …'

'You'll have to, in one way or another.'

'You might think so, I'm not sure even about that. But I think Wally and I need to be on the same hymn sheet about this, and I don't have a way of contacting him. No address or email, nothing. Can you help? You know everything and everyone.'

'Did you write to Hodder?'

'Surely, Miles, surely that …'

'You're right, yes, of course. You know what? Leave it with me.'

'Thanks so much, I'm very grateful.'

Before he could draw breath to reply, I'd rung off.

I'd begun a draft of a letter congratulating Wally on his day 'in the sun', the tone-deafness of which can only be explained by how uneasy I was writing to him in his Jamaican exile. Keep it simple. However great his transient celebrity, he is a simple soul, and all the better for it. Aside from a sniffy piece in the *Speccy*, most of his notices have been positive. Interviews were scheduled on Zoom, as the possibility of in-person appearances was moot, at least for the moment. When the plague has lifted somewhat, and Wally is free to travel, he would still be unable to enter the UK due to the circumstances of his deportation. This was iniquitous, and I'd offered to help him in any way to return, if even briefly, to what is his native land, a brown citizen of this unwhite island.

I informed him that though I have been approached to do something with or about him, I had refused, and that I hoped he would understand this. The success was entirely his, and I had no desire to feature in it. Though I signed this missive, 'James', I was not surprised when his return letter, a week later, addressed me more formally. In prison he'd called me Darky, which was now manifestly inappropriate.

*Dear James Darke,*

*I am so pleased to hear from you. Life here in Jamaica is pleasant enough, though I am not a beach bum, and have no taste for rum or weed. The people are welcoming, and I have a few distant relatives who have taken me to their hearts. There is much publicity in the local papers, and I – me, Wally! – am on TV and in the newspapers. People in the street hug me with tears in their eyes, and say that I have told their story as well as my own.*

*I would not call it a homecoming. England is my home, and I will keep trying to return. Until I do, I am grateful for my success, my health, and the warmth of my reception.*

*And I thank you too, once again and from the bottom of my heart, for your literary and emotional encouragement. I know what that has meant. You probably do too, at least a little. But that's between us, and I agree that an appearance together, of any sort, would do no good, and might go wrong in any number of ways.*

*So, until I see you again, which please God will happen one day, very warm regards from your old mate,*

*Wally*

I read and reread this, making my way easily across his recognisable hand, which seemed, somehow, exactly the right vehicle for such simple sentiments. I am furious at the treatment he'd been subjected to, this unfortunate subject of Her Majesty: his parents shipped to England on a disguised slave ship, their son shipped back to the West Indies as if a slave of old, required by Empire to cut sugar cane or to pick cotton. He had described and subverted all of that but it didn't give him his life back. He'd have to fight for that, and though no optimist, I felt a stirring belief that he would prevail. I'm told that goodness and right sometimes do, though few examples spring to mind.

Like Wally, I have to make the best of things, though unlike him I don't have many things left. When I contemplate returning to my poor little Africans, and wonder what will happen next, the increasing answer is: nothing. Not merely because I have reached an aesthetic impasse – the first part of my story is told by the mother, but the rest is about ONE, and I don't know, quite, how to alter the narration and point of view. I have reread what I have written so far, and though it is fit for its lowly purpose, I'm not sure I care. What do my imaginary Black friends matter when my real one is suffering?

Bronya insists that I need exercise, and that we should go for an amble every morning, promising a treat at the kiosk in the park if I am a good boy. They offer a surprisingly adequate coffee ice-cream, which may act, Bronya has acutely surmised, as an incentive, though my more substantial motive is to make her (and Lucy) shut up. Stroll! Amble! Repeat as Prescribed! They worry that I am declining in health and energy. They are right. That's my fate, and goal. But I am attached to my elegant walking stick, swanking it in the local environs. There's nobody quite like me out there, not these days, the others like me are long dead.

There's nothing left. My Blacks, singular and plural, can make their own way, and I, mine, were there only way to make. What is left is merely time to kill, until it kills me. No reason not to stroll a little, drink and smoke a lot, in readiness for and anticipation of the day. On our first, gentle foray into the wilderness of the park, as I ambled, puffed, and cut a figure, we approached the café next to the newsagent's, and sitting in the front window at a Formica table, hunched over a mug of tea, was the boy to whom I'd given the cigarettes months ago. He looked worse, if that was possible, his hair matted, wearing the same clothes, only filthier. Wretched, lost, pitiable. He'd been not on, but in, my mind since our brief acquaintance outside the newsagent's. I felt sorry not to have done more for him, found some slight way to come to his aid. I should have, though there was a restraint and pride in him that I felt I should honour. I am unclear whether that was a moral mistake or a triumph of emotional acuity.

I stopped short, and Bronya had gone ahead a few paces before she noticed I was no longer at her side. She looked back, and I walked forward to join her.

'That's him,' I said. 'The boy I told you about, in the window drinking tea.'

She turned to walk back.

'Don't! We don't want to embarrass him. Let's carry on.'

Bronya caught my eye, as if she wished to say something, but didn't. She's learning.

On our way home from the park, we reached the café, and motioning to Bronya, I put on my mask, itself a sign of serious intent, and entered the premises, which smelled of sweat, tannic tea and powdered coffee, overcooked cheap sausages and bacon. There was a greasy fat fellow in a filthy apron behind the counter.

'Morning! What's yours?'

'Some information, please. About twenty minutes ago there was a boy at the front table, drinking tea ...'

He looked at me suspiciously, up and down.

'Oh, yeah, what's it to you?'

'I met him a few months ago, and I'd felt sorry for him. I'd like to do him a good turn ...'

The counter man's suspicion deepened and darkened.

'What sort of "good turn"?' He pronounced the phrase with a scowl. I was too grand to use the term 'a favour'!

'If he comes in regularly ...'

I received a brief nod of acquiescence: 'For a cuppa, yeah.'

'. . . I'd like to leave some money with you so that he can have a good meal. He seems wretchedly poor.'

'That he is. What's it to you, though? Who're you?'

'Just a man who once gave him some cigarettes, he'll remember.'

The suspicion that I was trying to procure the boy was unsustainable even in a mind as suspicious as his.

'Aye. I'll tell him, he comes in most days, like. For a cuppa. I give it him free, he's a nice lad, had a rough time.'

I took out my wallet and extracted five twenty-pound notes.

'Can this be for his expenses? But only for him, mind you.'

'Bit peculiar, like, not sure I'm easy about this . . .'

'I'd be so grateful.'

He considered this for a moment, studied my face for signs of psychosis or perversion, took the notes, put them in the drawer in the cash register, and tore a piece of paper off the receipt book.

'I'll keep a tab,' he said.

Bronya looked at me quizzically when I came out the door.

'I'll tell you later,' I said. 'Let's get home, I'm longing for a decent coffee.'

Without my requesting or even much noticing it, Bronya is more often here than wherever her there might be. She now spends three nights at the house, perhaps more, I never quite notice. She is anxious to use this time profitably, by which, thank God, she does not mean *together*. Or might she? Who knows such things?

She and I have all too little in common. Separated by gender, age, country, education, class and inclination, we are as mismatched as any computer could produce, and I stutter and cast about for topics in which we might share an interest. Going for walks is an adequate activity, as it requires only the smallest of talk. We discuss Lucy and the children, now in some metaphoric manner her family, as well as the news, which we watch on the BBC, and we share our copy of *The Times*. She often watches telly in the evening, inviting me to join her, which I rarely do. Most programmes are fatuous and demotic, catering to the risible 'taste' of both the proletariat (quiz shows and soap operas) and the middle class (dramas about costumes and documentaries about fish). Yet there are evenings to pass, and while we sometimes read, neither of us has, quite, the stamina to do much of that. Bronya calls it 'Covid-head', a term she's picked up on the wireless, which is apparently a syndrome that makes it impossible to concentrate. I call that being old and bored.

Lucy has suggested a boxed set, now rebranded as a Series. I have looked into this, and demurred, either you waste time watching a few episodes before you realise it's rubbish, or you watch quite a lot, until the writers and producers run out of ideas, and introduce a licentious green alien into the heroine's arms. Undaunted, Bronya has suggested a plausible procedure: each of us picks a telly programme that we have loved, and introduces the other to it. We agree in advance that we will each give it a fair go, however strong our initial distaste.

My choice, which will not only recall past pleasures, but introduce Bronya to a wide and improving world of reference, was *Civilisation,* by Kenneth (later Lord) Clark. I first watched this at Oxford, and was entranced by the elegant ease and mastery of the presenter, one of the great and good who knew both how to talk and what to talk about. Bronya would surely profit from exposure to this quintessential example of urbane Englishness, and when the various viral fogs have lifted, we might go to the galleries and museums together. A capital idea! When I told Bronya about it she said she often visited the National Gallery and Tate Britain on her few days off – like Rudy she is mad about Blake – and sometimes the new Tate: 'Great spaces! And good coffee!'

I don't know if I was disappointed to hear that she had toes in these waters, I'd rather fancied playing Henry Higgins to her Eliza, but I regularly underestimated her intelligence and cultural range.

Having first encountered her as a cleaner, which to my class and generation is not a job but a category of being, I found it hard to adjust my view, to credit her education and learning. Yet her choice of telly programme hardly reflected this high ground, instead it was firmly anchored in the mud. She wished us to watch the first episode – and more, she hoped – of the adventures of the rag-and-bone men, *Steptoe and Son*. How funny, how painful, how appropriate: Civilisation: High and Not at All!

She announced her surprising choice – how did Bronya know about *Steptoe*? Surely it didn't have reruns in Sofia? – in a tone both puckish and incipiently defensive, and reacted at once to my involuntary moue of distaste.

'Good actors! Makes you laugh and cry!'

'I've heard of it. Let's give it a go. What are the rules, do you think? I suggest we start with the first episode of each series, and see if we fancy more. If not, there are plenty of other possibilities.'

When we lived in Oxford, Suzy watched telly to take her mind off her accumulating troubles. When 'blocked' in her writing, and increasingly despondent, she would plonk herself in front of the box after supper, and finish off our bottle of wine. She hardly smiled during that period, but the one thing that would make her coil and recoil with laughter and tears was *Steptoe and Son*. She adored the lugubrious, self-improving Harry H. Corbett and his scabrous father Wilfrid Brambell, whose expression suggested that someone had just used his face to scratch their piles. She was entranced by the quickness of the repartee, and the tragic situation. More satisfying than a play by Beckett, she maintained, because the characters were recognisably real, and alive. It was her eccentric belief that Beckett's plays were staged in purgatory, his persons already dead but still chuntering on, not being but waiting, talking of nothing from nowhere. Steptoe was better!

*The foul rag and bone shop of the heart!* Low may also be high, it's been known to happen, from Shakespeare to Wordsworth, but from my very first exposure to the Steptoes (a more resonant title) I loathed it with a visceral, cringing distaste. The first episode began with the weary son returning their horse to its stable, entering the scrapheap that he calls home. He is immediately upbraided by his father: the day's takings are paltry, he doesn't work hard enough, he hasn't fed the horse properly! We are not at the beginning of a drama but smack in the middle of it. Harold shivers, shudders, and says he's hungry too.

It was astonishing, I'd never seen anything like it, and as scene followed scene it was clear that there was something monumental about it, this generational archetype of antipathy and misunderstanding, audaciously crossing the Elizabethans with the theatre of the absurd: the extravagance, the showy cruelty. I hated it.

'Turn it off!' I begged, but Suzy was already entranced.

The intensity of my reaction surprised and disappointed my wife, as I soon absented myself to read a calming book while listening to soothing music. Jane Austen and Mozart, nothing in the least disturbing there, as far an aesthetic distance as possible from the vulgar mayhem on the screen.

Never one to let things pass, Suzy quizzed me about my reaction.

'You didn't like it? Fine, it's a matter of taste, I suppose . . .' When she said such things, what she meant was that she had it and I did not: Steptoe was not her *taste*, like a mushroom, it was demonstrably *good*! Failure to reach this conclusion was a failure of discrimination.

'I don't know . . . It maddens me to see those ugly people grubbing in the dirt like dung beetles, infesting each other's psyches. *Hell is other people!*'

To my surprise, she left it, and me, alone in my fug and stew.

That evening, I dreamed of my father, which was rare. I hardly ever thought about the old bastard, saw little of him when I was a boy, and nothing in my manhood, by which time he'd buggered off to Australia, never to return. Or even to write.

In the dream I was a little boy and I'd done something very bad. Hid under my bed, as he stomped round the room, shouting for me to come out. I was going to be punished!

I awoke in a sweat, terrified and shaking, and Suzy held me in her arms.

'You're just dreaming!' she said.

'Yes. Sorry! Go back to sleep.'

Practised in having bad dreams, waking often to write them down, Suzy knew not to insist that I talk about it, rubbed my shoulders and back until I relaxed, and eventually drifted off.

In the morning I had a lie-in, and she appeared with one of her badly made cups of coffee, with a couple of Hobnobs on the saucer.

'Are you OK? Did you get back to sleep?'

'Yes. Thanks.' I sat up to take a long, dangerous slurp of coffee, spilling only a little on the bedclothes, and ate a biscuit in three bites. Washed it down.

I'm no Interpreter of Dreams, though God knows I'd had a bellyful of Suzy's, and participated unwillingly in her lengthy, self-engrossed attempts to unpick them: image by image, feeling (or 'affect') dissected and interrogated, and related to other dreams and the ongoing themes of her therapy. The connection was clear: I had watched *Steptoe and Son,* and then dreamed of my father. Darke and Son.

The apparent difference between the fathers (one a rag-and-bone man, the other a military one) might make one doubt any meaningful similarity, but the parallels were clear: a querulous working-class father, angrily trapped in the wrong life, all spit and no polish, is the sire of an unworthy, ambitious son, who is anxious to improve his situation, his prospects, domicile and accent. To move out, and on. What could such a father do but feel judged, and nourish an aversion to his upwardly mobile scion? And what might such a son feel, other than the bruising of this constant disapproval, and the urge to escape?

Harold's detestation of his father is almost complete, though leavened by very occasional moments of pity and tenderness, these occasional aberrations merely highlight how estranged he is. He is later to confront Albert in words that caught my father's nature exactly: 'A dyed-in-the-wool, fascist, reactionary, squalid little "know your place", "don't rise above yourself", "don't get out of your hole" – complacent little turd.' The implication is clear, vulgar and not funny: what happens when you get out of your hole? You're a piece of shit. That was me, as a child. I have few memories of my early years, but not few enough. I neither wish to revisit my past, nor to escape it, if I could I would erase it entirely, have come into my world fully formed and unparented, a free spirit.

Oxford was a long time ago, presumably long enough to revisit the Steptoes without shuddering with distaste. It would test how far I'd come, or if I was still mired in the Oedipal swamp. Anyway, it was Bronya's choice, that was the agreement. Me in my way, her in hers? Aye, there's the rub. My way is better than hers. Not a matter of taste but of discrimination, as Suzy had argued, no steptoeing round that.

Civilisation! For our Opening Night, I suggested that we began with a meal worthy of the topic, which I would cook and serve, after which we could watch our episode adequately fed and watered. To my surprise, Bronya countered with the observation that since the first episode of *Steptoe* begins with the very subject of feeding and watering, before her screening, she would provide a 'tea', how linguistically accurate of her, appropriate to the appetites, taste, and means of her subjects. Instead of my freshly shucked oysters and beef Wellington, she would offer whelks in vinegar, sausages and mash and mushy peas; champers and claret with mine, Newcastle Brown with hers; passion-fruit crème brûlée for mine, sticky toffee pudding for hers.

Bronya suggested that we dress in character for our screenings, which was pushing her luck. Not my sort of thing, not at all, though at Suzy's insistence, I'd been to a few fancy dress parties at Oxford, and presented myself as a Roman centurion, when the theme allowed it. Though I made a fuss, actually it was modestly enjoyable under my helmet, sword at my side. She always dressed as a hard-boiled detective from the noir world. I suggested that she occasionally change the look, and go as a hard-boiled egg, a good one. This elegant double witticism was apparently not funny.

But of course it was, and the smile prompted by the memory made me drop my guard, and to my surprise, I found myself agreeing to Bronya's proposal. What is happening to me? I suppose it's my incipient role model: I will make an admirable Kenneth Clark, I rather fancy that. But given that there are no women in his series, on screening night Bronya will need to dress as an artistic subject rather than an actual artist. Ingres's erotically charged *Grande Odalisque* popped to mind, and was rather hard to shift. But what a humiliation it would be, reciprocally, for me to impersonate Albert Steptoe. Or perhaps I'd be better as Harold, so deep was my (unconfessed) identification with him. Bronya could do either, she has rather a dramatic nature, though all too few opportunities to display it. And so she ends, at the last, as my live-in father?

On the fateful day, I spent the afternoon in the kitchen preparing the pastry for the beef Wellington, searing the foie gras, prepping the leeks, red capsicums and Jersey Royals, assembling the crème brûlée. I chilled a bottle of Perrier-Jouet Belle Époque 2006, and decanted a 1985 Lynch-Bages, in the hope that Bronya might appreciate them, or might learn to. Having finished these chores, I repaired to my bedroom to put on a dark grey suit, white shirt and tie, with black brogues, and slicked back what is left of my hair, preparing my version of K, as he was called, or J, as I will be. I wondered how Bronya would find a female role model in K's masculine world.

Never underestimate an intelligent Bulgarian. When she made

her entrance – no other phrase will do – Bronya was dressed in a flowing white shirt and black skirt, a floppy black cap perched jauntily on her head, carrying a casually but artistically assembled bunch of orange lilies.

I peered at her quizzically.

'You look wonderful!' I said.

'You do too,' she said. 'Mr Kenneth Clark!'

'That's Lord Clark to you,' I said, unable to keep the words from my lips, and immediately ashamed.

She looked at me carefully, up and down.

'Only better-looking. He has fat cheeks and wattle-neck, and tilts his head with eyes half-closed . . .'

'Does he? How do you know? I thought we were starting from the beginning, after dinner!'

'Yes, yes, we start watching. But I do some homeworks . . .'

'Bronya dear, that's cheating!'

'We never made rule. And anyway I would break it, and be glad. Because you know what?'

'What?'

'No women in his fancy-pants Art World, just in his bed. No woman artist, no sculptor, no architect, no no no. Whole civilisation is about big fat men and big fat museums, and big fat money!'

'I don't remember. I suppose that might be right. But who're you dressed up as?'

'Natalia Goncharova!'

'Welcome to my home, Natalia. Would you like a glass of champagne?'

I did not add, *whoever the hell you are,* my ignorance was assumed if not verified. I could google her after the festivities were over.

'Perhaps I might bring a vase for your flowers?'

'Thank you. Is gift.'

I'd lit a fire, and we sat by it with our flutes full, then empty, then full once again. Neither of us remained in character, that's not how you do fancy dress. Our excellent dinner passed companionably, and Bronya appreciated the Lynch-Bages, without needing to say so, sniffed, looked at the colour in the glass, took a preliminary taste, and another fuller one. Smiled and nodded. She's coming on.

While Bronya unset the table and began the clearing up, which she insisted on, as I'd done the cooking, I quickly googled Natalia Goncharova, clicked on images, and studied the pictures. Russian. A proper painter, no question about it: Bronya had dressed as one of the self-portraits. A nicely made point. I fiddled about looking for other underestimated women painters, but didn't find any to hang on the best wall, if that isn't an unpleasantly ambiguous formulation. I was reminded of Suzy's dismissal of women artists and writers: none of the highest standard, none to put beside the transcendent male geniuses. Try saying that aloud these days, you'd get eaten for breakfast, and made to do the washing-up after.

After the richness of the food and the excesses of the wine, I was embarrassed to find that Lord Clark soon had me dozing fitfully in front of the telly. Turning my head to apologise to Bronya, I found that she was asleep, her head resting on my shoulder.

On reflection, it would be an offence against credibility, even of nature, for me to dress as a younger character and Bronya as an older one. My role has to be Albert Steptoe. I will not, of course, twist my face into knots, spit and declaim, but I can stop shaving for a couple of days, mess my hair artlessly, don a crumpled old shirt from the laundry basket, and cover it with two oversized cardigans. Go out in the rain in some old cords, muddy my shoes, and recycle them for my performance. Smoke some frayed rollies, I'll bet I can still do one.

'When you dress like someone you feel like them,' Suzy said, when she got herself up as Humphrey Bogart. This was astute of her: in my Roman garb I felt delightfully imperious. Perhaps my incarnation as old Father Steptoe may be enlightening with regard to the privations and resentments of the lower orders? Or of my own. I'm quite looking forward to Bronya's enactment of Harold, and of the psychic complexity of reversing my position with regard to my own father. Might I begin to understand how he felt? I hope not. He's better off dead. Both of us are.

# Chapter 13

There's no sense in it, yet it nags. I need to get it out of my head, onto the screen, and into the ether. Get it over with. I'm making a fool of myself: not the dreaded Gampster, the even worse Japester. What remains to be done? 1) Settle on a title; 2) Provide an indication of what is to come; 3) Write the covering letter; 4) Stir and keep simmering; 5) Send.

I'd begun with the witless provisional title *A Simple Story*, and fooled about with various other possibilities, none of them good – by which I mean bad – enough. Given that I need something immediate and eye-catching in my email subject line, I have settled on *TRANS/Formation of ONE*. This is so blatant that it might well appeal to the tone-deaf virtue-signallers of the young generation. Surely, one of them with the requisite tin ear will be sufficiently intrigued to read the email? And having done so, the attachment?

I haven't the stomach to write more consecutive text, and anyway it is probably better to give an idea of how the faux-narrative faux-unfolds. So I have drafted an outline, what I will call a Precis, which seems both more naive and more pretentious, of what is to come.

Once I give myself over to this, or perhaps I mean it gives itself over to me, it's hard to stop. After tea I drafted the rest.

Precis of Chapter 2

ONE is now living in the big city, in a room with two young girls and a boy. They lounge on a broken sofa and mattresses on the floor, though all are clean and well-dressed. The door is constantly guarded by a moustachioed man with a gun, who brings food as necessary and supervises visits to the toilet and shower. When one of the children is required by a visitor they are introduced to the client, and ushered into a bedroom.

The Manager of the House of Joy is a swarthy Arab with brown teeth who sits downstairs in the evenings drinking coffee and smoking his hookah, ready to greet his customers, solicit their choices, and take their money. In the quieter periods during the day his wife performs these duties. The children are more frightened of her. If a customer complains of unenthusiastic attitude, or an uncompliant response, the offending child is beaten afterwards, though no marks show.

ONE has kept her name, because she is most in demand, and fetches the highest price. In the morning she washes, applies lipstick and face powder, does her hair, and dresses in a silk saree and matching slippers. She has been taught not to cry. Every week she is taken to a local doctor, who in exchange for her services, gives her ointments to allay the swelling and occasional bleeding, and pills for discomfort and pain.

One night, just before the children were wearily slipping into sleep, they were awoken by a man shouting, and the murmur of Manager attempting to placate him.

'No, I am sorry we are closed, sir! Please come back tomorrow, we will make you very happy ...'

'Now!' shouted the drunken man. 'I want it now. I pay extra!'

Those were the magic words, and ONE heard the steps coming towards the door. She recognised the voice, could not mistake it. Banbo, her father. ONE quickly drank the full glass of dirty water on the table, and lay down behind it.

The two men entered the room, and the drunken man looked over the cowering children.

'Stand up!' Banbo studied each, though ONE kept her head down, and in this female incarnation was not recognised, though she was studied carefully.

'This one!' he said, pointing. Manager drew him aside, and spoke to him quietly. First, a very high price, second, the particulars of what he might find once he took the pretty girl to bed.

The father laughed.

Pointing to ONE he put out his hand.

ONE rose and approached Manager, and whispered in his ear. The man looked angry.

'This child has been ill. Has fever and diarrhoea this hour, is no good ...'

'Never mind. You wash her up!'

Banbo turned his back, and the two men faced towards the door. When they could not see her, ONE forced two fingers down her throat, and immediately fell to her knees, retching and vomiting.

Manager turned to ONE.

'Clean up. Tomorrow you will be beaten.'


ONE has secured a bundle of books from Aziz, one of her few kind and clean regular visitors, who has a simple book stall in the market.

Her favourite book, which she has read twice, is the enthralling Anne of Green Gables, about a poor orphan girl who is brave and who finds a home with a brother and sister who have a farm in Canada. Whatever her many troubles she is bright and happy, because she has Imagination. Sometimes she lives in a world of Stories of her own. ONE has tried to learn from this, but her only story is now her own, though she has no one to tell it to.


That flowed trippingly off the tongue, sufficient to allow a break for a glass of champagne – I deserved it! – and a small cigar. Suitably refreshed and rewarded, I carried on, eager to know what might happen next.

Precis of Chapter 3

The children are listless. Something is happening. The telly flickers with images of fires and conflict, of armed crowds and soldiers in the streets. One day they hear shots, see crowds running down the street, and people fleeing from the shops and houses.

ONE opens the door gently, just enough to see into the hallway. The chair is empty, their guard has vanished. She gestures to the others. The reception room on the ground floor is empty, the door open, a hookah with its charcoal alight. ONE peeks outside. There is no one seated at the table in front.

She readies herself to rush away, but not before embracing the others.

'Good luck!' she says. 'May God be with you always!'

Ducking into the street, ONE makes her way slowly and carefully towards the indoor market, her back against whatever walls she can utilise. After a frightening, slow half-hour, during which ONE has frequently hidden beneath tables or inside abandoned shops, she enters the empty market, and makes her way down a dusty alleyway to Aziz's book stall. To her delight and surprise the proprietor is there, boxing up his stock lest it be looted or set afire. He looks up to see the distressed, filthy figure of ONE, rises, and takes her into his arms.

'Come, come!' he says, stroking her hair. 'You're safe now, safe with me. I know where to go!'

ONE cries and cries. Her heart is full and breaking.

I considered a second glass of champers, but demurred. It might encourage a certain ease in my prose, an expansiveness that could so easily descend into intelligence and wit. Best carry on. I can sense a need to get it over with, as if the smoke and alcohol were having a laxative effect, which is appropriate for the job at hand.

Precis of Chapter 4

No one knows how many have died, and for what purpose. In the countryside villages have been burnt, women and children massacred, the boys taken away to play at soldiers, raping and killing. ONE has sought anxiously for news of her village, there are rumours that it has been destroyed, and that many are dead.

ONE tends the shelves of Aziz's book stall, arranges the books, deals with customers. At first she argued with Aziz, who thought it more seemly that she dress as a boy, though it was as herself that she cooked and warmed his bed in the room behind the stall. But ONE was adamant. She is a girl, and has always been a girl. A girl with a male member, an embolo, which she hates, and dreams of losing.

Over the long hot days ONE sits in the shade at the rear, reading and reading, interrupted only by the pesky flies and an occasional browser, with whom she is keen to chat.

'He is very good, Mr Greene Graham,' she would say, pointing to a bedraggled paperback. 'This one is set in Africa! Very exciting!'

The customer, who taught at the local school before it was bombed, looked at ONE with quick interest.

'What is it about?'

'It is a very sad story about a man. He cannot find God and God cannot find him, though both are trying.'

'Tell me,' said the teacher, 'who are you? I have not seen you at school. How old are you?'

'Fifteen, sir. I came to the city one year ago. I left my village, and have not gone to school since. I miss it very much, but there was much trouble there.'

The teacher smiled.

'I can imagine,' he said. 'What is your name?'

'I am called ONE.'

'Well, ONE you are, and shall be. I am Mr Mohammed, and I

would be pleased if you recommend some more reading to me, and perhaps, if you wish, sometimes to sit and talk about books. Would you like that?'

ONE's eyes glistened, and she nodded her head in assent, and gratitude.

It's been an agreeable hour and a half, putting this together, but of course (as Truman Capote said about Jack Kerouac) it's not writing, it's typing. And it's not as good, even, as the unrolling screeds of that rat-infested beatnik. I think of my lackadaisical effort as writing by numbers, filling in blanks. Anyone with half a brain and a sufficiently sardonic streak could do similarly or (if they knew even a little about the various subjects) much better.

Am I ready to go? I've now got over 2,000 words of narrative diversity, and have cobbled an arresting covering letter.

*Dear Publisher,*

*My name is Mayeso Ndipo Wakuda, and I come from Malawi in East Africa. I now live in Sudan. I attended the University of Khartoum, and received my Masters Degree with Distinction in Creative Writing, in 2018. I was the top student in my year. For my course requirement I submitted a short story which my Honourable Professor recommended for publication in our College Magazine. He also encouraged me to continue with it, saying that it has, in his esteemed opinion, the capacity to form the basis of a novel 'of quality and importance'.*

*I am writing to ask if you might consider the publication of this novel, and attach some passages from it. I would be most grateful if you could tell me if it is of sufficient quality.*

*Sincerely yours,*

*Mayeso Ndipo Wakuda*

I need to do some research about which publishers are partial to ethnic offerings, and send out my emails. I imagine them being fielded by an archetypical Sensitive Young Girl – the sort of SYGnette bobbing on the edges of a publishing pool, age late twenties perhaps, an Oxbridge graduate with a First in English, family connections and money, in charge of unsolicited submissions. I presume hundreds of these arrive every month, and get deleted. The submissions, I mean. I hope mine is sufficiently arresting to be noticed. It is presumably the desire of every SYGnette to make an Important Discovery, after which she will rise from her pile of slush and swan off to the Ivy to swallow an expensive fish with an impressed gander in her wake.

Enough? Too much? Suzy used to say that the funnier I found my incessant punning and japey jokes, the less funny they were, having only the audience of one. Or ONE, if I might say. She called this process 'Darke slays Darke!' and would put her finger down her throat in case I missed the point. I didn't, nor have I mended my ways. I may have a solipsist's audience, but it is discriminating and easy to satisfy.

My project hums and recurs, and gives me no peace. When I sit and hover my fingers, thinking of Lucy and Rudy, or sometimes Bronya, they do not reach for the keyboard, just tremble above it, waiting for the return of ONE. This is mildly embarrassing, as if she were a potential earworm anxious to re-insert her nonsense into my head. Surely the point of a joke is that it ends? That it has a punchline?

But ONE is not a joke, she's a hoax. That's different, though I don't know much about hoaxes, save for my own personality, which has been one from the earliest days, as if I were Harold Steptoe: Improved Version. My father, like old Albert, despised me for this, gave me a lot of the 'too big for your britches' guff (and more) though he colluded, at my mother's insistence and on my grandparents' tab, in my improvement, sent me to the prep and public schools that honed my accent and refined my nature, made me, what I yearned to be, *not* a Daddy's boy. He regarded the emerging product as an implicit criticism of his nature, felt judged, eclipsed and humiliated in my increasingly polished presence. Made it clear to me that I was a fraud.

He was right, I felt a fraud too. This is England, you are where you came from and how you began, we do not believe in self-improvement, however much we pursue it ourselves and for our children. It takes a few generations to escape the taint of upward mobility. I was a working-class boy from Lancashire. When my peers learned this, that my parents were unexceptionally ordinary, their behaviour towards me shifted. I was not one of them.

So revisiting the Steptoes in their complexly laden setting and relations reawakened a wash of feeling in me, and I prefer my feelings latent and unacknowledged. Denial and repression are the twin pillars of civilised behaviour, English style. Sitting in front of the telly – this time *before* eating – Bronya was at my side, both of us dressed to the minus-nines. My soul shivered as I heard, for the first time in some fifty years, the jangly musical introduction to an episode of *Steptoe*, which caused more feeling in me than a rendition of 'God Save the Queen'.

Bronya knew nothing of this, as the first episode of *Steptoe* rolled onto the screen, the black as black can be, the white as white. Crude to the point of stereotype, and all the more effective for it. As the jingle began to play, Bronya smiled widely and laughed.

'I remember this, is so perfect!' and began to hum along.

I suppressed a shocking impulse to punch her on the nose.

Over supper, which we shovelled in with our paper serviettes tucked into our shirts, Harold/Bronya quizzed me about my reaction to the episode. I tried to explain, told her about watching it with Suzy, and my reaction to my first exposure to Albert and Harold. Which I was surprised to find was still within me, aching still.

'I know,' she said slowly. 'I could see. And you know what? You are right. I felt it too ...'

'What do you mean?'

'The cruelty. Is too harsh. Dickens would say is *Bleak House*! I don't want to watch it again, no more!'

'Thank you, dear Bronya. That makes me feel better. I thought perhaps it was just me ...'

'Is not!'

'And you know what? Revisiting things puts them in perspective. Or perhaps it is we who change and not the things?'

'Is dialectic!'

'I don't know anything about that. But I do know that watching Kenneth Clark, I felt not my old abject admiration but a huge Fuck You, fuck you and your pompous self-confidence, your assembled trinkets and their fancy housing, fuck you all!'

Bronya threw her head back and spluttered.

'Is right. Fuck Steppytoes and Clarkytoes! What we do next?'

Wednesday night is now Designated Film Night. Bronya and I had agreed, after some friendly negotiation, on the following six films, which could be reviewed as necessary, assuming that we were still in our right places.

James: *The Third Man*, *The Lady Vanishes*, *The Lavender Hill Mob*.
Bronya: *Babette's Feast*, *Il Postino*, *The Great Beauty*.

On such evenings, as we sat companionably shelling and nibbling pistachios, sharing a bottle of wine chosen to go with *le cinéma du jour*, I felt increasingly odd. The feeling was difficult to locate, and to name. It was as if I were becoming ill, experiencing a slow seepage of being, an organic loss. It took weeks before I understood the process, when I noticed that I was simply enjoying the films, my usual rush to critical judgement not so much in abeyance – I was not suppressing adverse reactions – as simply absent. My pleasure was the thing in itself, chortling at my old English favourites, and finding a way to enjoy the more sophisticated Continental flavours of Bronya's offerings, I popped my pistachios, sipped my wine, sank into the warmth of the sofa and the air. I had an impulse to hold Bronya's hand.

I felt satisfied and empty, or perhaps I mean emptied. The scorn was draining from me as if a lifetime wound were slowly releasing its infection, and a surprising and hardly recognisable feeling of well-being was slowly taking its place. I was puzzled by this, being over-reliant upon the former and unaccustomed to the latter. I do not wish to be released from scornfulness, which is the foundation and generating impulse of my moral being. Without the vigorous opposition which vice should stimulate in a virtuous mind, I am rendered ordinary, an ineffectual opponent of the folly of my fellow man.

Yet what I observed, as I levitated my spirit to the ceiling and gazed down at my figure on the sofa, was an elderly Englishman, unexceptional in any way, enjoying himself. I was neither moved nor surprised by this vision; it had the mere force of perceived truth. Was this what I was becoming, this I who was not me? Not Henry to her Eliza, but Darby to her Joan?

Such feelings are meant to try us, and I failed to keep up the good work. For every *zug* that nature offers us, there is an accompanying *zwang*. Or do I mean dark and light? When the internal planes shift, the land masses above may alter but they do not become unrecognisable. James Darke I was, and am. I say this in reaction to my experiences with Bronya, in acknowledgement, appreciation and fear. But whatever it means, however I continue to acknowledge the dark side and to reside in my habitual attitudes, they are no longer compelling, and can fade over time, as the juices that sustain them cease their imperious flow. The journey of my soul upon this earth is ending. What is done, is done. Were I to cease from this day, nothing of value would be lost, nothing worth regretting. I'll carry on for a time, write a bit more until it runs out, and there's nothing more to write. This journal is, and always has been, a book about nothing, which seems beautiful to me.

Nothing will come of this. I like that. Nothing will come of that. I like this.

# Chapter 14

*Civilisation,* as aired and recommended by the BBC, was introduced by a dolorous burst on an impressive organ, playing sacred music in sanctification of its subject. In the first episode, Kenneth Clark, the self-installed High Priest of High Art, introduces and contrasts two images: the first, the carved wooden prow of a ninth-century Viking ship, primitive but intensely memorable, the second the (to him, greatly preferable) Greek statue of the Apollo Belvedere, an idealised male nude whose organ is as small as the accompanying organ music is big.

I gazed surreptitiously at Bronya as the image of the statue appeared. Would she focus, as a man would, on the incongruous little willy on the muscular body?

'Is absurd,' she chortled. 'I can't believe it!'

I began to explain that the classic Greek sculptors rightly regarded male genitalia as ugly, and diminished them as best they could, before I was interrupted.

'No, not that. Big one, little one, no matters. What is funny is Mr Clark making such big fuss about this rotten statue, so like, what you say, on chocolate box?'

'Well, usually they have beds of pretty roses on them, not naked men, but . . .'

'You know what I mean! Once you get big Civilisation in your head you can't see straight any more. Just same old, same old. Recycling stuff.'

This may or may not have been fair, but I felt oddly reassured by Bronya's lack of interest in poor Apollo B's minuscule willy. No man, raised on the contemporary glorification of penile length and breadth, can look at such a work of art without self-referencing. For those large of organ, a feeling of immense smugness must pertain, while for those with lesser genitals, some relief perhaps at this Hellenic baby-dick. Small is beautiful!

When I was at school, showers after games were a torment as I, and many of my fellows, buffed and fluffed our naked organs locked in the loos before emerging to immerse ourselves in the cold flow, which merely reaffirmed and exacerbated our shrinkage, until we hurried desperately, still damp, into our underpants. The culture of the school yard subliminally reflected the physical calibrations of the changing room: even when a boy was a poor sportsman, if he was envied in the showers, he was esteemed accordingly. He had a cock. Lesser beings had willies.

I spent many private moments of boy-time stretching and pulling, which never got me beyond five inches fully topped up. I don't know how the other dick-builders fared in their erection businesses, but when I first saw some primitive porn at school I was astonished by the lengths some men can go to. The revealed organs were disgusting, it was hard to imagine a woman responding with anything but terror at the prospect of imminent immolation.

This makes me, now, sympathetic to ONE's phallo-phobia, though I'm happy enough to retain mine own so long as it confines itself to urinary duty. Not that it does that very well either, I have multiple daily dribbles, not all of them into the appropriate vessel, and now think of a strongly flowing stream as something in a bad Wordsworth poem, rather than over a lavatory. The only credit I offer my penis, now, is that at least it stays flaccid. These years of celibacy have been a welcome relief. Images of lovemaking with Suzy no longer arouse me, and I inwardly gaze at them with the same cultural bemusement that one might look at various native rites and dances on a Pacific atoll.

Of course, school was only school, and while humiliations were regular, there was plenty of time for me to outgrow, or minimally to shrug them off. The few women with intimate acquaintance of my penis did not giggle when it was introduced, which I hope was more than a form of good breeding. I didn't laugh at small breasts or wobbly bottoms, even when a tad disappointed by them. We are all made differently.

But not as differently as pertained in prison. We showered in clumps of men under trickles of lukewarm water. It was almost impossible not to be jostled front or rear, usually a matter of mere proximity. Of course I never felt under imminent threat of physical assault, there were finer specimens than me huddled there, a few of them distinctly available. The first time I was exposed in and to the communal showers was profoundly shocking. I'd never seen anything like it, or them, the swaying sausages of the conspicuously over-endowed. There was much banter about this amongst the inmates. I lowered my eyes and self-esteem.

I am worried, as this by no means gratuitous preamble might suggest, by the problem of ONE, who does not care whether her vitals are small or large, who has hated them since a very young age, and whose fondest dream is to have them removed, and replaced, by a snip-and-gouge surgeon. During her incarceration and repeated rapes in Manager's House of Joy, she was penetrated and bruised, and hated it accordingly. But the grossest humiliation was when one of her ardent clients took her organ into his mouth, and sucked it, willy-nilly, to climax.

Nature prevailed, but ONE paid for the transient organic relief with her profound distress of being treated in this manner. She was not a boy, her abiding fantasy was of no longer having a male body,

235

looking instead into the glass to envisage the body of ONE, with breasts, a pubic area uninfected by outward manifestation, and a smile on her face. When she looked at her naked form in the cracked mirror of the bathroom, she would tuck her organ between her legs, and see what she longed to see, if only for a few gratifying moments, her future revealed in the dusty and broken glass.

How this transition could be accomplished, without means or contacts, is unclear to me, but then again I have no need to work it out, my sample chapters being fit for purpose. But still, having brought such a being into the world, like God, it is my role, surely, to see that she is all right. Or is it? That other God, the heavenly Lordy one, is a conspicuous and consistent flop in looking after his creatures. Prayers and supplications requesting a transformation from illness into health, woe into happiness, much less boy into girl, are answered or ignored randomly, without regard to merit. Bad men float, good ones drown.

I am no author, but in amateurishly donning the cloak of creativity, I wish to treat my subject fairly, according to her nature. ONE must prosper, in answer to the contemporary political demand that the politically righteous be rewarded. I found it surprisingly easy transforming ONE from boy to girl, once I understood the linguistic situation. It's a matter of the movable 's' – he becomes she, she becomes he. Though in drafting my precis chapters I initially referred to ONE as he, I soon returned to add the requisite letter, until it became a matter of habit. Boy then girl. He then she. That is how it happened on the keyboard, and is nowadays meant to happen in the home, the school yard, the office, the bedroom: what is now trans-formed is not a noun, but a person.

But ONE, however snipped and gouged, will come to understand that she is not a real she, just some modern and socially acknowledged, even admired, iteration of femaleness. ONE – I understand her, she's mine – has an abiding ache, which can never be assuaged. She may be penetrated in her new organic guise, and receive some pleasure from the act. But no trans-formation will supply her with a uterus and the capacity to conceive. ONE is a woman, if a woman at all, who will never become a mother. She may have trans-formed her body, but not her heart, she has wounded that. She once adored her little ones, the brothers and sisters who she will hardly see again, and her only chance to become a parent was thrown away in post-operative biological waste, perhaps to be devoured by a scavenger dog at the local dump.

A well-earned indulgence after a week of toil, it was once called a lie-in. On Sunday mornings in Oxford I would get up to brew Cona coffee, make Hovis toast with Lurpak butter and Bonne Maman marmalade, and bring it to bed with the Sunday papers. Suzy and I would eat, read, shower and brush our teeth, make love, perhaps drift off for a snooze, before getting out of bed satisfied and restored, feeling guilty and giggly as prep-school children, as if we'd got away with breaking some rule.

Whatever that rule might have been, it certainly doesn't pertain any more. Every day is lie-in day, and Bronya encourages this indolence, in the hope that it may be followed by a short stroll after I have risen. Each morning she knocks at the door at about ten, and when invited to come in, which she always is – I can hardly sleep more than a few hours in the nights, hence my need for extra rest, or so I justify myself – she enters with a tray bearing a flat white, buttered sourdough toast with unsalted Normandy butter and bitter Seville orange marmalade. She has placed my daily pills in a small glass, and watches, like the prison warders before her, as I swallow them. Under her arm, our copy of *The Times*, which she has arranged to have delivered.

Of course, I do my part, it's only fair. I sit up, put two extra pillows behind my back, and lean against the bedstead in upright fashion, so as not to spill coffee down my pyjama front and onto the sheets, which makes for less laundry. Bronya appreciates this. I can see her restraining the urge to fluff and readjust the pillows to save strain on my neck, and to straighten the bedclothes, either of which would be a touch too far. Usually, she just smiles benignly, as one would at a toddler in bed with a light fever, and takes her leave.

'Bronya, thank you. This is lovely, it always is. Will you sit for a moment?'

She looked puzzled. Did I mean, on the bed?

'Bring the armchair over, it's not heavy.'

She lifted the ugly blue Parker Knoll chair (inherited from Suzy's parents, Lucy won't allow me to throw it away) from the corner, and passed carefully by the side table that holds my framed photos of Suzy. I have several times reminded her to dust their silver frames but she wanted nothing to do with them, and was oddly hostile to any talk of Suzy herself. She had read Suzy's novels, but never mentioned them. When I asked why, she shrugged her shoulders.

'No,' I said. 'Be frank, I'm interested to know what you think.'

'Think? No need to think, is like fast food, in one end and out the other, not serious nourishing . . .'

I was rather shocked, and seeing my expression she halted.

'. . . but just my opinion, you know, just maybe not for me, my taste.'

'Say what you think. Suzy is long gone, and I am not so attached to her memory that I cannot hear criticism of her.'

In fact, I rather like it, but of course did not say so.

'OK. Not a good writer, just smart girl with big eyes and bosoms, not so big heart!'

This was a half-truth, and I inwardly applauded Bronya for getting this far. Suzy's problem was not that she lacked heart, but that her employment of it was entirely self-referring. She had plenty of heart when it was beating in and for her, 100,000 times a day; she was forever moved by the contemplation of her own emotional vicissitudes. She loved crying, and composed many tear-soaked scenes both in her fiction and in her life, gifted herself the extravagance of salt-watering distress.

Her other love affair was with the observed world, though not with the language necessary to describe it. She cared about right seeing, as a painter might, but less passionately about right saying. She had no feeling for the potential poetry of prose. Finding the right words in the right order is the quest of any writer worth taking seriously. Since all writing is autobiography, why not give as good an account of yourself as possible?

Bronya carried the ugly heirloom to the head of the bed, sat down, and looked up quizzically.

'Oh, Bronya, wait a moment. This is so rude of me!'

I pushed the tray to the side of the counterpane carefully – no stains, no extra laundry – and began to get up.

'Wait! What?'

'I can't eat my breakfast while you have nothing. I will make you a flat white. Just hold on ...'

She recognised this for the civilised, hence insincere, gesture that it was, and stood up to stop me from rising.

'Is very kind, I had already. Tell me what you want to talk about.'

'About? Well, nothing. Just a chat perhaps?'

We do plenty of chatting, it's hard to avoid, living in such close proximity. But never in the mornings – I am barely coherent for the first few hours of my waking day – and certainly never in my bedroom. I could have breached my subject, and perhaps her defences, later in the day, but I felt, which is curious, that sitting partially unclothed in my bed I had the psychological upper hand. This was astute of me, but wrong.

'I had a long conversation yesterday with Lucy ...' I began.

Though Bronya did not respond with as much as a nod, I knew that she would know this.

'... and I am a little, concerned you might call it, at how very much she knows about me, how I am eating and feeling, whether I have had my exercise, worn my mask, washed my hands frequently, exhibited any signs of headaches or fever ...'

'Yes.'

'She knows these things because you tell her. Every day. And I am not happy about this! I am not a child, or an invalid. Nor am I mentally incompetent. This constant perusal and reporting is invasive, and I am surely entitled to my privacy ...'

Bronya looked down at her lap for a time.

'Why am I here?' she said. 'Why?'

'That is what I am beginning to wonder. Not as a spy, that would be intolerable!'

I could feel one of my tachycardia spells coming on, put my flat white to the side, and tried not to pant.

'I am here. Lucy paying me to look after you! I am not lodger, not friend coming to stay for super nice visit. No, I am employee, just like old time, when I was cleaner. Now I do more than that, but position is the same, only now you are not boss, Lucy is. You don't remember that? Lucy is boss. You insisted she pays! And now you are surprised that I do my job properly, and report to her!'

Bronya has a strong voice at the most relaxed of times, so it's hard to judge when she has raised it. She doesn't need to, when roused she has an authority surprising in one so far removed from her cultural roots. Or perhaps because of them.

I hadn't expected this admonition, however fair it may have been. I would have demanded compliance if I had any justification for doing so. *I am so sorry, Mr James, I will not tittle-tattle with Miss Lucy any more. You are right, sir!* I lay back, picked up the glass of mineral water from my bedside, took a long swallow. It felt as if a herd of gerbils were playing rounders inside my chest.

'You know . . .' I managed to keep my voice and emotions under control, I am not English for no reason or benefit, 'I am not sure this is working out.'

'And you are wrong! Again, wrong. Wrong, wrong, wrongest as can be wrong!'

'What? What do you mean? I just . . .'

'You doing what you always do. Always do, Lucy says. You run away! You fire me once, now you do it again? Funny thing is you don't just need me here, you like me being here, is fact! We have good times together. Eat, talk, laugh, watch films, read books. Sit by fire. Too many, too much, right? Too many! And when it gets close you run away, close the door, lock it, lock your heart. No Bronya, no Lucy, no Rudy! You go to prison because that is where you have always been!'

'Wait, that is a little . . .'

'What am I here? Is your place, lord and master! What am I? Servant? No, thanks. Employee? No. Friend? Lodger? Not. Haha! What am I? What do you think, what do you call me? Tell me!'

'I don't know. I don't like these categories. I call you Bronya . . .'

'And I am not knowing my place because is your place! Do you think of this?'

I didn't answer. Anything I might say would make it worse. Saying nothing did as well.

'No love! It frightens you, to be too close, because you afraid that your heart will be broken, again, like little abandoned boy, so sad.'

If I had spoken to my parents like this I would have been thrashed for my impertinence. It was intolerable, it had to stop before it got unimaginably worse. Though perhaps that was what I was inadvertently seeking: a walkout, a strike, a withdrawal of labour. The return of my home, my solitude: my life.

'Bronya, let's leave it, please! I'm very sorry.'

'You bet I leave it!' said Bronya, rising, lifting the chair as if it were a feather, thumping it back into its place, and stomping out of the room. Bronya is a first-class stomper, but unlike many such she does not slam doors. There's that to be grateful for.

I stayed in bed for the rest of the day, rather hoping for a belated and chastened delivery of lunch, but no such arrived. When I dressed it was almost suppertime. There were no noises in the house, and the lights were out downstairs. No sign of Bronya. I went back up the stairs to the landing, and knocked at the door of her room. No answer. I turned the knob and pulled the door open slightly.

'Bronya? Are you there?'

She was not. I hesitated for a moment – I have never entered her room since she began to stay over – and finally went in, feeling guilty and exposed. I needed to see. Her bed was made, her plastic hair brushes and a matching hand mirror were on her dresser, together with three framed photographs, one of an elderly couple seated primly on a dowdy settee in a room out of a Soviet film set, one of Toe-mass looking handsome and upright, wearing his black linen suit, and one of her and Toe-mass together, laughing, somewhere in Piccadilly. In the bathroom her toothbrush and paste were in place. A few clothes hung in the wardrobe, her bits and pieces in the chest of drawers. There was no sign of withdrawal, after all she spends some nights of the week with me, I mean in my house, and others in her other place. She will have personal stuff in both places. That's the arrangement, and I was under the impression that it worked.

So, she'd gone home, if that is the right phrase, is it? Gone home? Or is my home now her home too? How did that happen? It seems empty without her. Empty? Could it be that, having played Henry to her Eliza for these many months, I've grown accustomed to her face? If it could happen to that bloated buffoon Higgins, then it might happen to James Darke. Could happen, however unlikely, however undesirable. I closed the door quietly, so as not to disturb the air. Had a strong impulse to text her with the simple words 'Come home, please', but resisted it. She would return, of course she would, I am her job. She doesn't have to like it, or me, she has to do it.

I have behaved badly. I always do when I'm frightened, it's been my life's work. The next morning I rang my florist's to arrange delivery of an oversize offering of extravagant blooms, but they were closed. The florist's, that is, not the blooms. Or both: almost everything is, especially me. I'm sick of all of it, unto death. I felt too ill to eat, but managed a dozen smoked oysters on poppy-seed crispbread, an endive salad, and a glass of Te Koko Sauvignon Blanc, and rose from the table feeling restored. I forgive myself. I forgive Bronya. We'll live to fight another day.

I'm having second thoughts, third, fourth … uncovering doubts where I thought none existed. Scruples are such a bore. My jolly jape is ready for the posting, I've created email and Twitter accounts for my dear author, all I need now is to decide to whom to send the proposal. If the publisher is too small, some worthy mummy-and-puppy outfit serving the needs of the diverse writers of the world in all their gendered tinty complexity, then an enthusiastic response from a gullible SYGnette will inevitably cause distress, embarrassment, and perhaps loss of a job, as the name of the press is held up for ridicule for countenancing such an obviously concocted, risible proposal. But if, by way of contrast, I send it to one of the major publishing houses, it's most likely to end up be-sogged in a pile of slush. Who knew that a jolly hoax could be so complicated?

Oh, dear. It's worse than that. Working through my list of esteemed literary publishers, none seem to accept unsolicited manuscripts. Too bloody grand to open their doors, hearts, and minds to the huddled scribblers of the world, burning sufficient midnight oil to cause a world shortage. I thought that publishing houses existed partially to raise flocks of SYGnettes, downy from college, yearning to make names for themselves converting piles of slush into realms of gold. But reading unsolicited manuscripts is lower even than such an upwardly mobile bird would wish to descend.

The online advice? Get an agent. But many of those, on enquiry, do not accept unsolicited stuff either, like the grand Wily Coyote. The answer would be Miles, I'd love to implicate him. But he has demurred: too little to gain, he says, and too much to lose. Publishers are sensitive about being mocked and made fools of by uppity agents, the relationship is sufficiently strained already: *More!* says the agent. *Less!* says the publisher. And that, more-or-less, is how it staggers along, in mutual distrust and recrimination.

Which seems right to me. Having perused the dreary websites and doughy corporate self-descriptions of agents and publishers alike, I distrust and dislike them all. Pompous imbeciles pimping their brand! With the future of literature in such hands, God alone knows how many a flower is born to blush unseen, and waste its sweetness on the desert air. How many mute inglorious Miltons rest in obscurity, how many Mayeso Ndipo Wakudas? Most of the classics of our literature were rejected by the majority of the publishers to whom they were submitted. How many further were rejected by them all? In this madding crowd, what chance has my poor dark heroine to transfer her story into print? If the industry has any residual sanity, the right answer is: none.

Fuck it. Fuck them. Just because they say *don't* doesn't mean I can't. I'll email all the bloated publishers, and the grandiose Wily Coyote as well. My subject line will be crucial, before I get tossed into the electronic bin. I'll make a change to my submission, and add a subtitle, play the race card as well as the gender one. Extra-diversity! TRANS/formation of ONE: An African ... *what*?

Tragedy? Tale? Readers prefer to be uplifted, especially in this psychosexual arena, and uplifted readers mean uplifted sales. An African *Triumph*? Perfect!

It's done, whooshed into the ether.

Note to self: do not sit in front of computer awaiting responses. If any, they will take days, or weeks.

Four hours. Nothing yet.

The law has once again intervened in my life. As I sauntered and puffed alongside Bronya yesterday afternoon, we were stopped by a disapproving bobby, enquiring if I were one of the Underlyingly Challenged who should not be darkening the viral landscape, lest it darken them. Of course not, I replied, asserting that I was fit as a fiddle, and wished him good day as I shuffled into the near distance. Unimpressed, he impertinently asked Bronya who she was, and how we came to be together, and suggested he accompany us home. On the way, he failed to keep his social distance and held my upper arm, as if to offer needed support, surely not in case I made a run for it.

On the doorstep he paused to write down our details, threatening a fine and further consequences if I had contravened the terms of my (un)managed isolation. I subsequently had another visit, and a strict admonition to keep myself to myself, indoors. Bronya managed to convince him that we were a bubble, about which he was sceptical, but let it pass. I clearly need looking after, and what's done is done. Henceforth I am forbidden to venture out, bliss, I'm bored with out. Even in doesn't interest me very much, not any more.

What else is almost done is this journal. Days go by without need of an entry, life placid and unremarkable, nothing to notate or to remark, nothing to complain about, no past or incipient bruising, neither haunting memory nor thought of the future. Day goes by day, Bronya and I companionable, Lucy and the family in regular unremarkable touch. Rudy sends pictures and says he is cooking, and 'writing something'. I'm not. My African story is still afloat in the ether.

Happiness may be relatively uncommon, but it is dull, no one writes about it. Generically, the novel is a chronicle of human distress, and the journal a pit into which self-obsessed anxiety may be poured. Diaries used to have a dinky lock and key. Nowadays they can be done online and password protected. Rudy taught me how to do that.

The time I spend at my computer, however, has increased. Bronya thinks I am pecking away, as writer-chickens do, but that's over now. I have to do my final gathering, I cannot bear to leave Lucy and Bronya with a distressing set of mysteries and loose ends. I have created a yellow desktop file entitled 'PERSONAL AFFAIRS', which has a subsection, if that is what it is called, which will contain letters to Lucy and to Rudy, and even a note to Amelie, to be opened after my death. They bear as full and full-hearted a testament of love as I can manage; unaccustomed as I have been to such effusions, I kept them as concise as blurred vision would allow.

My short farewell to Amelie was just a hug and kiss goodbye, not one of those 'Read this when you are sixteen, it's from your long-dead and totally forgotten grandfather' letters that you find in soppy novels. My missive to Rudy, to my surprise, flowed trippingly off the keyboard. Our relations are now so tender, so grounded in affection and mutual respect, that I found the words and the tone easily enough, at the cost of a few not unwelcome tears. My farewell closed with the words:

'O He gives to us His joy / That our grief He may destroy.'

He would of course recognise the reference to *Songs of Innocence*.

Ah, but then, then what? Lucy. I could feel myself freezing at the keyboard, my fingers incipiently cramping. She wouldn't come, I couldn't summon her inwardly, the bruising from our recent arguments still tender. Rising from my desk I went downstairs to fetch our family photographs from the bottom drawer of the Georgian bureau, and carried the relevant ones back to my study. In her last year Suzy purchased several leather albums from Smythson, and arranged the photos chronologically.

And there she was, our Lucy, from the earliest days in her mother's arms, on the slides at the park, dressed up in her beret and scarf, playing games at school, loping in the countryside with Suzy, going up to uni, graduating, marrying, conceiving, mothering. I gazed intently at the pictures, and the more I studied them the less they revealed. They did not catalyse feeling, they paralysed it. Whether this is because I am not a visual person, as Suzy never tired of reminding me, or whether I lack the necessary sentimentality to gush over family pictures, I would not care to say. They took me away from Lucy. They were not her.

The images provoked neither feelings nor words. What promotes words for me is other words. Make a start. Get something down, then make it work. I sat, composed and studied, wrote and rewrote, as if revising for my Finals, a most inappropriate catalyst. It is one thing to write about Chaucer and Milton, quite another to write to Lucy. To say farewell. To try to say more than that, of course. But the overwhelming futile desire to say the one thing needful, pressed me, and silenced what is left of my spirit.

What does one talk of when one talks about love? I know too little of it. Was raised without affection by distant and uninterested parents, and in my later acquaintance with the subject, got barely passing marks. Suzy did the emoting for us both, she enjoyed wringing an occasional expression of affection from me, said that it ensured that it was heartfelt. I liked to believe that the problem was not so much with my heart, but with my tongue.

And with my daughter? So much to say, but as Rudy wisely observed, so much to *do*, or to have done, or to have failed to do … I've never walked the dog. Trying to compose myself and my words, I know it is too late, and I am incapable of the right constructions grammatical and emotional. Why, just because I am soon to shuffle off, why would I suddenly become other than I always have been? I now have the urgent need, or requirement, to say what is in me and fills my heart, yet I look inward as at an empty room. I am wrung out, worn out, finished. It is too late. The dying are enjoined to accept bedside testimony of love, and to offer it in return. But dying suborns all one's energy and focus. It is not demonstrative. Final words do not come, the more I strive for them, the more false they seem.

*Lucy.* Lucy has been everything to me, from the squalling moment of her arrival to the squalling moments of her adulthood, feisty, demanding, entirely her own person, and so often mine too. I was, from the beginning, rather in awe of her infant zeal, and as she matured that feeling grew into both respect and a degree of trepidation. She fought with her mother, and they were close, but she most needed me, exactly because she perceived that she never had me, not quite, not adequately. Not to have and not to hold.

*Dear dear one,*

*My time has come, and I do not regret it. I've had my day. And now your time has come round at last, and you will have yours. I am so proud of you, of what you have come to believe and to exemplify. The world as you understand it is new to me. I can see why it is necessary, indeed inevitable. May you find joy in it, and may it profit from your generosity of spirit. My chest is filled to bursting. I have loved you so much, and my mind and spirit will fill with your dear image and voice as I drift off easefully.*

*You are my legacy. Think of me sometimes, and kindly, and without tears. Forgive me my trespasses. We shall always be together. Love is like that, isn't it?*

*Dad*

Not enough, perhaps, not accurate, quite. It is impossible both to evoke overwhelming feeling, and to contain it. This is, alas, the best I can do.

I rose from my desk and filled a whisky glass with Glenmorangie, neat, and drank it in three swallows, sat back in my chair to let it do its work, and returned to my computer. To lighten up, and have a bit of fun, I began to compose a little piece in anticipation of my demise. An obituary, like any form of biography, is a crass and impertinent work of fiction. When I asked myself what I was most proud of, the first of my exploits to come to mind was the Easter pageant that Suzy and I played at Oxford, in which we invented a Christian sect that celebrated Christ's fall and rise by making absolutely divine passion-fruit soufflés, and having an ecstatic celebration. This sect, named the Soufflarians, apparently exists to this day, and there are references to it in several books about Oxford, none of which attribute the origin of the ritual to Suzy and to me. It still slays me.

Other than that? Just me and the history of my life, one damn thing following another, same as most. Good and bad, attached and detached, articulate and inarticulate, moral and immoral. A man, that's what, not so very unlike others. More honest, perhaps. I once thought a desirable quality. Perhaps I might be buried beside Suzy in that Oxfordshire churchyard? Her headstone reads 'WRITER', which she would have found bloodless. For mine own, in deference to her post-mortem disappointment, I could quote one of her favourite sayings, and inscribe 'FUCK 'EM IF THEY CAN'T TAKE A JOKE'. Lucy would disapprove, and anyway the vicar would intervene. A jolly Talmudic scholar might endorse such a proposition, especially if it was inscribed in Hebrew, but Christians have no sense of humour.

Done, it's done now. I've rather enjoyed composing the separate files containing my will, a clear statement of my finances with the names of my lawyer and accountants, and a list of my shares, bank accounts, paintings, and other financial assets. My estate will come to something over 7 million pounds, depending on the value of the house, the state of the stock market, and various exchange rates. I have done as advised with regard to minimising tax, set up a trust for the family, stipulated a few charitable donations and a sufficient amount for Bronya to buy a modest flat in London.

When I told her of this plan, she was shocked and tearful, waved her hand as if to shoo me away, and said that of course she could not accept any money from me.

'Is so good of you, no, but I, no, I cannot ...'

'Dear Bronya,' I said, wishing but unable to take her hand, 'it is not so very much money, there's plenty, and Lucy will be delighted for you.'

'Is her money! Her and children's!'

'It is most assuredly not. It is my money. Of course she will have most of it, because it is mine to give. If I wished I could leave it to a cats' home ...'

Bronya looked up anxiously and wiped her eyes, wondering what I could possibly be talking about.

'No, no, not literally, what I mean is that until I shuffle off, what's mine is still mine. And I would be so grateful if you would accept a small amount of it.'

'But, but ...' she began, uncertainly. Stood up and paced round the kitchen, poured some mineral water, and offered a glass to me.

'You see, James,' she continued, '... is not the same any more.'

'I don't understand.'

'England. Not same. Naughty boys throw us out of pram like toys. Country doesn't want or need me, need us. I stay because you are here, and are my family. I discuss this with Lucy and she says when the time comes, go! Is best, is right. Toe-mass is waiting. My parents waiting. I go home, like frog, back to puddle, spend rest of my life. Feels better already.'

The implication was clear. She would of course stay until I die, wants to look after me, and help me though my final days.

'Bronya, of course you're right, England's become a nasty country, always has been really, smug and insular, full of people like me, who cannot see in front of their faces and histories, and want to preserve England for the English. It needs revisiting and rewriting, all that Empire and Commonwealth nonsense, it has poisoned us.'

She took my hand.

'No. Not you!'

'I voted for Brexit!'

'But you learn. Are sorry?'

'Of course. Very.' I squeezed her fingers gently. 'Would three hundred thousand pounds buy somewhere nice in Sofia?'

She did not reply, turned away, put the glasses in the dishwasher.

I presume it will. Not having anticipated Bronya's decision to return to Bulgaria, I hadn't done my research. After we left the kitchen, Bronya still crying, I did some judicious googling: *Real estate sales in Bulgaria*. The answer was yes, of course it will.

I will leave funeral and memorial details to Lucy, as they have nothing to do with me. Suzy obsessed over such guff right until the end, when it didn't matter and she let it go. I don't care, and have no need to be formally remembered, though fondly would be agreeable. If that's not too much to hope for.

# PART FOUR

# *The End*

Now my charms are all o'erthrown,
And what strength I have's mine own,
Which is most faint . . .
As you from crimes would pardon'd be,
Let your indulgence set me free.

*The Tempest*, Act V

# Chapter 15

I spend a lot of time in bed, it would be lovely if it were lovely, but it's curiously exhausting. I sleep fitfully in the evenings, nap during the day, propped up by Bronya on pillows and cushions, sometimes with my swollen ankles and legs raised beneath the covers. I read, listen to podcasts and talking books, watch the telly on the bedroom wall, have coffee, drinks, and slight yummy treats during the day. I now have an iPad, Bronya taught me how to make it go, for my journal entries if I wish. It's titchy and uncomfortable, so I try to keep it short. I don't have much to say any more.

I dress for dinner, which is of course essential, once that goes everything is in danger of slipping. Afterwards Bronya sits by the side of the bed, and we listen to music or read our book, having decided that it would be agreeable to peruse the same text at the same time, and then to discuss it. She chooses. I no longer prefer one book to another, they're in the past. But I like to know what engages her. She has chosen *The Picture of Dorian Gray*. I hadn't read it for over forty years, and renewed acquaintance reminds me of why. Florid, stuffy as a closet. But I don't make a fuss.

Very occasionally, when I can summon the strength in the afternoon, we sneak through the exit at the back of the garden and giggle ourselves out for fifteen or twenty minutes, enough to buy the *Evening Standard* and get a bit of fresh air, which Bronya says she needs. I prefer mine stale. There's no sign of our censorious bobby. Bronya worries, but I say, 'What's he going to do, send us to prison?' Bronya laughs uneasily.

'Been there, you done that?'

'You may well say.'

I have, though, some saying still to do, my days may be limited, but my jolly jape needs to burst into the full light of the moon. I have now composed it as a pamphlet, and ordered copies to be typeset by the private press printer who set my *De Profundis*. He has sufficiently reactionary views that he will be happy once again to be on board, though he insists that his name and that of his press must be suppressed.

It has been almost as easy to write my pamphlet as it was to compose Mayeso's awful fiction. Not thinking hard or clearly, or writing attentively, have the great benefit of saving time.

# THE DIVERSITY CIRCUS

## A Story of Our Times
## James Darke

Occasional Pamphlet Number 3
The Reichenbach Press, 2022

I am an elderly white man, highly educated, and with a few residual marbles, and I read rather a lot, which is one of the few remaining pleasures of advanced age. I read English at Oxford, and during my career as a public school teacher taught a wide range of canonic authors from the jolly Chaucer to the glowering Hughes.

I follow the reviews of current books in the broadsheets and literary magazines, though I find their contents increasingly puzzling. Ten years ago, reading the Book Sections, I was certain to come across the old gang of English novelists, who though getting on in years, still commanded attention: Barnes, Byatt, Ishiguro, McEwan, Swift. The Booker lot. Nowadays I peruse the book reviews, and all is changed. Most are written by obscure young journalists, the majority of whom are women. Nor do I recognise the names of most of the authors whose books are reviewed, many of them drawn from what Conrad called 'the dark places of the Earth'. How could it be possible that so many and such various 'new voices' have pushed to the front of the literary lists and pages, in so short a time? Where were they? Who are they? Are they of any genuine merit?

I am, to my shame, the owner of a Kindle device, on which I download multiple samples of 'newly discovered writers' of various colours and persuasions, so that I can give them each as many minutes of screen time as they deserve. Once I read enough of this searing, heart-rending guff, one thing became clear. Most of these authors are published because they are different from, and a replacement for, the culture of 'old white men', alive or preferably dead.

The New Diverse have a mission. Their aims are writ large on every page: to act as the carthorses for the heavy ideas of the moment. Black writers achingly reveal that their lives matter, abused women tell their stories and cast the first of many stones, sexual deviants proclaim the awesome naturalness of their predilections, the mentally retarded or psychopathic describe stunning inward lives. Each book a chronicle of triumphant victimhood. All offer the same message: you, reader, are cloistered, ignorant and prejudiced, you need to be educated!

In 1959, the crusty C. P. Snow posited the Two Cultures of science and the humanities, which were by no means as distinct and embattled as the two cultures today: of art and politics. I am a reader and sometimes writer. I value discrimination, the eye, ear and heart that tries to see things, each and every thing, as it truly is. Blake refers to 'the holiness of minute particulars', and warns that 'to generalise is to be an idiot'. That is the voice of the artist. And to such a person politics is not so much anathema as deeply and uncomfortably alien. And hence my aversion to, and my increasing contempt for, the contemporary world of social media-driven causes, for mass movements, for mottos that violently yoke different entities under one simple heading and headline. This reduces our beautiful palette of subtle differences of tones and hues to crass comparators, makes persons into groups and then into mobs, thinking into sloganising, and requires the suspension – in those who retain such faculties – of scepticism, curiosity, and discrimination.

Those authors whose fictions portray and promote the causes of the day are not writers, but lobbyists, and their fictions are rarely worth taking seriously. Their supposed art is merely politics. It is polemic, not writing, the wolves howl, the multicoloured parrots flock and squawk. *Poor You! Me Too!*

But it's too easy, easy as can be, constructing simple stories in praise of the self-proclaimed victims of our degraded times. Make your characters representative of whatever ideological snake-oil you are peddling. All one need do is to address the relevant diversity issues. Tick, tick, tick, tick. Today's publishers can't get enough of such twaddle, which they do merely by lowering their standards.

Even I, I thought to myself one day, even I could write such nonsense. And thus, over the space of a few hours, I composed a story of some 2,500 words, allegedly by a young East African transsexual whose name, Mayeso Ndipo Wakuda, translates from Chichewa as 'Test from God and Dark(e)'. My faux-narrative concerns the first child – known as ONE – in a large impoverished family with a war-scarred former boy soldier as a father. ONE often dresses as a woman, and tells stories to his younger siblings, theatrical and compelling. Soon bullied by the local village thugs, ONE flees, and becomes a trans-child prostitute in the big city. War flares up, and ONE makes her escape. She is befriended by a client/mentor, and builds a refuge for herself in books, like her heroine Anne of Green Gables, only poor. S/he features as the hero/ine of *TRANS/Formation of ONE: An African Triumph*.

I make no apologies for the risible fatuousness of this, its utter predictability. That's the point of it, which should immediately be recognised by anyone with half a brain, and a decent ear. If the *New Statesman* had a competition to write a parody of an African novel, my entry wouldn't even get an Honourable Mention. Discharge, more likely.

Mayeso Ndipo Wakuda composed a letter to twelve of the esteemed literary publishers in the UK, citing an invented degree in Creative Writing from the University of Khartoum, asking for her submission to be considered for publication. Though large publishing houses warn that they do not accept unsolicited manuscripts, I thought that my title alone, sitting boldly in the email subject line, might catch a gullible and sympathetic eye. I consulted the retired literary agent Miles McAllister, who assured me that this would be the case, and that my hoax was a spiffing idea. 'Go for it!' he counselled.

Though publishers no longer have slush piles, they continue to employ bevies of upwardly mobile young women graduates, who are exploited and underpaid. They dream, each of them, of doing something significant, something to get themselves noticed, and promoted to a lunching presence. To discover someone or something! My assumption was not merely that one such would be moved by my jolly jape, so topical, diverse as buggery, if that still is. Which would confirm (what seems so obvious to anyone who is still functioning intellectually) that the publishing industry has gone bonkers, and is now in thrall to the outraged social media types who have as much respect for nuanced argument as they do for freedom of speech. Talk about the wretched of the Earth!

In response to my letter pleading for a literary hearing, four publishing firms did not answer at all, four others recommended that I procure the services of an agent, and I had encouraging replies from the rest, of which the following was the most enthusiastic:

> *This is a very moving and promising project. While I cannot offer more than support at this point, if you are able to send me further chapters, and perhaps an indication of how the novel develops, that might enable*

*us to consider publication. We would need, of course, to know more about you, where you live and what you are now doing, as well as an author's picture. I'm sure you've led a remarkable life!*

An email correspondence ensued, and it became apparent that Mayeso was on to a winner! I withhold the names of the interested publisher and sensitive young editor, because it is not my purpose to humiliate particular persons. I wish to humiliate the whole industry, and through them the much larger cacophony of illiterate know-it-alls who are driving the market for the kind of diverse rubbish that I provided. Who believe that freedom to speak the truth is essential, as long as it is only they who exercise it.

It is the day of the rabblement. Publishers take fatuous moral positions about the prescribed and proscribed topics, preen in self-regard, then return to their normal activities, promoting myriad grisly novels about serial killing, murder both individual and mass, torture, sexual abuse, rape and paedophilia, suicides and self-mutilation. The authors and publishers of these works are not required to take a moral position about their subjects, to disavow or to apologise for them. *Warning: Hannibal Lecter is a Cannibal. Eating People is Wrong.* Quite the reverse. Airport shops are shelved with biblio-gore, freely available for perusal by the impressionable child or a morally undiscriminating adult.

But write and disseminate a single phrase such as 'Trans women are men!' and the wolves attack, teeth bared, ready for the kill. Now there's a subject for a good thriller. This moral confusion, this nonsense, is so pernicious that scorn is inadequate, what is required is contempt. The writers, publishers, and media who parrot the latest 'woke' nonsense, then disseminate their murderous thrillers, are not abashed but self-celebrating. One bestselling gore-fest replaces another, while modest and more worthy attempts at truth-telling fall away unnoticed, or worse than that, noticed, vilified, and censored. If this only happened on social media, that would be acceptable, it is the natural home of idiots and zealots. But once that hive is buzzing furiously, the publishers and their editors cringe, censor, and begin to fill out their apology slips.

I haven't long to live, and have more or less lost the desire to do so. My dream of an Open Society, equally receptive to ideas and to persons, has now closed. I've done the few things I have to do, of which this final expression of intellectual and moral desolation is the final outburst. My day is gone, my days are almost over. The civilisation in which I was formed has faded, and been replaced by something that does not deserve the name. It may not have a lot longer to live than I do.

I find this impossible to regret.

\*　　\*　　\*

When they arrived in the post, some weeks later, my pamphlets looked elegant. Ignoring Bronya's inquisitive gaze, I unwrapped the large parcel, and laid the copies on my desk. I had originally conceived a bijou limited edition of twenty-five signed copies, but my jape required that the recipients believed that multiple copies would be in circulation, and hence that if they wished to frame a response they'd better do it quickly. I had thus stated, on the rear cover, that one thousand copies had been printed, though in fact I only did one hundred. After all, most examples would go out by email.

None will go to friends and family, hardly my target audience. Lucy would be horrified, Bronya perplexed and saddened, my few friends have abandoned me, or more often I, them. I certainly want Miles to have a copy, and the sanctimonious Archie and Miss Mayfly on *The Times*. I will send hard copy to the editors to whom I sent my spurious submission, and the many literary agents to whom I did not.

Why only them? Why stop there? I compiled an extensive list of UK magazines and newspapers, and then the many in America, where the diversity hounds are baying and braying, and emailed copies. Then, of course, to the major international wire services, and selected media outlets. It was rather fun. By the time a couple of days had passed, I had emailed over three hundred pieces of e-kindling, and waited for the conflagration.

Without divulging anything about the contents, I asked Bronya to post a basket full of the hard copies, and she, bless her, knowing that I didn't want to discuss the matter, did not accede to the pressing impulse to enquire, unlike any other woman I have encountered. Over dinner that evening she was uncommonly quiet, surely for some reasons of her own, about which I didn't ask. We are starting to understand each other.

It wasn't fair of me, I knew that, and by the time we were eating our after-dinner Belgian chocolate truffles, I fessed up, and showed her a copy of the pamphlet. She took a quick look at the title page, and said, 'I read it later.'

After supper, though, I did not invite her to watch the news on telly, or perhaps to read for a time, as I was feeling unwell and headachy, went directly to bed, took two sleeping pills, and managed a night's blessed unconsciousness, troubled by neither thoughts nor dreams, gone into that nowhere from which we come and to which we shall return, rounded with a sleep.

I don't believe phones ring in different ways, the same phone I mean, surely it can't change its tone to reflect the feelings of the caller, but when mine began to trill and shrill early on Wednesday afternoon, it seemed more than usually ominous. The bell tolls for me? That, and more. It was Lucy, and she answered my faux-cheery greeting with a splutter and a loud voice.

'Dad! I can't fucking believe it! What do you think you're doing? What have you done?'

'Good morning, my darling. Are you referring to my little pamphlet? How'd you get hold of one? I purposely didn't send it to you ...'

'Of course I've seen it. Are you naive, as well as bigoted and callous? I'm appalled, and profoundly embarrassed! You have no idea of the modern world, flailing about because your dinosaur world has been overtaken, and you're now extinct. Boo hoo! Things change! That's what happens. People change, values change, new ideas replace old ones. New people replace old ones. Why insult them? It is SO offensive, this bad-mouthing of everyone who is not an elderly white male Oxbridge graduate ...'

'Darling, my only alternative to being "an elderly white male Oxbridge graduate" is being a dead one ...'

'That's not even remotely funny!'

'I suspected you might not approve. You know, sometimes people rather misread my tone. I can be a bit provocative, I know that, I mean to be, but it's all a bit puckish really, a way that I can amuse myself and perhaps a few others ...'

'Crap! And dishonest! It's all very well, you being a high literary curmudgeon, offended by the best ideas of your time. But that's crap too!'

'I don't know what you mean. It's a fair characterisation, I suppose, but ...'

'But! Your stupid pamphlet is a perfect example of what it is attacking. You claim to be an *arts* person, particularising and discriminating, whatever fancy names you call it. You're appalled by the crass simplifications of politics? But what is your fucking pamphlet but a political statement! A manifesto in homage to the past? You disregard and distort the evidence, make one false statement after another, do not honour the words and arguments of your opponents. Our beliefs and arguments are relentlessly mocked, your own assumptions are taken as gospel!'

'Slow down, stop shouting. You're clearly an opponent. Tell me what you mean. Give details!'

'One instance: your characterisation of the book sections and reviews! Not my sort of thing, but I've gone and done my homework. And you've totally distorted the picture. Yes, there are a few – not enough – new women writers and it is more inclusive racially and sexually, but there is still a preponderance of white male voices in almost all of the papers and journals. I've done a spreadsheet. Let me read you the figures …'

'Darling Lucy, spare me, please. I will take your word for it …'

'You fucking won't. You'll hide behind a grumpy old man persona, which allows you to say anything and take responsibility for nothing!'

'Oh, deary me. So I do, it's rather freeing to the spirit, I find!'

'Don't you start with me! The old Oxford manner! I understand that you think like that, and you think you're amusing, and so superior, attacking the ideas and feelings that so many people hold dear. It's a bigger and more compassionate world now. It has more and more different people in it, and more voices are being heard! It's not "diverse", it's *inclusive*! You're against that, are you? Have you any idea how offensive your "pamphlet" is?'

'I'm not entirely sure that I do, or that I care. I felt the need to have a final go at some of the new …'

'More crap! You think because you can find one gullible editor you have "humiliated" an entire industry! What kind of megalomaniac nonsense is that! Bad books get published all the time! So what?'

This was followed by a strangled expostulation that appeared to have some curses embedded in it, and she rang off. I looked at my phone for some time, as if it might be glowing with some overheated substance. But it was only an Indignation, after all, Lucy can do them every bit as well as I. In the old days, when rational discourse was still possible, one might have suggested that a forum or panel be established in which debates might be held. The Dinosaurs against the Diversities, one side would have measured argument, the other rage and slogans. I suspect they might come to blows.

I don't suppose it is a rule, spoken or otherwise, but I feel that a person who hangs up on a phone call has the obligation to make the next one, to be conciliatory in the minimal way of re-establishing connection. For the next week no such phone call ensued. I could sometimes hear Bronya chattering sotto voce with Lucy, but I didn't enquire, and Bronya kept her counsel. Until this morning, when she delivered my flat white to my bedside table.

'We talk maybe a few minutes?'

Before I could answer she had hauled over the Parker Knoll chair, and placed it by the head of my bed. Sat down heavily.

'I too read *Diversity Circus*. Lucy is very upset, you should call her, make it better ...'

'Bronya, I think that she ought ...'

'... but first I want to ask question. Is all right?'

'Of course!'

'I understand. You think like that, perhaps always did, more so when you come out from prison with your ... what you call it, insulting great writers?'

'My *De Profundis*.'

'Yes. I remember. You publish it, little bit. And now you do this, publish this. What I do not understand is ...'

She paused and thought for a moment, leant forwards.

'... why you are so angry. And why you want to hurt people? Is so unnecessary. Cruel!'

'Bronya dear, it distresses me that you should think this. It is most emphatically not my intention to be cruel. I am angry because I am so disappointed to see my fellow man behaving so foolishly. Scorn and satire work by exaggeration, and by striking attitudes more firmly than everyday discourse allows. It is directed against the follies of the day. Of course, if you are one of the fools responsible for such follies, you will not see the funny side of it. But if you're a halfway reasonable being, satire should make you stop to reflect, that's how it catches attention ...'

As I said this, at more length than I intended because I was feeling under attack, I could see Bronya's eyes closing, a somatic withdrawal registering in the tilt of her head and posture. Lucy and she have accused me of 'mansplaining', which apparently describes the extended explanations that a rational male may offer to an irrational female.

'I'm so sorry to go on. Am I boring you?'

She recalled herself together with a tiny shudder, and looked at me steadily.

'Not boring. It makes me sad. You, you make me so sad.'

'I'm sorry about that, Bronya ...'

'I too am sorry,' she said. 'I do not understand why you think any of this is funny. Is not. Is sad, and you, you should think and think, and then be ashamed to cause pain for no best reasons.' She stood up abruptly, replaced the chair, and left the room.

There is most assuredly something to think about here, though I won't. I made my decision, wrote and published my final wilful testament, and if others find it offensive, that's their business. I still think it's funny, and apt. And that it needed saying.

Curiously, unexpectedly and somewhat disappointingly, I soon heard from Miles, whose reputation and career my little *jeu d'e-mauvais sprit* had attempted to undermine. Indeed, not long after the distribution of my pamphlet, his name was replaced on his formerly eponymous agency, and he was relieved of his place on the board. Yet he bore me no ill will, which he reserved, however whimsically, for his young colleagues, who 'are from a different enclosure in the universal human zoo. I'm in a smelly dark house with the few mastodons and dinosaurs. They are prowling with the wolves and flocking with the parrots.'

McAllister was unrepentant, as he said in an interview in the *Telegraph:* 'Darke's was a very witty idea, and it had back-room approbation amongst my generation of agents and publishers. This diversity nonsense has got out of hand, and the young'uns need to have training not merely in inclusivity, but in freedom of expression.' There was, he went on to observe, a wonderful irony in my final project: 'James is incapable of writing badly. His TRANS/ formation proposal is rather moving. Suitably completed and edited, it might have made a fascinating novel.'

I have no idea if there is any truth in this. I rather hope not. Could it be that Mayeso was struggling to free herself from hoax person to storyteller? To be heard, even through as unlikely a conduit as myself? Perhaps – can this still be true in this stupid age? – sometimes you need *not* to know something in order fully to imagine it. *Darling, why don't you try acting?* That's what novelists do, when they're any good. They act like someone else. They don't merely transcribe their limited and often uninterrogated personal experiences, they find a way to speak and to think and to be as a child, a woman, a soldier, an Indian, a hunchback. That is appropriately what novelists do, they *appropriate*.

The notion of my poor doddery self reinvented as an African novelist of non-binary persuasion is enough to tip one into madness, or hysteria. I stayed in bed the next day, the headache undiminished by medicaments of any kind, throbbing and intense. Bronya offered a thermometer, but my temperature was normal, and no further symptoms have appeared. Save the odd one that, when she brought my morning coffee, I rejected it after a single sip, she'd made it so badly that it had no taste.

Bronya looked alarmed.

# Chapter 16

It would be wrong, if I am being pedantic, to describe the reaction to my pamphlet as 'instantaneous', that is certainly impossible, but it was quick, and vociferous. If I might be pardoned the phrase, a lot of shit was soon flying from a lot of fans. It was *The Times* who came out first, with a news-page exposé, penned as I had hoped by the dreadful Archie, who had the advantage of having read both *The Diversity Circus*, but also my *De Profundis*, which had so traumatised the fluttering Mayfly.

The case against me was there to be made, if you were sufficiently modern, tone-deaf and brain-dead, and he made it with a vengeance. I was accused of every ideological sin under the broiling diversity sun. I am racist, misogynist, anti-trans, hostile to LGBT alphabet soup, the whole kit and caboodle. I am incapable of understanding that reparations are being paid, and that the world is changing, for the better, before my dimming elderly eyes. Over the next week multiple responses to my story, most of them hostile, appeared round the globe. A few at least gave me the benefit of my arguments, and quoted them at some length, but most simply had fun tacking me to my self-erected cross.

They need hardly have bothered. Feeling increasingly ill, I did not take to my bed, it took to me, and I had hardly the energy to bask in the glow of the many fires that were burning indignantly.

I turned off my phone, and instructed Bronya not to respond to the doorbell. But of course there was Lucy to deal with, because the major way for the Outraged to respond was through the Foundation. Bronya rang her to leave this short statement on my behalf, which would be all that I would say on the matter:

'I rest my case.'

I held Bronya's hand, reassured her. Nothing to be frightened of, just the dratted virus. I'd expected it, perhaps sought it out, we found each other. For once in my life, I'm a good host. It's not the end, is it, not yet, just the beginning of the end. I can live with that, for now. I don't know whether to tell Lucy. Or do I mean: how to tell her? Perhaps that's Bronya's responsibility? I can't stand a fuss.

Lucy cries and says I am a big troublemaker. I hope so, I whispered. Bronya held the Alexa machine but I didn't want. To see. Be seen. A few words all either of us manage. Words our legacy. No need for more, there's enough of them about already. As if they matter. Nothing nothing nothing to regret. Did a good thing, laughed, was jolly once. Leave them to it. No Lives Matter. But some matter more? They do. Do they? Does it matter, matter cannot be created or destroyed. We're all here, still, here in the universal molecular constructions, elegantly gloopy.

Suzy Superior Suzy. What's left of you? Was I ever good enough, bad enough? Was she? Her and her many Miles. On the clock. That would be funny. She said I had good taste that was bad. Now I don't have any taste at all. Is that what funny, ironic ... say ... what does it matter. Nothing is better or worse, nothing. Nothing to admire nothing to dismiss. Nothing to eat or to drink all same nothing.

Bronya opens the curtains, there's nothing but the night. I want to see a star shooting but my eyes are glazed with darkness. I rub away at them until she takes my cold hands in hers facing me under the bedclothes puts them between her legs. Warm soon. Kind, her kind, her kindness, her warmth.

I was awakened by shouting in the night. Sat up in terror, someone was holding on to me, pushing me down. I cried for help.

'Let go! Let me go!'

'Shhhh,' came her voice, firm and soothing. 'Is dream, is nightmare. Shhh you now.' She clung to me until I stopped thrashing, let me rest back against the sheets, weeping.

'Is only dream. OK now.'

She cuddled round me. In a few minutes I was breathing regularly, though my heart was skipping and reeling.

'You go back to sleep now.'

I murmured my acquiescence, lay on my side, still. Soon Bronya was once again asleep, but the image and overwhelming grief filled my spirit.

There was a funeral, and a bier with a corpse on it, covered with a shroud. Round it a crowd of young people in white gowns were weeping. A priest came and lifted the sheet, and lying there on the pallet was the body of ONE, some years older now, grown fat and jowly, showing the shadow of a bullet hole on her temple, amateurishly filled with paste.

The priest bent over the body in prayer.

'May he rest in peace, and enter life eternal.'

The crowd keened and howled. I tried not to join them, and failed. I was awash, but not cleansed, with fear and pity, and remorse.

Bronya cuddled me back to sleep.


What sustains me, us then us alive, what keeps us in the is-land? Nothing does or will. I thought this was what I'm ready for I'm not. The cells are making a last stand. Must quell their rebellion. Not up to them it's up to me, still, awhile. How long how long how long?

Time is gone now. Time past, time passing. Nothing to it really nothing at all. Sleep dream sleep. Where am I where am I now? Who?

Last night so cold. She brought extra blankets I shivered she got under the covers and cuddled, warmer soon. Not enough air to go round. Gasping. Her arms round me, 'Aaah, there's nothing to you,' she said.

'Never has been,' I said.

'You shush you. You sleep soon.'

Her breasts against my back. My hand reached to touch her shoulder. Warmer later then hot again, my hollow fires burnt to black. Coughing ashes, dust, matter.

She knows. What to do? That he knows that. Upon the midnight.

Teatime soon sweetness and honey, all the rest my honey my sweetness soon.

I'll drink to that.

# Acknowledgements

I trust it is neither implausible nor whimsical to offer my thanks to James Darke himself, who unexpectedly entered my life some seven years ago, and has visited irregularly since. This, the final novel of the Darke trilogy, finds him in a more than usually combative, invasive and puckish mood, and I presume many readers will find his views uncongenial. I do too, sometimes. But James Darke is a fictional character, and entitled to be as he is. However challenging and discomfiting his irascible and often wrong-headed company has been, it has also been intensely stimulating. I'm still fond of the old curmudgeon, who has helped me to fill, to enjoy, and to make sense of this late period of my life.

I have some real people to thank as well. As ever, my sister Ruthie has contributed her sharp mind, eyes and ears, in spite of the fact that she has never warmed to my hero. All the more admirable, then, that she should have given so generously. I am lucky in my preliminary readers, and the final text has benefited enormously from the knowledge, critical acuity and enthusiasm of Bob DeMaria, Warwick Gould, Declan Kiely, Cliff and Gill Leach, Erik Martiny, Sandy Neubauer, Christina Padden, and Tom Wright. I am particularly grateful to the inimitable Stephen Stratford, who edited the text so wisely and enthusiastically, and who suddenly and tragically died a few weeks later. He was an inspiring man.

As ever, my agent and friend Peter Straus, publisher and friend Andreas Campomar, wife and friend Belinda Kitchin, have been supportive, critically astute, and by no means easy to please. I like that. I am grateful, too, for the efficiency and warmth of the team at Constable, especially to Holly Blood, Mary Chamberlain, Claire Chesser and Jess Gulliver.

Special and most heartfelt thanks, though, go to my nephew Matthew Greenberg, who has enthusiastically read the Darke series in its many drafts and revisions. From the very start he understood James Darke, loved his complexity and passion, intelligence and sense of humour, and added to them with his own. I am delighted to dedicate this book to him, in gratitude and with love.